Praise for the works of

Pony Dakota

Pony Dakota is a story filled with suspense, intrigue and new beginnings. Nat Burns has done an amazing job using suspense, comical wit and superior writing skills to bring two women, who are polar opposites, together toward a common goal. I would recommend it to anyone who enjoys loving and romantic relationships between women.

-Karen Badger, *Badger Bliss Books*

Pony Dakota is a profound story of the resiliency of a woman's heart. A budding romance strives to bloom in a landscape of anonymity, notoriety, and past relationship abuse. This great read is a triumphant journey filled with humor and the stumbling blocks we all face when exploring new love.

-S. Y. Thompson, Author

Rosemary

Really good science fiction romance.

-Patricia B., *NetGalley*

The Liaison

The entire story just flows so seamlessly from one scenario to the next. I really love the detailed description of the New Mexico landscape and I really enjoyed the way the author brought the numerous characters to life with the use of witty dialogue and by giving them quirky personalities. This story is going to have you hooked from the beginning. I was caught up in Lily's world as she struggled with the death of her father, disbelief about the huge task she was about to undertake and guilt over the tough but necessary choices she had to make. I was just blown away by the appearance of the extraterrestrial beings and their relationship with the people on Earth. If you enjoy stories about other life forms, women in uniform, breathtaking landscapes with a dash of romance thrown in for good measure, then this is definitely the story for you!

-The Lesbian Review

This book was really interesting. That really is the best way to describe it. When I was reading it, I wasn't saying "wow, I really liked this" but I was absolutely hooked from the first few pages. This book interested and entertained me enough that I would want to read another from the series. It's a pretty big wide open premise that could produce some exciting new stories.

-Lex Kent's Reviews, goodreads

Pony Dakota

Nat Burns

Other Bella Books by Nat Burns

The Book of Eleanor
Family Issue
House of Cards
Identity
Lights of the Heart
Nether Regions
Poison Flowers
The Quality of Blue
Two Weeks in August

The Desert Willow Series
The Liaison
Rosemary

About the Author

After decades as an award-winning journalist, it was natural for Nat Burns to turn to fiction. After a long history of freelance writing and a corporate career as an editorial systems analyst, she's now a full-time novelist and editor. This latest book, *Pony Dakota*, is her eighteenth novel in the lesbian genre.

Nat's debut novel, *Two Weeks in August*, won a 2011 Alice B Committee Lavender Certificate for new writers. Her novel, *The Book of Eleanor*, won a Goldie award in 2013. In 2024, she won the Alice B Medal for a career distinguished by consistently well-written stories about lesbians.

Nat is a member of several writing groups, including the Golden Crown Literary Society and she now serves on the board of the Opus Literary Alliance. She lives in Albuquerque, New Mexico with her partner, Chris.

Pony Dakota

Nat Burns

BELLA
BOOKS

2024

First Edition - 2024

Editor: Heather Flournoy

ISBN: 978-1-64247-568-5

PUBLISHER'S NOTE

Acknowledgements

I once lived for more than thirty years on a wonderful 175-acre farm in rural Virginia. I now live in the city of Albuquerque, New Mexico. The old adage that writers should write what they know is certainly appropriate in this case and it's been fun taking my characters into these places that I know so well. Taking them to the wilds of the Virginia mountains was almost like going back there myself, only better. You really never can go home again but in the fictional worlds of our stories, we certainly can.

Many thanks to editor Heather Flournoy who did a great job cleaning up my overlooked manuscript messes. She has such a good eye for catching boo-boos. I'd also like to acknowledge my dear Chris and the many friends who listened patiently as I worked out plot ideas on their tired shoulders and who offered helpful suggestions along the way. Thank you.

Dedication

This book is dedicated to the Shelter for Help in Emergency and the tree of purple ribbons that used to be on the courthouse lawn. Each ribbon, tied to the tree, marked one person whose life was taken by domestic violence.

Each year the shelter responds to more than 1,500 hotline calls, provides more than 5,000 nights of safe shelter to more than 200 women and children, and assists many other victims of domestic violence through outreach services.

The Shelter for Help in Emergency is the only agency in the city of Charlottesville and the five surrounding counties of Albemarle, Fluvanna, Greene, Louisa, and Nelson providing comprehensive services to women and children who are victims of domestic violence.

I was blessed to work as a volunteer for several years and saw firsthand the wonderful services SHE provides.

CHAPTER ONE

Ms. Bebe Simmons

Bebe Simmons paused on the sidewalk and stared up at the heavy glass doors. The *very heavy* glass doors. Even after more than fifteen years of passing through them, they were still formidable. She so longed for a simple employee entrance around the back, one that offered easier access from the parking area.

Her gaze fixed on the bright process blue of The Workflow Editorial Initiative logo and she scowled. "Bloody Monday," she muttered, mounting the two wide steps to reach the doors.

Her Monday morning had been an aggravating one, beginning with a frayed seam in a favorite blouse. Later, a bread-eating toaster caused her to momentarily misplace her keys, then completely forget her favorite e-reader, waiting patiently on the kitchen counter.

Now this door. Of course, she realized that, for security reasons, this needed to be the only ingress to the building and oh, sure, fire codes dictated the many exits that were available, but they only provided escape, not entry. Ridiculous.

Shifting the strap of her briefcase closer to her neck, she passed her cup of coffee to her left hand, freeing her right hand, and the card key, to tackle the door. Her sunglasses naturally chose that moment to slip from their perch on her head, and instead of opening the door as intended, she was forced to catch the sunglasses with that free hand. Placing the end of a temple piece between her teeth, she finally tapped her card key onto the reader then grasped the door handle and tugged. Even one side of the double doors was hefty and though she was tall enough at sixty-six inches, she didn't weigh all that much, so she only made a wide enough slit to slip through. Once safely in the entryway, she paused, dropped her card key into the front pocket of her briefcase, and smoothed the blazer collar that had been mussed by the strap.

Bebe noted that the outer door hadn't been key-locked, which meant that receptionist Ada Lawrence, had already arrived. Which meant small talk. Socializing. Bebe sighed. Not her favorite thing. She much preferred the written word and all the magic that those dark glyphs brought to her psyche. Although she knew, intellectually, that humans were supposed to be social creatures, tribal even, being so never seemed to work for her. It wasn't fear exactly, only that she found socializing with others to be a nuisance, something that took her away from the written pages that were her passion.

"Oh, honey, I woulda helped you with that mean old door. Why didn't you push the buzzer to let me know you were out there?" Ada was eyeing her quizzically. She stood, as usual, behind the black half-moon of the counter in the reception area. The TWEI logo was centered on the face of the counter and each end of the half-moon had a crystal vase filled with clear gel beads and fresh flowers. Ada had gone with creamy white Easter lilies as they were just about to step into the month of April.

Bebe smiled and took the sunglasses from between her teeth so she could reply. "Well, seemed to me that freeing a finger to press the buzzer would be just as good as opening the door. Besides, you have enough to do."

Ada laughed and ran her fingers through her short mop of graying curls, a process that lasted long enough that Bebe was mesmerized. Obviously, the receptionist was making sure her hair was air-drying properly, each curl exactly where it belonged. She was one woman who made sure she was dressed to the nines every day, with the appropriate cosmetics to match.

To the nines. Now that was an interesting phrase. Some people thought that it originated with a British military regiment called The Nines, which in the 1850s was renowned for their smart appearance. Bebe, in her readings, had discovered that the phrase was actually used in the 1830s. The first recorded use, however, was *as to the nines*, a phrase from the 1700s. Later, *to the nines* and *dressed to the nines* were both used to indicate a perfect appearance.

"Barbara? Are you okay? You kinda drifted away there for a minute." Ada was studying her with a deeply concerned, motherly expression in her dull blue eyes.

Bebe grinned quickly to set Ada's concern aside. "You know me, Ada. Just woolgathering."

Ada shook her head and waved one hand, the metal-flake pink nail polish reflecting the bright morning sunlight blazing in through the glass wall of the entryway. "Oh, Lord, child. Don't I know all about that. My Paulie says I'm a complete airhead most days, off in my own little world."

"Hmm, between you me and the wall, sometimes our own little world beats the heck out of the real world," Bebe responded archly.

"You got that right. I think our United States government has plumb done lost its mind, if you ask me."

She moved from behind the reception desk, her short rectangular body seemingly propelled on wheels instead of plump, stubby legs.

"Let me get the elevator for you, at least," she said sweetly, pausing at the elevator doors and pressing the call button. The machine whirred to life as Bebe moved closer. She waited, sipping her coffee. She was trying to remember the name of

Ada's son. She knew society's mores dictated that she ask after him. She gave up trying to remember.

"So, your boy? He's doing well?"

"Silas?" Ada looked as though a lamp behind her face had been switched on. "Oh, he's doing great. Suzy, too."

"And that grandbaby?"

The elevator doors swished open with a loud ding of arrival and Bebe braced them open with her foot. She watched Ada expectantly. She didn't have to wait long.

"I swear that sweet baby girl gains a pound every couple days," Ada said, beaming proudly. "Suzy must produce some good, rich milk."

Bebe hated that the childhood obesity statistics from last month's *Glucose, The Journal of Note* were the first thought that popped into her mind. She stepped into the elevator. "Well, you enjoy that baby and keep her healthy."

The doors closed and Bebe finally allowed relief to flow across her. She leaned her back against the cool elevator car wall and sighed. Alone at last.

CHAPTER TWO

Bebe Tolerates Ralph

Ralph Browning, one of the editorial managers for TWEI, was not among the few people Bebe tolerated well. In fact, in his presence she had to consciously prevent her top lip from curling in distaste. And here he was, his large form framed by her office door.

She sighed and turned her chair to face him. "Good morning, Ralph. What can I help you with?"

He cleared his throat. "Remember last week when we talked about spacing shortages on the bottom floor?"

Bebe glanced toward the new desk that had been installed the past Friday. "Yep, sure do. And I told you my opinion."

Ralph held up a forestalling palm. "I know, I know. And I promise we'll move her out once a station opens up in programming."

"Her? So, you've hired someone?"

"I did, Friday. She's a hotshot from back East. Six composite degrees in computer science and theory."

Bebe let loose a low whistle, secretly excited that a new egghead type might prove less annoying than the teen slacker she'd been expecting. "That's good. She's not doing design, though, because most of that's been done. For all my journals at least. I told Thomas to leave those layouts alone."

Ralph patted his left hand against the doorjamb nervously. "Oh no, she's just going to be the forensic troubleshooter. Seems like her training made her the perfect candidate for that job."

Bebe leaned back in her chair and squinted at Ralph, wondering what he wasn't telling her. "Forensic. I agree. So, when's she coming in?"

"This morning. That's why I'm giving you a heads-up. She should be here soon." Ralph moved across to the empty desk and rearranged the office phone set and the large dark green desk blotter that were both standard issue at TWEI.

"It's dark in this corner," he mused, backing up and studying the setup. "I think I'll have Ada order her a lamp. Desk or floor?"

"Good idea. I'd go with a focused floor lamp," Bebe muttered as she turned back to her computer screen which had finally loaded the journal she was supposed to be editing. The compositor responsible for laying out her journal pages had laid in a graph upside down. On the front page, under the abstract. Didn't these people read—or at least look at—what they were laying out? Her aggravation level soared. First Ralph, now this.

"Well, who is she?" she snapped, eyeing the upside-down graph. Then she bit her bottom lip in regret for taking out her anger on the manager. Ralph, fortunately, seemed oblivious to her ire.

"Her name's Emma. She moved from the East Coast about eight years ago. Living in the city here now, of course. And you should see her." He was absently rummaging in the long center desk drawer of the new desk, organizing and straightening the office-issued items inside. "She's really pretty."

Bebe wondered why Ralph had mentioned Emma's appearance. Was he matchmaking? Not many people knew of Bebe's sexual preference, and she'd certainly never mentioned it to the manager. "Pretty, huh? The guys downstairs will be happy about that." She studied him, seeking answers as to why he'd pointed that out.

He moved back to the doorway and peered out onto the editorial floor. Stan Ramey moved past, a sheaf of papers grasped in one hand. He nodded genially to Ralph and waved a forefinger at Bebe. Bebe didn't bother returning the wave as Stan was moving too fast.

"How many people are you planning on adding to the staff?" Bebe asked Ralph's broad back. She lifted a pencil and seesawed it between two fingers as she awaited his reply.

He turned with a sigh. "Not sure. I've asked Dam how many more he needs downstairs, but he hasn't told me yet."

"How about on this floor? We have a pretty close-knit family, and I'd hate to see that disrupted by adding on too many new people." Bebe nibbled her bottom lip thoughtfully. "Everything seems to be on schedule with no picket lines pending due to overwork."

"No plans for that yet." He grinned at her, uncharacteristically. "You're safe from the marauding hordes."

Bebe grunted and Ralph lingered. Unusual for him, as he liked manifesting an air of busy productivity. His gaze kept finding the desk as if visually measuring its merit.

Bebe sighed, but knew she had to make niceties with him if he hung around. "So, Easter. Any plans?"

He rocked back on his heels a few times as though seriously pondering her question. "My mother lives in Los Lunas so I'll be heading that way. My sis Martha and her family, and my brother and his kids always come, so it's a full house."

Los Lunas. Bebe knew it was a village of about fifteen thousand. Just half an hour south of Albuquerque. She'd taken a pleasant Sunday drive down there once and had dined at a supposedly haunted colonial mansion, but the ghosts had eluded her that day.

"Did you see that Thomas gave us Friday off? It'll be a good long weekend for you to spend there."

"Hmm, well, yeah, but there's six grandkids ranging from a baby to about ten. I don't think I'll be hanging around on purpose."

"I totally understand," Bebe said. She, too, thought being forced to be around children one of the worst situations one could be in. Even teens were obnoxious and best avoided.

"All right. Back to it. I'll bring her by in a little while so you can meet her, and she can get set up," he said before finally wandering away from her doorway.

Bebe took a deep breath and let it out slowly, heartily glad he'd gone away. She looked at the manuscript again and growled at her machine. She slowly checked the rest of the paper, making sure the abstract, introduction, and body were entered correctly. There were three other pieces of art—a graph and two photos—which all seemed upright and appropriately placed. Thank goodness. She flipped back to the first page, shaking her head at the all too obvious error. Her compositor, Sheila Grant, had been with TWEI a long time. And had been laying out Bebe's journals for most of that time. She also had a background in science. Worry about Sheila's state of mind percolated through her, but she shrugged it off. Everyone had a bad day now and again. Nevertheless, she lifted the phone handset and dialed Sheila's desk. Sheila had to make it right.

CHAPTER THREE

Emma Arrives

Emma Vernon was thinking about her remaining fifty dollars. She'd hidden it in the back fold of her wallet so there was no way Donna could get to it even if she found her, but she worried anyway. She worried if it would buy her enough food to last until her first paycheck. She also worried about what Ms. Donna Marsh would do if she found out about that first paycheck and where it had come from.

Renting and minimally furnishing the apartment had taken most of the bonus-padded savings she had managed to hide away in a locked drawer at her old job, so she was, at this time, pretty much running on fumes financially. Thank goodness her bus pass was still fully loaded with a month of rides. At least she could get to work for a while with no issue.

Escaping the short but entangled life she and Donna had lived together had been covert and fraught with anxiety. First, she had set up a postal box at a packaging store on the other side of town, using that packaging store address on everything that she could change. Then she'd completely done away with her own name, using a new first initial and her cousin's middle name on every document that she could replace. For more than a month she'd raced home from work early to get to the mailbox and sort out any important mail, or any address change notifications, before Donna came home. She'd smartly left some of her inconsequential sales-type items mixed in with Donna's in the box so her mail wouldn't be conspicuously absent.

She would eventually use the address at her new apartment, but she wanted to wait as long as possible, maybe even more than a year or two, to remove any chance that Donna could associate a singular location with her physical address.

Luckily, most of her billing and identification was online. Though she hadn't changed her name on everything digital— just adding "in the care of E. Vernon" as primary to all addresses—she had changed all her access codes and passwords, even setting up new email addresses and discarding all her old ones.

Thank goodness she'd never combined their checking accounts. It hadn't stopped Donna from accessing hers, using purloined passwords and PINs, then berating her about what she spent her money on. Somehow she'd discover every new PIN or password when Emma changed them. But, because Donna's name wasn't on the accounts, it had been easy to cash out and close them. Luckily, her new bank had stringent security parameters and Emma felt secure that, even though Donna might discover the new bank and find Emma's account, there was no way she could access it and find out where Emma spent her funds. She'd made sure of that.

Emma was so engrossed in ticking boxes in her mind that she walked right past the TWEI building. When she reached the end of the sidewalk, she stared in puzzlement at the cross street, briefly wondering where she was. Looking back, she spied the wide concrete steps she'd pinpointed from the bus window and shook her head with some exasperation. If she was going to successfully pull off this escape plan, she'd better get her act together.

Hurrying back along the block, she bounded up the steps and pulled on the right side of the double glass doors. Nothing happened, only a dull clank sounding as the lock resisted. Emma pursed her lips and sudden fear arced through her. She lifted her eyes to the name of the business, double-checking that she was in the right place. The words *The Workflow Editorial Initiative* were written under the TWEI logo. This building was the correct one. So, she tried the left side. Nothing. Then her gaze found a doorbell with a card reader set into the doorframe, and she pressed it as she breathed a sigh of relief. A piercing buzz broke the uncanny street silence of the Albuquerque industrial park.

"Oh, good grief," she muttered, glancing around nervously.

A short, rotund figure appeared behind the glass and the door whispered open.

"Are you Ms. Vernon?" the woman queried, one plump, pink-tipped hand struggling to hold the door open. "From the job fair?"

Emma took a deep breath, trying to get used to her new name.

The woman was watching her expectantly with pale inquisitive eyes, her curly hair moving in a gentle breeze.

"Yes, that's me," Emma said.

"Oh, good," the woman said. "I figured you'd get the position when I saw you talking to Ralph at our table. He was so into you. Well, welcome to The Workflow Editorial Initiative! I know you're just going to love being part of our little publishing family." She pushed the door wider, ushering Emma inside.

Emma stepped through into a pleasant, flower-scented foyer with a curved reception desk on one side and a rank of chairs filling a small waiting area.

"My name's Ada and I've been here for about five years now and I can't recommend a better place to work." She shuffled to the reception desk and, lifting a phone handset, pressed a button on the base. "Ms. Vernon is here. Thank you, sir."

She replaced the handset and turned a curious gaze back to Emma. "Ralph—Mr. Browning—should be right down. You can have a seat if you like."

"Thanks." Emma felt nervousness swamp her again. Could she actually do this? Reclaim and reinvent her entire life? The idea of it had terrified her repeatedly since it had possessed her.

When had the idea taken hold of her? Maybe when Donna had decided on living her own more secretive life while still micromanaging Emma's. Maybe it was the incorrigible flirting with every woman they encountered. Maybe it was the few times she'd found Donna in another woman's embrace. There were so many things. Emma absently lifted a hand to her left cheek, remembering the pain. The physical abuse had finally sealed her decision, although living together and feeling so alone, like she was still single but with a harsh parental figure, had already festered into a psychological blister.

Donna had seemed so wonderful...in the beginning. The abuse had started with simple things. Donna had expressed dislike for Emma's best friend, Alice Shumaker, and had slowly coerced Emma into pulling away from her. She repeatedly pointed out that Alice, an exotic dancer, would ruin Emma's reputation and credibility. She had also ingratiated herself into making friends with Emma's coworkers in the New Mexico Practical College's computer department where Emma had been working for more than seven years. Emma soon realized it was so these coworkers would inadvertently spy on her and report back to Donna.

One day, having finally gotten past the bliss of a new relationship, Emma realized that she'd been carved away from her earlier life into one of solitude, with only a suspicious Donna as friend and confidant. The idea of her own gullibility had terrified her. How had an intelligent, together woman fallen into such a cycle of abuse, of control? How had she allowed this to happen when she knew better?

"Hello, Ms. Vernon." Ralph Browning's voice drew her from reverie, and she had a sudden spasm of fear. Remembering quickly that he could not hear or know her thoughts, she stood and lifted her backpack with her left hand as her right reached to shake the one he'd extended. He was a big man, with big hands, and she felt absolutely swallowed by the handshake.

"Hello, sir, it's very good to see you again."

"And you're doing well?" He arched one brow in query.

"Oh, yes, sir. Ready to take on a new adventure."

Ralph smiled as she knew he would. Their interview the past Friday had been cordial and flirtatious, and Emma understood that some pandering to the manager would help her land the job. It had been an easy sell. Her credentials, though with a name altered by her computer skills, were true and impeccable, the name issue flying under his radar as he was intentionally charmed by her.

"Well, adventure it might be as we implement some of the proprietary software Thomas has designed. His ideas are cutting edge and I look forward to seeing what you can do with them," Ralph said, moving them slowly toward the elevators.

"So, not just troubleshooting problems then?" Emma asked as the elevator door opened.

They stepped inside and he pressed the down button. "Oh, I think it'll be mostly that at first, but Thomas is a genius and his continued innovations to medical publishing are winning awards left and right." He paused as the elevator doors opened. "He's like one of those mad scientist inventors, locked away and changing the world one invention at a time."

Emma widened her eyes as she thought about working for a company created by a mad scientist genius. "Sounds interesting," she murmured.

CHAPTER FOUR

Emma Meets Bebe

The expansive programmer den was dim, as most usually were, only illuminated by safety lights and the many dozens of computer monitors filed neatly on desks along each side of the wide central walkway. It was quiet, too, the humming silence broken only by an occasional murmured comment. Emma had expected all of this, finding security and comfort in the familiarity of the coder environment.

"So, this is where the magic happens," Ralph said proudly, his deep voice fracturing the quiet peace of the room. "When you have a job to troubleshoot, you'll come find who wrote that module of code and go through it with them."

Eyes turned their way and Emma sensed an air of annoyance, no doubt nurtured by Ralph's obvious attitude of superiority. The gazes morphed into curiosity as much as aggravation, thankfully, and Emma tentatively smiled at a few of the watching faces and found a grin readily returned. She was glad to see a handful of stations peopled by female coders. For too many years, programming—or software engineering as it was called these days—had been a male-dominated field. It was a relief to see that this company was progressive in its hiring practices. The clothing was even coder casual, as many were in long shorts and T-shirts.

They moved a few feet forward and stopped next to a larger station about halfway down on the left. A wood-grain placard on the right side of the desk, in front of one of three busily processing monitors, proclaimed that this particular station was used by Adam Pacheco. The man sitting at the left-oriented main screen, probably Adam, turned toward them as they approached. His deep brown eyes studied Emma from the toes of her ballet flats to the top of her head, finally settling on her face. He didn't appear unfriendly, just curious. He winked at Ralph and turned his gaze back to Emma. "So. This is our new superstar? She's a bitty bit of a thing, ain't she?"

"Now, Dam, there's no need to pick on her already," Ralph said, his voice stern.

Dam held up a forestalling palm toward Ralph. He extended his right hand to Emma, who took it.

He smiled a real smile as they shook hands. "Welcome aboard, Miss Emma. I'm Dam, and I take care of this motley crew of software crafters. It'll be great having you to help us get out of some tight spots. Sometimes it's just a little overwhelming, like pitching peace to the Hatfields and the McCoys."

Emma couldn't help the broad grin that stretched her features. She was inexplicably comforted by the oddly tall Native American man. "I promise to do my best," she said.

Dam smiled. "That's what we want to hear. Come on and meet the rest. Don't worry if you forget the names. Most answer to 'hey, bro' or 'dude,' so you're covered."

Tilda, Daniel, Stewart, Bobby Ray, Dotty. The names came to her in a kaleidoscope of images and handshakes. Most of the engineers were welcoming enough, but she was oddly relieved when Ralph pulled her away to the elevator. Blessed quiet surrounded them for a brief minute before Ralph broke it.

"Nice group, aren't they?" he asked with a small smile.

Emma agreed with a nod. "Yes, they are. Did you have a hand in setting them up?"

"Not so much." He was frowning now. "Most were Thomas's friends from college or their brainiac kids. The friends were in tech classes together, and after graduation, when he decided to start TWEI, they pretty much all signed on."

"And brought their friends along, I bet," Emma offered. "Now, remind me again. Who's Thomas, a designer?"

"Oh, he's the owner. He and his bud, Spence Turner, set this place up in the late nineties. He wanders around from time to time when he's in town. You'll meet him."

"Oh, right. Did you go to college with him, too?"

"No, no. I'm not from Albuquerque. Though I did CNM Community College remote in Los Lunas. Saw a posting there for the editorial office manager job with TWEI, and here I am, four years later."

"Wow, four years."

He nodded. "It's been a nice ride. The company is fair and no one's in your face all the time."

"A good thing, for sure. So, where are we going now?"

"To your station. Unfortunately, it's not down with Dam's bunch. We seem to be outgrowing our building, at least on the lower level, so you're in with one of our senior editors. It's just temporary, as they are reconfiguring and expanding the bottom-level workstations."

Emma shrugged. "No problem. As long as I have a terminal with a good monitor, I'm a happy girl."

Ralph turned a fond gaze toward her. "Well, I will do everything in my power to keep you as happy as I can."

Not sure whether it was the fawning gaze or the words, but Emma suddenly felt uncomfortable. "Um, I appreciate that."

The elevator door opened with a cheerful ding, and they stepped out into a wide, high-ceilinged, spacious room. It was filled with passing workers hurrying along with their important papers or electronic tablets, and it was bordered on all sides by glass-fronted offices. Two long conference tables, end to end, bisected the large open central area and were surrounded by two dozen black cushioned office chairs. Their bottom supports reminded Emma of spiky insect legs. Two employees sat huddled at the end of one of the tables, studying a printed journal. They glanced up and smiled at Emma as she and Ralph passed by.

"This is our first editorial floor, where the medical journals are managed. We publish trade and science publications up on the next floor, and the corporate offices are up top. The layout people are on the first floor, above the coders who are basement level."

Emma was not surprised by that. Software engineers and their machines needed dimness and coolness and often occupied basement-level offices. She was surprised at the variety of the TWEI publications, however.

"This is a big firm, bigger than I expected," Emma said. She was impressed by the orderliness of the editorial floor and how the high windows above the offices let in that beautiful New Mexico sunlight. The space had been decorated tastefully as well, with large baskets of greenery and huge ceramic pots with Native American designs placed at evenly spaced intervals.

"Oh, sure, it's grown a lot. Thomas and his friend from high school, Albie Knapp, started publishing a little out-and-about local magazine in his garage back in the day. Now look at it. The two of them, along with Spence, the moneyman, have brought medical publishing into the digital arena."

"They must have been true visionaries to have seen the trends coming," Emma said quietly. "New computer software have become the norm everywhere, especially in the field of publishing. It takes a lot of the grunt work out."

The two had moved forward and now stood outside one of the wide center offices along the right side.

"This is where you'll be," Ralph said. "For now."

He tapped on the closed half-glass door and then ushered her into the office. She was met with two workstations, a vacant one on the left, against the side wall, that she assumed would be hers. The other one, facing the door, was occupied by a small, thin woman who was dominated by a mass of very long, very dark hair braided and laid forward across one shoulder. She stood and Emma saw that she wore a white button-down blouse atop dark trousers, and a matching dark blazer was draped across the back of her chair. The woman lifted her gaze to look at her and Emma was mesmerized by the deep gray of the woman's eyes. They were like storm clouds that were preparing to spawn a killer tornado.

"And this is your office mate. Emma Vernon, meet Barbara Simmons, senior editor for a handful of our most successful medical journals."

"You can call me Bebe, most everyone does," Bebe said quietly as she extended her hand across the desk. Wispy, escaping hair surrounded those stormy eyes, softening them some. Her squarish face was bisected by an expressive mouth that now broke into a tremulous smile.

Why, she's nervous, Emma thought with some surprise. Her heart went out to this beautiful editor, and she knew—well, hoped—that they'd get along well.

CHAPTER FIVE

Red Hair and Religion

"You have red hair," Bebe blurted out after Ralph had made his strangely reluctant departure.

Emma, busy unloading her backpack at her desk, glanced up as though surprised. One hand almost made its way up to smooth that brilliant hair, self-consciously. She caught it before it touched, however. Instead, she sighed then smiled ruefully. "Yep, ginger to the bone, I guess. My mama is second-generation Irish, so I come by it honest."

"Oh, right," Bebe said as she quickly took in Emma's dark-blue tunic shirt and black dress slacks.

She nodded and hurriedly turned back to her computer screen, embarrassed and sad to have caused the new girl discomfort. Yet her eyes could not dart completely away from the figure moving thoughtfully in her peripheral vision.

Red hair and freckles had never been something she'd been attracted to, but on this small, squarely built person, she found it fascinating. The hair was certainly a crowning glory, as many people called it, thick, heavy-looking, and the color of polished copper. Emma had pulled it back into a hefty ponytail, but it spread across one shoulder like a metallic shawl. Her pale, luminous skin, heavily decorated with freckles, perfectly framed eyes that were a surprising shade of meadow green.

"That makes sense. Ireland has the highest number of red-haired people per capita in the world. Ten percent. And it's the rarest natural hair color in humans," she said finally, even as she wondered why she felt a need to turn toward and engage with her new coworker. Just being polite, she told herself, yet she continued to ramble on. "It's an autosomal recessive. Even if the parents don't possess red hair themselves, both can be carriers for the gene and have a redheaded child."

"Not an issue in my case, as both my parents bear the red of Ireland, though my father has Scots in his background," Emma said, adjusting the height of her office chair. She smiled at Bebe. "No recessive there."

Bebe returned the friendly smile. "You had no choice, for sure. Are your siblings gingers, too?"

Emma sat on the seat of the chair and bounced up and down as though testing for sturdiness. "A brother and a sister, both gingers. My sister has the lighter brassy red while my brother is a deep auburn, like our mam."

"And you're somewhere in the middle."

"Yep. Plain old copper." She appeared childlike as she used the toe of one shoe to set the office chair into a slow spin. One hand extended and used the edge of the desk to keep the chair moving around in a fixed circle.

Bebe was entertained and a low chuckle escaped her. "Are you having fun?"

Emma stopped the chair in midspin and her cheeks flamed crimson as she turned toward Bebe.

"Oh, sorry. Forgot myself for a moment."

Bebe covered her mouth with one hand to squelch the merriment that threatened to escape. "Well, you can continue to amuse yourself. It's not like they've given you any work to do yet," she said in a calm, level voice.

Emma tilted her head as though weighing Bebe's words. "True. Guess it'll give me time to settle in. If I stop playing, that is."

The cute, mischievous head tilt did Bebe in, and she was swamped with a sudden, almost painful attraction for the computer whiz. Her breath caught in her throat, and she felt despair close around her heart, crushing it. The last thing Bebe Simmons needed was a romantic entanglement. It would pull her into the real world with all its complications and irritations. No, she was having none of that.

She turned away abruptly, focusing on her monitor screen. "Well, back to work for me. You just play away 'til you have something to do."

Silence fell and Bebe felt even more uncomfortable. Was Emma watching her?

Crowning glory. Her mind tasted the phrase and turned it purposefully. The most glorious, beautiful thing about something. Or someone. Oddly enough, it had originated in the Bible, not one of Bebe's favorite books. In Paul's first letter to the Corinthians, he stated that if a woman had long hair, then it was a glory to her. That was it. That one mention was enough for the phrase to creep and then nestle into the English language. Very strange.

Bebe snuck a sideways glance at Emma, who was fiddling with her computer mouse and frowning at her screen. It didn't matter whether Emma had long hair or short, the shiny, beguiling color of her hair would always be a glory.

Glory. The word meant honor. Indeed, Emma was blessed. The image of glory was usually depicted as a brilliant aura around a saint's head, bearing a deep relationship with the Christian monotheism—or God. Bebe wondered what faith Emma believed in. She so hoped that she wasn't one of those rabid Christians spouting praises to their Lord at every turn. She sighed. Well, that would certainly temper the attraction she was feeling for her.

Bebe had been raised in an agnostic household. Her parents had been Mensa-level scholars and had seen the Bible as just another treatise written by man. They decided that there was certainly nothing holy about it, even if inspired to be written. Especially the New Testament, which had been penned some sixty years after the death of Jesus.

Also, Bebe's mother had told her many times that there was absolutely no historical proof that a person known as Jesus had actually lived. That most likely the Jesus touted by Christians was a composite of several religious figures that had lived during and before that time, even Siddhartha Gautama, known as the Buddha. The idea of that didn't lessen the Christian faith, however, and there were a lot of fraudulent facts floating around which they also saw as gospel. Somewhat troubling that their surface knowledge was more than enough to sustain an entire religion and didn't warrant further discovery.

Friends of Bebe's at her private school had been raised in Christian households. This had led little Barbara to do her own extensive research. Eventually siding with her parents, she had learned early on never to disclose what she believed and never to even discuss religion with those who believed differently. She didn't need the hassle.

One more quick glance at Emma and Bebe found herself hoping her new coworker's intelligence and knowledge would win out in her system of belief.

CHAPTER SIX

The Computer Whiz Kid

The machine assigned to her workstation was rudimentary at best. She wondered if Dam had participated in this poor setup and realized that she would be heartily disappointed in the programming department if that were true. She recalled the warm intelligence radiating from his deep brown eyes, however, and decided that it had to have been set up by an underling in Dam's department. Or more likely it was simply still factory issue and only needed a bit of TLC to get up and running to its full potential. The tender loving care of computers was Emma's specialty, and after sighing, she dug in.

The company servers provided base-level antivirus and malware software only, and Emma's first step was beefing that up on her workstation machine by adding her own proprietary program. Linking to her webpage, she did a back tunnel into her private server and brought over Gallop, the cutting-edge software she'd developed more than five years ago. She held her breath as it loaded on this machine's hard drive, unsure if it would be read as intrusive and set off fail-safes or even alarms. Often it would be picked up by sniffer programs used by employers to spy on their employees. When it finished with no alerts, not even a blip on the company radar, she breathed out and implemented a three-time-a-day dedicated scan with any alerts going straight to her website email. Because the scan portion of the software was web-based but set up on this machine, it would bypass any intrusion alerts onto TWEI company servers.

She pulled a peripheral hard drive from her pack and plugged it into the USB port on the front of the tall central processor. Accessing the drive, she pulled the macros she regularly used for forensic work from the drive onto the company desktop and tucked them away into a folder she created and linked to the company cloud. Her coworkers at the college had been excited by the innovations Emma had developed and they'd quickly become public domain. There had even been a magazine article about the wunderkind who'd created them.

Emma pulled at her bottom lip with her teeth. She hoped that the public domain status of the macros wouldn't set off any concerns with the engineers downstairs, and she certainly hoped no one at TWEI would stumble across the article. She glanced at Bebe, who'd set up an e-book reader next to her machine. She seemed to be reading as she waited for her computer to process something.

Emma idly wondered what duties Bebe handled, exactly. No doubt as senior medical editor, she was responsible for verifying the journal content as well as supervising the physical layout that actually appeared in her publications. A tough job, requiring a lot of medical *and* publishing knowledge. She wondered how long Bebe had been employed by TWEI and made a mental note to ask her sometime.

She turned back to her monitor and lost herself in researching the tree hierarchy that the founder of the company had set up. It was pretty standard, but it appeared as though he'd branched off into sub-roots that Emma had personally decided were necessary for a good business foundation. The college atmosphere she'd dealt with before was much less stringent, so she hadn't been too bothered by the lack there. Seeing those changes here though brought a sense of excitement and order that was immensely satisfying to her.

"Good job, Mr. Thomas," she muttered.

"Hmm?" Bebe responded absently. She swiveled in her chair and looked at Emma. "Did you say something?" Her cool gray gaze moved from Emma's computer screen to Emma and back again. "Is there something wrong?"

"Oh, not at all," Emma replied quickly. "I was just admiring the nifty software that my new boss has developed."

Bebe smiled, and light from the window nestled into her stormy eyes. "It's pretty impressive, isn't it? I mean, only he would think of breaking down a scientific paper into its base components and then allowing the writers to use those elemental modules to compose their research in. Then to put all the disparate modules back together into a completed body of research, ready for publication."

"For sure. That seems like it totally cuts out the middleman. Didn't you editors used to have to divide the papers into scientific format before you published?"

Bebe nodded. "We did, and that was a real pain. Sometimes doctors and scientists would lump their introductions in with their hypotheses. And forget about them making a coherent, stand-alone conclusion." She rolled her eyes heavenward. "Brilliance sometimes leads to chaos, seems like."

Emma laughed. Bebe was so interesting to listen to. "Sounds like you've been in this business a long time." Her statement rose into an indirect inquiry.

Bebe responded as expected. "Oh yes, I've been here at TWEI since the earliest days, years and years ago now."

"But you seem so young!" Emma exclaimed, embarrassing herself.

Luckily Bebe took it as a compliment. "Thank you, I think. So, this young person is hungry. How about you? Want to break for lunch?"

"Sure! Is there a lunchroom? Ralph didn't point it out when we toured the building."

Bebe stood and stretched her lithe form. She opened a bottom drawer and pulled out a silver, insulated lunch bag.

Relieved that packing lunch was socially acceptable here, Emma fetched her smaller yellow lunch bag from her pack.

"There's a huge one, a cafeteria, on the top floor," Bebe explained.

Emma saw that Bebe's hand hovered uncertainly above her reader. She sensed that Bebe, no doubt, preferred to spend her lunchtime reading. When the hand pulled away, leaving the reader on the desk, Emma felt a sense of warmth and gratitude. Bebe was trying to help make her comfortable in what could have been a new, unfamiliar situation. She smiled.

"Sounds great. Let's go. You lead the way." She made sure her wallet was still in her back pocket and then gestured Bebe toward the office doorway.

CHAPTER SEVEN

An Enduring Classic

Bebe knew she needed to make small talk in the elevator but, for some odd reason, silence felt okay when she was with Emma. She pondered the reasons as she watched the elevator floors change.

Quite often her natural silences made people uncomfortable, so she was forced to generate conversation when she actually had nothing to say. She found this just as stressful as causing prolonged silences. Maybe even more so. With Emma, it was different. She felt no such pressure on either front. She wondered if Emma might be an introvert—computer types often were—because she knew that introverts such as herself needed quiet time to recharge their social batteries.

This idea excited her, and she glanced curiously at Emma just as the elevator door opened with a crisp chime.

"I like this elevator sound," Emma said as they stepped off it. "I stayed in a hotel once that had an elevator that announced every floor in this little kiddy voice. It made me feel secure because I would easily forget to get off on my floor. I'm a bit of an airhead." She laughed at herself.

"Welcome to my world," Bebe said, laughing with her. "I start reading a book and the whole world disappears. I can't believe I haven't been run over by a bus yet."

"Wow, look at this place!" Emma exclaimed as they rounded the corner.

Bebe studied the overlarge cafeteria-styled room with a critical eye. Thomas had known that a lunchroom, or in this case, employee cafeteria, was much more than just a place to eat. Planning for eventual expansion, he'd hired a kick-ass designer who had blazed bright primary colors throughout the entire window-framed top floor. The designer had also added a huge carousel of brightly colored tables. Most offered seating for four or six as this floor also doubled as meeting rooms for various projects. A couple dozen or so smaller, more intimate two tops populated the outer perimeter. The food service itself could rival the busiest major hospital cafeterias. The designer had divided the service into hot and cold food, as well as hot and cold beverages. The choices seemed endless, and Bebe nodded. She and TWEI had nothing to be embarrassed about.

"Omigosh! Is that fresh fruit?"

Bebe laughed at Emma's amazement. "Yep. And there's juice, too. There's always a hot buffet line and some cold salad-type things every day, plus some service staff here during work hours."

"And fountain sodas? No way." Emma turned and eyed Bebe suspiciously. "Seriously?"

Bebe nodded. "And there's fresh iced tea all the time. My personal favorite."

Emma just shook her head. "Man, I can tell I'm going to go broke working in a place like this."

"Let's sit here." The room was sparsely populated as they were lunching early, and Bebe led Emma to a four-top off to one side. "You may want to sign up for the lunch plan that Thomas offers. Thirty dollars a month, deducted from your paycheck, and you get free lunch every day, all day," she offered. "I do it."

Emma looked at the bagged lunch that Bebe had placed on the tabletop. "But...you brought your lunch."

Bebe chuckled. "Well, I often do, but I get extras, like fruit or dessert or iced tea. And at a dollar a day, it's an amazing deal. One can't even get a drive-through drink for that anymore." She paused and took in a deep breath. "Um, can I get you an iced tea?"

"Oh, I can buy one," Emma said quickly. "I'll get it."

Bebe just shook her head. "Iced tea okay, or would you like something else? It's practically free for me, you know."

"Oh, all right," Emma conceded. "Thank you."

Bebe strode to the soda station and pulled two highball glasses off the shelf. She filled them half-full with ice then filled them with tea.

She set one down in front of Emma and was surprised when her office mate's face scrunched into a strange scowl upon seeing it. Bebe cautiously took a seat as Emma leaned forward.

"These are real glasses," she said quietly.

Bebe, relieved, looked at Emma, then at the glass and back at Emma. "Oh, yeah, Thomas and the TWEI board are really conscious about protecting the Earth." She pointed to an elaborate trash and recycling area. "See what I mean? He only buys biodegradable straws and even uses steam to sanitize all the dishes, to use less water. I think the man is trying to save the planet all by himself."

Emma lowered her head. "This company is amazing," she whispered.

"Are you okay?" Bebe asked.

When Emma lifted her head, her bright, wide smile almost blinded Bebe. "Oh, you bet! I've been hoping to come across a company like this. Thomas sounds like an amazing guy."

Bebe grunted as they both began unloading their lunch bags. Bebe made a quick trip to the rank of microwaves and returned a few minutes later, waving and smiling to coworkers and cafeteria staff.

"So, what's good today?" Emma asked, eyeing Bebe's warmed lunch.

"Just takeout left from last night. Vegetable fried rice. How about you?"

"Good old PB&J. A classic."

"Do you know the history of the peanut butter sandwich?" Bebe asked quietly.

Emma looked startled. "I never thought about it. Can you tell me?"

A warm glow filled Bebe. People were seldom interested in her eclectic, sometimes boring facts, so this was a treat. "Sure! Most people think it was the peanut guy, George Washington Carver, who created it, but it wasn't really. Though he did a lot of cool stuff with peanuts, the PB&J wasn't one of them."

Emma placed her sandwich neatly onto the folded wax paper it had been wrapped in. "I'm kinda guilty of assuming that, too. Who did do it?"

Bebe ripped open a packet of soy sauce and poured it onto her fried rice before continuing, "The first thing to come, which ushered in this type of sandwich, was factory-sliced bread. That was in the early 1900s. Now, in the late 1800s, this doctor in Missouri needed a way to get protein into his geriatric patients so he took peanuts and made a paste of them. Dr. John Kellogg, the cereal guy and health guru, was also using peanut paste at his sanitariums and was the first to actually patent the process. After it premiered at the next world's fair, sales took off and it began being commercially manufactured. On a small scale, of course."

Emma took a swallow of tea. "Wow. I've read about Dr. Kellogg but I thought he was just involved in cereal and other grains. I never knew about the peanut butter."

Bebe nodded, still chewing a bite of broccoli. "Oh, yeah. I think he had a finger in every pie and was just a brilliant, educated guy. A bit ahead of his time, but smart."

"So…he patented it?" Emma prompted as she took a large mouthful of sandwich.

"Yeah, he did." Bebe sat back and sighed. "That peanut butter was also promoted in Boston by a homemaker, this columnist named Julia Chandler. Writing about it, she made it hugely popular in the 1900s and this persisted through the Great Depression. Then, when World War II started, the military decided that peanut butter was a great food for the troops. It was portable and packed with protein and fat. The soldiers had already been using a Welch's grape spread for some time, on lots of things, but when they mixed the two on sliced bread, it was considered a perfect food."

"It is. All the vegan and vegetarian groups swear by it." Emma tore off a part of her sandwich and squished it between two fingers, watching the contents ooze out the sides.

Bebe watched her and noted again that there was a certain youthful air about Emma. Due to her extensive education, she had to be in her thirties. Yet she seemed so young and unjaded by life. Bebe found it refreshing, although it made her nervous. It was new, not part of her normal life experience. What she was used to. "Um, that's true. When the soldiers brought the idea home to their families after the war was over, I'm sure you can imagine how much they all liked it."

Emma grinned and waved the final quarter of her sandwich. "And still going strong today!"

Bebe had to return the grin. "Indeed. As you said, an enduring classic."

CHAPTER EIGHT

Troubleshooting

Emma was heartily glad that Bebe was being so kind. It would have been agony if she'd been tossed into the office of someone who treated her with indifference or even hostility. She was sure a situation like that, while she was so raw emotionally, would have thrown her right back into the trauma of her time with Donna. A charitable, caring person was what she needed most at the moment. If she couldn't be surrounded by the loving presence of her family, then Bebe would do. She swept a surreptitious glance Bebe's way and saw her scowling at the computer screen.

"Idiots!" Bebe shouted abruptly and left the office in a huff.

"Well, so much for kindness," Emma muttered with a short grunt of laughter.

She turned her attention back to work. Dam had given her some of his busy work, entering company invoices to help out the financial department, and she was just wrapping it up. Finished, she sat back and intertwined her fingers across her belly. She was just closing her eyes to give them a break when the office phone on her desk tinkled merrily.

"Vernon," Emma answered absently.

"Emma! It's Dotty from downstairs. Can you come see why this module I wrote won't load for this German client? He's getting really grumpy 'cause it's like the middle of the night for him or something and he wanted to get this done before going to bed."

"Sure," Emma replied. "Be right down."

Dam and Clara Reese, who worked tech support, were hovering at Dotty Anders's desk when Emma arrived. Dotty looked up at Emma and relief flooded her features. "He's off, but I'm supposed to call him back," she said as she nibbled on the end of a mechanical pencil.

"We've looked at it again and again, but he still keeps getting an error message when he tries to submit it. He says he's tried like eight times," Clara explained, nervously fiddling with the buttons on her shirt. "We're afraid the system will kick him out if he tries again and then he'll lose the entire submission."

"It will," Dam offered somberly. "Don't let him try again."

"I told him," Dotty muttered. She turned to the screen and pushed her glasses higher on her nose so she could better study the pages of code populating her screen.

"Up! Up!" Emma said, making a shooing motion with her hands. "I gotta see it to figure it out."

"Oh, right," Dotty said. She rose. "I'll get coffee. You want coffee, Emma?"

"I do," Emma replied as she seated herself and focused on the screen. "Three sugars, no milk."

"Let us know what you find out," Clara said. "I hope it's not too serious. We'll have to smooth some feathers, regardless."

"Will do," Emma muttered, glad that Clara and Dam had wandered away. She quickly copied the module of code then opened her webpage. She pasted the module into her proprietary diagnostic software and started the scan.

Dotty returned with the coffees and handed one to Emma. She pulled a nearby stool closer and watched as the scan went from line to line in the module. She pushed up her glasses and turned to Emma. "I swear the code was good. I ran it dozens of times and it worked every time. It was just a slight modification from our general module and it worked fine."

"Oh, I believe you," Emma said in a reassuring voice. "It feels like maybe it's something he's doing on his end. Is this the first time he's used it?"

"It is." Dotty nodded so hard the coffee in her cup sloshed dangerously close to the ceramic rim. "He's a new doctoral fellow who just got hired by this company that uses TWEI modules."

"Has the company had any problems?"

A small snuffling sound from the computer let Emma know that the original module had easily passed all the test scans.

"Your code is good," Emma said thoughtfully. "So, it's something he's doing. I need to access his submission. But it failed, right?" She looked at Dotty expectantly.

Dotty was twining a hair tie into her thick mane of blond hair, so she jutted her chin at the screen. "Bottom left. In the email. I had him send it to me because I knew we'd have to check it out."

Emma opened the email server and found the latest one. "You, my dear, are a genius," she muttered.

After opening the email attachment, she copied it and pasted it into her webpage scanner. It found the problem in seconds, sounding the mischievous giggle Emma had programmed it to play when an error was found. "Ahh, there it is!"

"What? What?" Dotty said, leaning forward while retrieving her cup of coffee.

"Hold on." Emma closed down her webpage, cleared the browser history, and then dragged the file attachment from Dotty's email account onto her desktop. She opened it and highlighted a section of the German author's submission. "See this, at the end of this line? It's a German character. I've seen it before, and it's often left out of the usual programming because it's not supposed to be used on an American paper. It's called an *eszett*. The software knows it's not supposed to be there, so it gives us an error message."

Dotty stared at Emma with wide eyes. "Clara and me read that several times, both of us, and somehow we missed it?"

Emma laughed. "That is so easy to do. Plus, see how it kind of blends in near this scientific formula? Your eyes probably just thought it fit as part of that."

"I guess." Dotty was watching Emma as though she'd just performed a miracle.

Emma sighed. She knew word of her feat would be spread through the whole company by the end of the day. This wasn't her first troubleshooting rodeo. "So, you can go ahead and submit this for him, as he was ready, obviously, to enter it, but make sure you send this to him with the eszett highlighted so he can know to watch out for it in the future."

"I will." Dotty nodded and her blond ponytail bounced against her shoulders. "Thank you for catching this. Do you think we should incorporate that symbol in the international modules?"

"I wouldn't," Emma replied. "He's publishing in an English-language journal, using American-based software. There's no place for a nonmathematical symbol here. It would set a bad precedent."

"I gotta go tell Clara." Dotty placed her cup on the desk and hurried off.

Emma rose slowly and lifted her own mug of coffee. She took a deep sip and decided that it was so good she'd take it upstairs with her.

At the first floor the elevator paused, and Ralph stepped aboard. He grinned at Emma. "Hello. It's good to see you. How are you settling in?"

Emma grimaced. Ralph had made it a point to stop by their office at least once a day to check in on her, the newest employee, always asking the same question. "I'm good, good. Was just down doing some troubleshooting with Dam's bunch."

"Well, I'm sure you were a solid help to them," he said, beaming at her.

"And I got coffee," Emma said, lifting the cup as if for proof.

"Ahh. Well, speaking of coffee, the two of us should go for coffee—and danish—sometime soon. Get away from the building for a while. I know a great little place, and I think it would do us both good to get—"

The elevator door opened at the editorial floor and Emma stepped out as quickly as she could. "Sounds great, Ralph. Thanks!"

She hurried down the hall and entered her office. Bebe was back at her desk, and she lifted a questioning gaze to Emma.

Emma took a deep breath as she gripped her coffee mug tightly. How could she tell Bebe how freaked out she was by Ralph's invitation? She decided that it was a bin of worms that needed to stay tightly shut. She moved to her workstation. "I was helping out downstairs," she said.

CHAPTER NINE

Barcode Readers

"Hey, I don't see a barcode reader anywhere," Emma said with a frown a few days later. She was eyeing Bebe's desk curiously.

"Hmm?" Bebe pulled her attention from her screen. "A what?"

"You know, they're used to track the manuscripts as they go through the system."

Bebe turned her chair so that she faced Emma. "You seem to be speaking some of that tech speak. I have no idea what you're talking about."

Emma's face looked as though a brick had fallen on it, her features flattening as she pondered Bebe's words. "Seriously, you have no idea what I'm talking about? That's criminal. How do you track your medical research through production?"

Bebe lifted a pencil and fiddled with it, her long fingers plucking at the barrel nervously. "Each submission gets a production code. Is that what you mean?"

Bebe saw Emma's mind working as she considered this new information. Silence fell heavy in the room. So much so that

Bebe worried that her own normal breathing would be too loud to Emma's ear.

"Ooookay, so let me get this straight. Each piece that comes in, all the components that make up the scientific paper, they each get a number. I am assuming the same number?"

"Well, yes, we add things on, like a suffix, to differentiate the individual items. Graphs are labeled with an additional number three at the end, so we know what the item is. I mean…" She paused. "You have to do that or there'd be total chaos." She would have thought that her last statement should have been easily evident to the sharp computer girl. She watched Emma for some clue of understanding. She spread her hands, waving the pencil.

"But you have no barcodes on anything?"

"Barcodes. Like in the grocery stores?" Bebe was remembering her usual store using a type of scanner on her bulk pack of paper towels. It was a fast thing.

"Exactly!" Emma leaned back, her frown finally replaced with a smile.

"But how would that help us? How would it fit into journal production? We don't buy anything. Not like that anyway."

Emma grinned more widely and did that damned adorable head tilt again. "You may not have noticed, or maybe didn't realize it, but the reason they use barcodes isn't just for sales. It's used for pricing regulation as well as inventory. You know, inventory."

Something was blooming in Bebe. There was this nagging idea that Emma was going to do or say something that was sure to change Bebe's daily reality. Fear swamped her, but there was a little bit of excitement as well. Bebe's long-dormant adventurous spirit rose up from its deep slumber and peered sleepily at Emma. "Inventory…"

Emma nodded enthusiastically and turned back to her computer. "Let me write Dam."

Bebe's thoughts whirled in the ensuing silence. Wow, she thought. Just wow.

Later that morning, Ralph joined Bebe, Dam, Emma, and Laretta Silver, senior head of tech support, at the long conference table just outside Bebe's office. Dam had brought a large laptop from downstairs, and he was setting it up on the table, Emma helping alongside.

"So, what's going on?" Ralph asked musingly, scratching under his chin. He moved close to Bebe so he wouldn't be heard by the other three.

"A new kind of hardware, I think," Bebe replied.

"Well, Thomas would have to approve anything like that and he's in Philadelphia right now."

Bebe hated the accusatory tone that manifested in his statement, and she turned her face away. "Yeah, I know, but let's see what all this is about before we get our panties into a wad."

The two computer techs sat back and rolled their chairs away from the table so Ralph, Laretta, and Bebe could see the screen.

"So sorry I'm late," Edie said loudly as she stepped through the elevator doors. "Stan had a new crisis that had to be dealt with downstairs."

"No worries," Ralph said as Edie stopped beside the conference table. "Have you met our newest computer whiz kid? Emma Vernon, this is Edie Wells, our senior science editor and third-floor manager. Edie, meet Emma."

Emma grinned and shook Edie's hand. "Nice to meet you finally," she said. "I've seen your name all over the website."

"Only in good postings, I hope," Edie replied with a chuckle. She nodded to Dam, Laretta, and Bebe. "Hey guys, what's up?"

"We were just getting ready to show you." Dam gripped the mouse and woke up the screen. "Our new wunderkind here has come up with an idea that may very well revolutionize how we all do our jobs." He paused a long second. "I gotta say, this is a downright brilliant idea. I still can't believe none of us thought of it. Guess we're not as on the ball tech-wise as we think we are."

Bebe was growing impatient. "So, what is it?" she ground out.

Dam called up a webpage which featured a strange flat-looking item. It was white plastic on top and had a gun-like grip.

"This, ladies and gents, is a barcode reader."

"Wait, like in the grocery? Or the hospital?" Edie said as her right hand absently rubbed her bald head. She suffered from alopecia and the hair loss often made her exposed scalp itch.

Dam and Emma shared a conspiratorial smile before he answered, "Yes, exactly. It reads barcodes. That's all it does, and these…"

He flipped to a new page which featured the reader alongside letter-sized pages of black barcodes. "These are barcode stickers. Each page has sequential alphanumeric barcodes—a master number plus a suffix letter A through Z—and you use one page per each scientific paper."

Emma pointed to the screen. "These stickers can be placed on each paper as it comes in. All art gets one—graphs, photos, tables, even source pages. It's placed on the back of each piece as they go to layout or to graphics. Each department will have a code reader and can scan each part into the system as they receive it."

"That way each person in the department can call it up by the scanner and see where the components are in the production process," Dam added.

Bebe felt excitement swell in her breast, her mind expanding with possibility. "That will save so much time. So many calls to other departments to check on progress," she mused quietly.

Emma smiled approvingly. "Yes! So glad you see it. Think about it—the whole production process could be completely digitized. No more writing numbers on the manuscripts, some of which can't be read easily. No more looking them up by typing in the numbers. The computer screen will simply populate with *all* the information about that manuscript when you scan the barcode with the reader."

"Oh, man," Ralph pointed out. "That has to be outrageously expensive. I mean, we'd need more than thirty readers and God knows how many of those label things."

"We crunched the numbers and we've already prepared a proposal for Thomas," Dam said. "Once we all agree on it, of course. It's only thirty-two hundred to start, including the reader software."

Edie gasped. "That's it? Really?"

"Why haven't we done this before?" Laretta asked, turning her gaze on Dam.

He shrugged. "Just overlooked it, I guess. It's relatively new in the publishing industry. Though lots of companies use it for inventory, of course."

"Tracking manuscripts is a new use for it," Emma added thoughtfully. "But from what I've seen and been reading about, this software is really making inroads. We even used it at my previous job for professor tracking. I predict it's going to be status quo pretty soon."

"It's perfect for what we do," Edie mused. "I can't wait to see how it saves time in our group."

"Absolutely," Emma agreed enthusiastically. "As I said, with just one check-in, you should be able to see where all your active manuscripts are in the system. And this is a great way to monitor individual progress. It's auto-dated, too, so you can see when something hits a bottleneck."

Dam shook his head as though impressed, then turned to Ralph. "So, should we run it by Thomas?"

"You already have." A pleasant male voice emanated from the flat, saucer-shaped communication device in the center of the table.

"Sorry, guys. I went ahead and dialed him in," Bebe said apologetically. "This seemed important, so I thought, why delay?"

"I give this a one-hundred percent go, Dam," Thomas said. "Ralph, can you work with Emma and Dam to get them ordered? Order as many as you think we'll need and just invoice them to equipment."

"Will do, boss," Ralph replied. "I think it really might be a plus to production."

"It sounds like it. Gotta love innovative technology. Signing off. Let me know if you need anything else." A soft click let them know that Thomas had disconnected the call.

Emma took a deep breath and looked at Bebe with wide eyes. "Was that...?"

Bebe grinned at Emma's obvious hero worship. "Yep, that was the man himself. Thomas."

"He sounds so young," Emma said.

"He is," Ralph agreed. "I told you he was some kind of a genius."

Bebe snorted. "Not hardly. I've seen him with mismatched socks and untied shoes."

Edie laughed and shot Bebe a thumbs-up. "I've heard that all the true geniuses do that. Must be a common trait if you wanna be part of the genius club."

"Wow!" Emma muttered. "Just wow."

CHAPTER TEN

Spaghetti Lunch

Using the new barcode reader was an amazing benefit to Bebe's workload. Nevertheless, implementing it required a learning curve, so it had been an exhausting morning. Bebe was heartily looking forward to some quiet downtime during lunch, but Emma was not about to help Bebe's exhaustion. She started in immediately.

"So, what do you know about the history of spaghetti?" she asked as she took the chair across from Bebe. "I have yummy leftovers from Tony Bello's."

"Tony Bello's. Is that the little hole-in-the-wall place on Menaul?" Bebe screwed up one eyebrow, trying to remember.

"That's the very place. Be right back." Emma hopped up and strode purposefully to the microwave. Bebe watched, entranced, as her legging-covered bum swayed under her long green tunic. Even her bright copper ponytail seemed to dance with each step. Emma turned after switching on the microwave and, catching Bebe's eye, smiled and winked.

Bebe, mortified, nervously smiled back then dropped her attention to her salad.

"Anyway," Emma continued when she returned several moments later. "Tony Bello's has the best spaghetti. I never get the meat sauce, though. I just get the yummy marinara. It's so good and he seasons it so well. I usually just get it to go...I'm not so keen on eating in restaurants alone."

"I'd go with you," Bebe offered quietly, eyes downcast.

Emma breathed out. "I would love that. I mean, I've been in Albuquerque a long time and have made some good friends, but...well, you know, everyone is so busy these days. Most of them have kids and husbands, too, so lots of responsibilities."

Bebe nodded in understanding. "Well, I'd ask if Tony is Italian, but I know that most Italy Italians don't eat the way American Italians do."

Emma's eyes grew large. "Omigosh, have you actually been to Italy?"

Bebe grinned. "Oh, yeah. My parents believed traveling in other countries provided a much better education than one could get in American schools. We went to Italy and across to Spain when I was like eleven years old."

Emma leaned forward, almost spilling her dish of noodles and sauce. "That is so amazingly cool. I have wanted to go overseas, like, my whole life."

"You should go. It's an amazing experience to see other cultures. Educational too, because it helps one decide what they want to incorporate into their lives. I mean, we *can* pick and choose. People can decide what's best for them, personally."

Emma tilted her head in that sweet, thinking way she had. "True. Like being an agnostic in a highly religious family."

Bebe chuckled. "Or an animal-rights vegan in a Texas barbecue family."

Emma pointed her fork at Bebe, nodding and trying to laugh with a mouthful of spaghetti.

"Anyway," Bebe said when the merriment had died down. "I can tell good old Tony Bello may not be from old Italia."

"How so?" Emma lifted a questioning gaze.

"You had to mix your spaghetti. And it's the main part of your meal."

Emma was still studying her face curiously, so she continued.

"In Italy, though there are some regional differences, spaghetti is more of an appetizer to prepare the diner for the main meal. And it is always mixed. The red sauce is mixed in with some of the starchy pasta water and it is always served tossed together. In a small portion."

"I never knew there was a difference," Emma said, poking at her meal with her fork.

Bebe smiled and swallowed a well-chewed bite of tomato. "See? More reason to travel."

Emma grinned, her bright gaze finding Bebe's. "Okay, smarty pants. Tell me more."

Bebe couldn't speak right away. Emma's friendly, beautiful gaze was overwhelming. It made Bebe momentarily speechless. Finally, she cleared her throat.

"Interestingly enough, spaghetti started out as more like a pizza. It was a thin eggy bread, rolled out, baked, and served with sauce and cheese on top."

"No way!" Emma covered her full mouth as she exclaimed.

Bebe laughed at her. "Way. Then someone thought about slicing it super thin and boiling it, in about the fifth century. No one seems to know why."

"Was that in Italy?"

Bebe watched closely as Emma spiraled spaghetti around the tines of her fork.

Bebe nodded. "I think the bread was, but the idea for long noodles is supposed to have come from China, where rice and millet noodles had been eaten as far back as anyone knows. Marco Polo supposedly was the one who brought the idea from Asia to Italy, though I'm not totally sold on that."

Emma sat back, still chewing. "So, spaghetti came from China. Very weird."

"Not so much, really. They had, like, rice noodles, but the wheat noodles came from the Middle East. They were sturdier and traveled better with those nomadic tribes."

"But who brought it to America? Everyone eats it here. Was it Italian immigrants? Or Asia or the Middle East?" Emma was watching Bebe curiously.

Bebe chuckled again. "It was probably Thomas Jefferson in the beginning. He loved spaghetti and made sure it was regularly made in his kitchen. He died before Italian immigrants caused a surge in its popularity later in that century."

"So, nineteenth century?"

"Yes, yes, of course," Bebe affirmed, spreading her hands in apology for her lack of clarity.

Finished with her spaghetti, Emma closed her empty container and pulled an apple from her bag. "I guess I'll never look at chow mein the same again."

Bebe focused on her salad, knowing a goofy smile was plastered to her features. Emma always seemed to have a unique way of phrasing things.

Emma was studying her. "So you, Miss Bebe. What is your stance on the whole spaghetti issue?"

Bebe glanced up. "What do you mean?"

Emma waved the apple. "You know. Love it, hate it, or indifferent to it?"

Bebe's eyebrows raised. She'd never defined her food preferences before. Well, beyond a passion for her mother's Watergate cake. "Now that I think about it, I really do love it. Even with garlic and olive oil, as opposed to tomato sauce. It's certainly a satisfying meal."

Emma scrunched up her nose. "I like it that way, too. Meat sauce is gross. Though my friend Alice would disagree. She's a huge carnivore. We disagree so much about that."

"Or agree to disagree?" Bebe queried.

Emma laughed. "Yeah. Something like that."

"So, is there any meat that you do like? Chicken?"

Emma tilted her head as she pondered the question. She was just so adorable, Bebe thought yet again.

"I don't mind the taste of chicken, and my mama makes me take two bites of turkey breast at every Thanksgiving, but until they change the meat farming industry, I will not give them my hard-earned dollars. I just won't support the abuse and suffering of animals."

Her face was in defiant mode, and even with lips pressed firmly together and green eyes afire and angry, Bebe still thought her beautiful. And her heart stuttered just a bit. In addition, she felt the exact same way about consuming meat and even animal-produced foods, rarely eating cheese and choosing to drink nondairy milks. "Thank you," she said absently.

"For what?" Emma took a bite from her apple and watched Bebe curiously while she chewed.

Bebe felt her cheeks grow ruddy with embarrassment. She hadn't intended the comment to be said aloud. "For…for caring about the animals," she said finally.

Emma shrugged. "If we don't, who will?"

CHAPTER ELEVEN

Dancing Leprechauns

Ralph was pacing back and forth in their office when the two returned after lunch. "And just where have you two been?" he asked in a strangely accusatory tone. His annoyance was palpable.

Bebe waved her lunch bag at him. "Eating lunch? Hello?"

He had the grace to look sheepish. Stuffing his hands in his trouser pockets, he rocked back on his heels. "Oh, sure, sure. Of course." He turned toward Emma. "How was it?"

Emma nodded as she took her seat, gaze never leaving him. "Good, good. Leftover spaghetti."

He looked toward Bebe. "I should come up there. You know, eat when you guys do. What time is that?" He glanced at his watch. "Noon, then?"

"That's just today," Emma said quickly.

"Right," Bebe agreed. "It's totally random, whenever we have a good breaking time."

He looked disappointed and Emma clenched her hands together, not sure what to expect.

He smiled widely. "Well, I'll just have to see if our paths cross from time to time."

"I thought you ate at your desk, most days," Bebe pointed out, pushing her lunch bag into a desk drawer. She was frowning as though displeased with him.

His lips curved downward. "Well, that's certainly not set in stone. I go upstairs sometimes. Might as well take advantage of that expensive cafeteria, don't you think?"

Bebe grunted and, using her mouse, brought the computer screen to life. She immersed herself in her email server, effectively dismissing any further conversation with Ralph.

As though oblivious to this dismissal, he moved closer to Emma's desk. Emma extended her right hand to her mouse, hoping to mirror Bebe's action but with a better result.

"So, Miss Emma. Are you still enjoying your time here with our little TWEI family?" His voice was low and even, as though sharing an intimate secret.

Emma briefly closed her eyes and sighed, hoping he wouldn't notice. He didn't.

"I'm doing well, Ralph. All is good. No problems. None at all," she reiterated for what seemed like the thousandth time.

Ralph settled into the rolling office chair on the other side of Emma's desk. Out of the corner of her eye, she noticed Bebe's concerned glance toward the office manager. Then Bebe's gaze flicked to Emma, but Emma couldn't parse out any information from it.

Ralph spoke again, his voice quiet and curious. "I remember that you're originally from Virginia, is that right?"

Emma knew they'd discussed this before but felt a responsibility to answer yet again. "Yes, sir. On the lower western border. My whole family settled there when they came from the old country. Been there ever since."

"Old country?" He had crossed one leg atop the other and now fiddled with the hem of his jeans. "Was that England?"

Emma spied an email from Bebe. She clicked it open and smiled. "No, sir. It's Ireland. My grandparents came from Ireland and settled in the mountains of Virginia."

What the hell? Bebe had written. *Tell him to go away.*

You tell him to go away. You have seniority, Emma typed in return.

Bebe chuckled, drawing Ralph's attention. Bebe waved one hand to brush his interest away.

"Ireland, yes. Well, that explains that beautiful head of hair you have. We don't see too many redheads here in New Mexico. Are there a lot of redheads in Virginia?" he asked, turning his attention back to Emma.

Bebe sent Emma a comically dancing leprechaun hugging a pot of gold. Emma had to swallow the peal of laughter that she wanted so badly to let escape. She coughed to cover it.

"Omigosh. Are you okay?" Ralph asked, concern ringing in his voice. He peered farther around the computer monitor on her desk to better see her face.

"No, no. I'm good," Emma managed to gasp out. She smiled at him, even though she knew her cheeks were beet red with merriment. "My huge family is made up of mostly redheads, so yes, there's lots of redheads in Virginia. At least that part of the state."

"You know." He settled back, entwining his two hands across his belly as if settling in for a long winter's nap. "You wouldn't know it by looking at me, but my family has blond running through it. My cousin Bertha is almost an albino, her hair is so light."

Guess I was wrong, Bebe wrote. *I had him pegged for a Bigfoot relative but as far as the research shows, there aren't any blond ones.*

Emma lost it. She stifled a huge giggle and squirmed in her chair. Ralph eyed her curiously as she cleared her throat, seeking control.

"Luckily her eyes were brown, so we knew she wasn't. An albino, I mean," he continued.

Edie, thankfully, chose that moment to stick her head into the room. She searched the room with heavily lined and mascaraed eyes, somewhat incongruous when paired with her baldness, finally spying Ralph. "Hey, boss. Gwyneth Farr is on the phone for you. She says we misspelled a word in the planetary issue last month and I disagree. She's not happy with talking to me about it. Can you come talk to her? We need a united front, I'm thinking."

Ralph rolled his eyes and gave Emma a long-suffering look. "No rest for the wicked."

He rose and stretched his tall form. "I guess I'll see you gals later. Maybe at lunch tomorrow."

Bebe and Emma stared at one another for a long beat after he left.

"Dancing leprechauns? Really?" Emma said.

Bebe shrugged and they both dissolved into unavoidable laughter.

"I wonder why he's been hanging around so much," Bebe said in a musing tone when they had quieted.

Emma had her suspicions—and apprehensions—but she wasn't going to share them with her coworker. *Never stir a tempest in a teapot* had been one of her mother's favorite sayings. She shrugged eloquently.

Bebe eyed her suspiciously. "I think he's gone a bit sweet on you, that's what I think."

Emma swallowed hard before replying. "Omigosh. I sure hope not."

"He's not too rough to look at, if you were interested." She watched Emma closely. "Wait, you're not married, are you?"

"Um, no, no, I'm not," Emma muttered, hurrying to change the subject. "But as they say in Virginia, a bear never poops where he eats. It's never a good idea to date a coworker." She stood. "Be right back. Gotta wash my hands."

She wiggled her fingers at Bebe and hurried from the room, her gaze fixated on her feet as she took each step toward the ladies' room.

CHAPTER TWELVE

That First Touch

"Are you guys going?" The question came from Laretta, who was sitting laid back in their extra office chair. She, Bebe, and the other managers had held their monthly meeting in the main editing floor meeting area earlier.

"I think it's kinda mandatory," Bebe murmured. She, too, was laid back in her chair, uncharacteristic for her.

"What is it?" Emma asked absently, gaze fixed on the streams of data populating her computer monitor. She had not been part of the editorial meeting. "Do the engineers need to come?"

"It's a big party," Laretta said, crossing her long, thin legs. "All the staff comes, all departments." Her voice grew playfully stern as she glared at Emma. "Including ours."

Emma turned and gazed at Laretta. Though the tech support manager was a woman of color with darker skin, she nevertheless had striking hazel eyes and modern, blunt-cut blond hair, straightened and shorn close on one side. "So, when is it?"

"Friday evening," Bebe said. "It's sort of an after Easter celebration."

Emma grinned. "Will there be a bunny there? With eggs full of candy?"

Laretta laughed. "Lordy, I hope not. With my three kids, all preteen, I got more than enough of that Easter foolishness."

"It's for us grown-ups," Bebe explained. "Drinking and dancing. Revelry to welcome spring."

"My innate pagan DNA thanks you. And TWEI," Emma replied. "Sounds like my sort of party."

"Pagan?" Laretta raised one eyebrow in quizzical curiosity. "Are you one of them demon followers? Am I gonna need to report you at my church on Sunday?"

Emma laughed, the merry sound brightening the room. "Not exactly. I'm just Irish, though some might say that the demonic assumption is correct."

It was Laretta's turn to laugh. She rose. "Well, back to it. You never know when that nasty Ralph-man might be creeping around."

Bebe laughed and nodded.

"Ralph doesn't seem to be too well-liked around here, does he?" Emma commented when Laretta had left, shutting the door behind her.

Bebe leaned forward and woke up her monitor with the mouse. "When he first came on board, he acted like he had something big to prove. Pranced around like he owned the place. Thomas finally got him to back off a little, otherwise there just might have been a mutiny. Laretta hasn't forgotten those days."

Emma sighed, feeling close enough to Bebe to share her thoughts. They'd occupied the same office for a little more than six weeks now, sharing a lunch table just about every day. Emma took the plunge. "I…" She cleared her throat. "I'm actually not too keen on the way he looks at me."

Bebe turned and fell forward in her chair, her upper body pointed expectantly at Emma. Her eyes had gone all stormy, and Emma suddenly wished she hadn't said a word. Bebe's elbows rested on her knees and her hands were clenched tightly together. Tension permeated the room. Her words were like bullets when she spoke. "We do not allow any sort of harassment here at TWEI. What has he done?"

"No. Nothing really," Emma replied hastily. "I guess he just creeps me out a little, you know?" She watched Bebe, her whole demeanor entreating her to just let it lie. "The way he, he comes around all the time."

Silence fell as the two regarded one another. Bebe finally spoke in a gentle tone. "Okay. Just know that you can tell me anything, okay? I, well, I'd like to think that we're friends now and that you could confide in me if you were having any sort of problem here."

Still sitting, Emma rolled her chair across the walk space between their desks until her knees were barely touching Bebe's. She took both Bebe's clenched hands in hers and heard Bebe's small gasp of surprise. "Yes, yes, I think we have become friends and I'm grateful for that."

The soft skin under her fingertips slowly penetrated her psyche and Emma looked down at their hands. She felt a very new and different feeling overtake her. And it was powerful. She wanted to kiss Bebe. She wanted to reach up and lay her palm under that thick dark braid and pull Bebe's face to hers. She wanted to inhale the smell of Bebe's pale skin, rub their noses together and finally their lips. She wanted to pull Bebe's nervous lips to hers, to taste their softness, to relax them and bring them to passion. She wanted all this, in a flash of desire, and her body betrayed her with a jolt of excitement in her very core. She dared not lift her gaze higher or Bebe would see. Bebe would know.

Gently, she released the hands with a friendly pat of reassurance. "I would tell you," she whispered. "I would."

She slowly rolled her chair back to her desk. "Thank you for helping me settle in here at TWEI. It means a lot," she said, staring at her monitor.

"It's been a pleasure," Bebe replied in a small, quiet voice.

CHAPTER THIRTEEN

Bebe Escapes Herself

The touch of Emma's hands on hers had unwound something deep inside Bebe. It felt like she'd found something she'd been missing. An answer to something she'd been asking for a long time.

But what had happened, really? It was just a friendly gesture.

But there had been that warmth of her skin, the interesting freckles atop the paleness inundating Bebe's gaze. She'd found herself trying to count those freckles as they trailed along Emma's forearm and up into her sleeve. There were so many, some lighter, some darker, and Bebe had been entranced by them. Maybe it was a way of keeping her from looking into Emma's eyes. If she did that, if she saw into Emma's soul, she could never go back to her calm, predictable life. Emma, with her light sandalwood scent, would be a firebrand scorching everything that Bebe cherished. She would demand and Bebe would gladly give.

No, there could be none of that.

Her glance slid across the office. Emma was thoughtfully sorting through new assignments Dam had brought to her earlier that morning.

What did she know about Emma? Her coworker wasn't exactly forthcoming with information about her private life. But then that was essentially the pot calling the kettle black, accusing Emma of a fault which she, herself, shared. Basically, hypocrisy. Bebe had so many things she absolutely kept to herself, for so many different reasons.

Bebe knew a pot and kettle would both be blackened by the same fire, as the Spaniards were well aware of when they coined the term back in the 1600s. So, why was Emma so secretive? What private thing was she hiding and why? Bebe only knew her own issues and wondered if or how they aligned with Emma's.

Years ago, somewhat troubled by her inability to connect with people, Bebe had sought the opinion of a therapist. The therapist had quickly labeled Bebe a loner and had pressed upon her that fighting loneliness required ongoing work. She said that making social connections was like becoming a battery that needed constant recharging. She made the word *loner* into a pejorative thing, something highly abnormal and maybe even criminal.

It didn't seem to matter that Bebe had explained time and again that she didn't suffer from loneliness, that her books and the characters within were more than enough company for her. The therapist still deemed her damaged somehow, saying it was against nature to remove oneself from the flux of society.

Bebe, after suffering the pangs of insecurity wrought by the doctor's judgment, gathered her tattered feathers about herself and fought back. Her defense was reasonable, to the point. People have the right to be alone. To live alone, to dine alone, and even work alone. Her parents had been an example as they were mostly loners. Their friendships were sporadic and included only a select few professional, monied couples. Her father had said from time to time that friendship quite often comes with more costs than benefits.

William Shakespeare, the playwright, had excellently portrayed this in his play about Timon, a wealthy Athenian. In the play, Timon lavished gifts upon his friends, all the while wining and dining them in luxurious surroundings. As time passed, his income dwindled, and his so-called friends quickly deserted him and he was forced to turn to manual labor. When this labor caused him to regain wealth, due to a lucky accident, those friends returned in droves, expecting him to once again lavish money on them as he'd done before. This time he sent the money-grubbers away, became a loner, and developed a hatred for his fellow man, finally seeing their true natures.

Bebe had, probably subconsciously, taken these ideas to heart. Not in a financial cost manner but more in an emotional way. She often found the process of being a close friend exhausting. No, overall, being mostly alone was a better existence for Bebe Simmons.

But then there was Emma. Bebe snuck another glance at her. The computer guru seemed restless, and alarm bells rang deep in Bebe's brain. Was Ralph more of a problem than Emma was letting on? Bebe had never liked the man, and she hoped this wasn't coloring her perception about what was happening between him and Emma.

Bebe felt overwhelmed and knew she had to escape the situation and especially her betraying thoughts. She brought up her email account and sent a quick note to Amy in the human resources office, letting her know that she had things to do and would be leaving early. The approval dinged right back as Bebe knew it would. She had more paid time off and sick leave than almost anyone else in the company. Next, she grabbed up her phone and sent a quick text to her friend Linda Royce.

Tea time? I need a break.

She didn't wait for an answer, instead turning to face Emma. She cleared her throat. "Hey, Emma. I'm gonna pop out early. I have some errands that can't wait. So, I guess I'll see you tomorrow?"

Emma smiled, and the sweetness of it shredded the edges of Bebe's heart. "Sure! Be safe out there amongst the English."

Bebe scrunched up her nose. "English? Oh, is that an Irish thing?"

Emma laughed and pivoted her chair so she could better see Bebe. "Not exactly. It's from one of my favorite movies about an Amish family heading out into a big city. The grandfather says this to his grandson and the grandson's mom. Oooh!" She brightened swiftly. "We'll have to watch it together. I think you'd like it."

Bebe relaxed her face and smiled. Emma. You had to…love her.

She took her lunch bag from her drawer and folded it into her briefcase, placing her reader next to it. "I'd really like that, Emma. We'll do that."

Bebe took one more nourishing glance at Emma's beautiful countenance before leaving the office and closing the door gently behind her.

CHAPTER FOURTEEN

Teasingly Sweet Tea

Linda had responded by the time Bebe reached her car, and she was heartily glad to discover that her friend could join her. Not that she would tell Linda what had been chipping away at her composure lately, as they remained only acquaintances, but at least spending quality, familiar time with Linda would skew her thoughts back to a more normal vein.

Teasingly Sweet was a small but elegantly appointed tearoom on the east side of Albuquerque. Bebe had first come there with her mother to celebrate important events as a child, and she had continued the tradition on her own, not even needing events to savor the delectable offerings.

She stepped into the cool, wood-paneled lobby and strode to the tall butcher block counter in the back right corner where she was greeted by a pleasant but unfamiliar young woman. "Hello. I'm sorry but I've neglected to make a reservation. Do you, by any chance, have any rooms free?" Bebe inquired hopefully.

"Tina, allow me to introduce my friend Bebe Simmons. She's one of our most cherished clients." Teasingly Sweet's owner, Kayt Evans, had approached from behind Bebe and laid one palm on the back of Bebe's blazer. The enticing herbal scent of tea seemed to follow Kayt, and Bebe took in a deep breath of it.

Bebe turned and hugged the short, plump proprietor. "Hello, Kayt. It's always so good to see you."

Kayt's hug was warm and comforting. She laughed as she let Bebe go. "You just say that 'cause I give you the best rooms in the place."

Tina laughed. "It's very nice to meet you, Ms. Simmons."

Bebe grinned at both ladies. "Well, the room may have something to do with it, but it is still always good to see you. And nice to meet you, Tina."

"She'll be in the coral room," Kayt told Tina as she led the way along a long, dimly lit hallway lined with curtained tea rooms on either side. The coral room was one of Bebe's favorites because the sofas were incredibly comfy and it was filled with adorable coral-hued stuffed animals just begging for a cuddle. Bebe fully realized the idea of cuddling stuffies, as they were called, was considered juvenile, but nevertheless, she found doing so during her tea times a perfect counterpoint to her somewhat sterile life.

"Ahh, this is wonderful," she said as Kayt ushered her in. "Will you ask Tina to be on the lookout for my friend Linda?"

"Is she the woman with short gray hair and the tortie glasses?" Kayt squinted one eye as though remembering.

Bebe laughed. "That would be her, the one that looks like a schoolteacher."

"Hey, I don't pigeonhole you into an editor box," a low voice said from the curtained doorway.

Bebe and Kayt both turned to face the newcomer.

"Hey, I'm a realist," Bebe quipped. "We yam what we yam."

Kayt laughed and gestured for Linda to come in as she stepped past her. "I'll send Charles to take your orders in a few. Enjoy!"

"Thanks, Kayt," Bebe said.

Linda pulled Bebe into a brief hug and placed her bag on the farthest sofa. "I just love it when she gives us this room," she said as she lifted a large coral-colored teddy bear with a bright blue bow tie on his neck. She hugged him as she took a seat on the sofa across from Bebe.

Bebe lifted an oversized rag doll from a nearby chair and seated herself across from Linda. "I'm glad you could get away," she said.

Linda pursed her mouth as she shifted her overlarge glasses farther up her nose. "Spring break. One of my favorite times."

"Not to mention that, as the boss, you get to come and go as you please."

"As if," Linda said with a derisive snort.

Bebe passed Linda one of the small, engraved menus and silence fell as they perused them. Deciding on Earl Grey tea, as usual, Bebe set the menu aside and studied her friend.

Linda was the dean of The Helen D. Mondragon School, an expensive private school for girls aged five to seventeen. Bebe had met Linda when they were both English majors at the University of Virginia. Seeing her in the library as often as herself, Bebe had been intrigued. Could it be that there was someone else as addicted to extensive knowledge as she? Their paths had physically crossed one day in an elevator on the grounds of the university and Linda had struck up a conversation. Discovering that Linda was also from New Mexico had cemented their cordial friendship. Linda was one of the most well-informed people that Bebe had ever encountered, and that was saying a lot.

After college, they had both, oddly enough, returned to New Mexico. Bebe had been first, returning to Albuquerque to work at TWEI and Linda sometime later, after marrying her Virginia boyfriend and spending a few years there near his family. During her first pregnancy, though, Linda had become homesick, and they had decided to move to the Rio Rancho area to be near her family. Now, three kids later and with a teaching degree under her belt, Linda ran the Mondragon School while her husband, Brent, worked at the Intel plant in Rio Rancho.

Linda set her menu aside. "Going for cinnamon tea today," she announced to the room. She adjusted her skirt over her ample thighs and sighed. "I need some spice."

Bebe grinned. "Oh, really. Brent not spicy enough for you these days?"

Linda gave her a churlish look. "He's plenty enough for me," she said in a low tone. "Now we just need to find a man for you. And it's not Earl Grey."

Bebe's mouth fell open in mock indignation. "How did you know what I was going to order?"

Linda grunted and shifted in her chair. "When don't you order Earl Grey?"

"It is my favorite," Bebe agreed thoughtfully. "Shall we do the full tea?"

"You bet, I'm starving. Lunch was a nonstarter today. Too much bookwork."

"I'm always a bit amazed at the amount of paperwork it takes to run a private school."

Charles arrived in the doorway. He looked like a stereotypical surfer boy but was probably just a New Mexico college student working his way through.

"Hello!" he chirped cheerfully. "I'm Charles, here to bring you some teasingly sweet joy."

Both women groaned at the intro and Charles was the first to laugh, drawing the other two into the merriment.

"Kayt did not tell you to say that!" Bebe said with some surety.

Charles looked sheepish and his cheeks pinkened. "True. I just thought I'd try it out. Not so good, huh?"

Linda just shook her head and exchanged a mischievous glance with Bebe. "I'm not so sure it jives with the tearoom aesthetic."

"Hmm, maybe not. So, finding my decorum, would you two like to know how the ordering works?"

"Oh no," Bebe said. "We're old hats at this. I'll start with a pot of Earl Grey and I'll decide later what the other two will be."

Linda nodded in agreement. "And I bet one of them will be the lemon," she added. "I'd like the Asian Cinnamon blend for my first pot, and we definitely want the full four-tier tea." She hugged her teddy closer, adjusting his position on her lap.

"I thought you two looked familiar," Charles said. "The teas sound wonderful. I'll have them sent right out."

"Old hat," Bebe said musingly after Charles had disappeared. "Some tearooms have Victorian hats that their patrons can wear while they have tea. That might be fun."

"Obviously, you've never worked with children. Head lice are real."

"Oh no. I'm sure they clean them." She nevertheless examined the huge doll she was cuddling to her chest. "Do you think these are okay?"

Linda shrugged. "Probably. I wouldn't worry too much about it. This place is spotless. I bet they fumigate it regularly."

Bebe nodded. "Yes, Kayt would do that. She likes things done a certain way."

"It shows. So, paperwork. You'd be amazed at the state-level crap that even a private school has to deal with."

"You should have moved to a Montessori platform so you could have more freedom." Bebe played with the doll's pinkish, yarn-like hair.

"Montessori are usually state schools these days. They have even more to file than I do. At least private schools don't have to report compulsory education findings to the state, but we do have to answer that issue on our charter. So, it can be a lot. Plus dealing with some crazy, entitled parents." The last was imparted in a whisper so as not to be overheard.

"Hello, ladies. Who gets the Earl Grey?" A pleasantly smiling college girl stood in the doorway, a pot of tea in each hand.

Bebe raised her hand and the young girl placed their pots on the table and covered them with thick, quilted cozies that she pulled from her apron pocket.

"Shall I pour?" she asked.

Bebe lifted her flowered china cup and allowed the server to fill it. As the server poured Linda's cinnamon tea, Bebe lifted two cubes of sugar from the bowl on the table and pushed the small creamer pitcher toward Linda.

"So, tell me what's been going on. Is work going well?" Linda asked, cradling her cup in her folded hands and sitting back. The bear responded to her movement and slid into the niche between Linda and the sofa arm.

Bebe crossed her legs and sighed, knowing where her thoughts would go. "Let's see. We have a new employee, a new software troubleshooter."

Linda sipped her tea, savoring the mouthful before swallowing it. "Troubleshooter, huh? Why did Thomas feel like he needed that?"

Bebe placed her teacup on the low table and pulled the rag doll closer to her chest. "It wasn't Thomas exactly. It was the editorial floor manager."

"That Ralph guy you told me about?" Linda pushed a strand of her short salt-and-pepper hair behind one ear.

Bebe nodded. "He's being creepy about her, though. Like hanging around all the time and asking her these inane questions."

Linda frowned. "We had a teacher like that once. He ended up in jail when he got too close to one of the girls. You might want to nip that in the bud as soon as you can."

Bebe took a deep breath. "What can I do? How did you handle it?"

"Here you go, ladies," Charles said, breezing into the room "I'll remind you, savory is on the bottom two tiers, scones are above that, then sweets on the top. Today's special is on the scone tier, Irish whiskey butter." He grinned and his eyes twinkled. "Let us know what you think of it. Remember, plates and extra silver are on the sideboard. I'll check in on you shortly, but give a shout if you need anything at all."

Then Charles was gone and Bebe watched as Linda chose a small shepherd's pie from the tall tea stand. "So, what should I do, really?"

"Watch him like a hawk," Linda advised around a mouthful of pastry.

CHAPTER FIFTEEN

Lunch and Liquid Aminos

Thursday rose with the hint of summer, and Emma's bus ride to work was hot even though fans fore and aft struggled mightily to move some air. Emma was busy moving some worrying thoughts around. She was dreading the mandated party slated for the next evening. She wasn't dwelling on what to wear and how she might be received by a larger group of coworkers. Instead, she was focused on the possibility of spending quality social time with her office mate. She realized now how Bebe continued to affect her. And agonized about how Bebe felt toward her. They'd never talked about sexual preference, of course, and Emma wondered what their friendship entailed. Bebe was hard to read beyond the superficial sharing of her esoteric knowledge. But did Emma really want more? She was at a precarious crossroad in her life. The escape from Donna had been harrowing, and getting involved with someone new might not be the best idea.

Emma shifted on her seat, glad she'd worn a sleeveless shirt and a light denim pair of jeans. She pushed a forefinger into her bottom lip as if she could anchor her restless thoughts.

And then there was the work thing. Another layer of impossibility. It was never a good idea to date in the workplace. This rankled her, as how else were career-dedicated workers supposed to *meet* dating material, if not at the job? She sighed. The whole idea of dating Bebe was ridiculous. So said her brain. Her hands, however, even a day later, still remembered the touch of Bebe's skin. Soft, warm, electric.

Emma pushed the disturbing thoughts aside as she exited the bus and walked the short distance to TWEI. She just couldn't shape her mind into professional mode today. She idly wondered where Bebe had disappeared to yesterday. Did she have a partner, a husband? Strange how that subject had never come up during their busily chatted lunches. She knew a bit about Bebe's parents, especially how their advice had shaped many of Bebe's actions, but little more than that. Tapping her card key on the reader and pulling open the tall glass panels, she vowed to divert Bebe's interesting tales toward a more personal level.

The morning was a busy one, with Bebe opening packages of manuscripts and pasting on barcodes while Emma was busy with several new code sequences for data entry that she'd been sent. Unfortunately, her fast scans wouldn't work on these as she had to test run each segment manually and fix any problems she encountered. Lunch was a welcome respite.

"What is that you're spraying on? Soy sauce?" Bebe eyed Emma's rice dish curiously.

"Oh no, soy sauce is fermented. This is a special, lighter concoction made by one of my favorite companies." She turned so Bebe could see the yellow label. "It is so much better than soy sauce, and with less sodium."

"Really? I don't think I've seen that before. Liquid aminos? Sounds kinda weird." She frowned.

"Here, try some." She held the spray bottle above Bebe's salad and, after receiving a nod of permission, lightly sprayed a top leaf with the sauce. Bebe eyed the brown liquid suspiciously, then gingerly lifted the lettuce to her mouth.

Emma smiled expectantly as Bebe's dark eyes lit with pleasure as she chewed.

"Oh, my gosh. That is so good! Wait, I gotta look this up." She pulled out her phone and tapped it eagerly.

"It's made from soy—" Emma began but Bebe quickly interrupted.

"It's a liquid protein concentrate which uses acids." She looked at Emma while lifting an eyebrow. "Acids?"

"Keep reading," Emma ordered. "The acid is neutralized with baking soda."

"On soybeans, which leaves concentrated amino acids that are more nutritious than soy sauce, with slightly, only slightly, less sodium. Soy sauce is different in that it adds extra salt."

"As you probably know," Emma added. "Amino acids are the building blocks of protein. Consuming them is important for good health, especially if you follow a vegan or vegetarian diet."

"Hmm," Bebe continued. "Liquid aminos have sixteen amino acids. Your body needs twenty different amino acids to grow and function properly."

"Yep, and aminos are also rich in umami, that savory fifth taste."

Bebe leaned and turned the bottle so she could read the label more closely. "Nope, no coconuts. Some are made from coconuts."

"Yes, but they're fermented. I like these better, more minimally processed," Emma said.

Bebe licked her lips. "This really does taste good."

"It's sort of like soy sauce, as they have the same base, but I think it's lighter. Also, there's no wheat added to this so it's even gluten free. It's made from only two ingredients—soybeans and purified water—so it's vegan and contains no chemicals, coloring, or preservatives."

Bebe pushed her bowl closer to Emma. "Might I have some more, please, sir?"

Emma grinned. "Of course, you silly Oliver Twist. The correct phrase is 'please, sir, I want some more.'"

"Please, ma'am, I want some more." Bebe watched as Emma freely sprayed her salad, then pulled her bowl close again. "You should do a TV commercial for this stuff."

"Speaking of soy sauce," Bebe said sometime later. "Did you know it was originally created as a way to have more salty taste when salt was super expensive?"

Emma looked at Bebe's angular face, enjoying how her cheeks pinkened when she was imparting some new nugget of knowledge. "No, I didn't. Makes sense though. Soybeans are more plentiful."

"They put it, the soybeans, in with fish and a little salt. They let it ferment for about six months and it became this goopy paste that they added to food, like we do ketchup."

"Goopy?"

Bebe frowned in mock annoyance. "Well, thick and...and moldy-like from the grains they added."

Emma curled her lip in distaste.

"Hey, this was more than two thousand years ago. Mold was important back then. So, by the time of the Han dynasty, they started fermenting mostly just soybeans because they developed a separate recipe for their fish sauce."

"I can't believe you know all this. I mean, do you even cook?" Emma watched Bebe closely.

Bebe had the grace to look sheepish. "Um, no, but that's beside the point. Ancient archaeological digs gave us most of this info. If I can continue now? By the time of the Song dynasty, like 1200 anno domini, the term *soy sauce* had become the accepted name for it."

"So, it became vegetarian at that point?" Emma closed her empty food container and pulled a fruit cup from her lunch bag.

"It did, especially when Buddhism came to Japan from China in the seventh century. From there, it spread to other Asian countries, like Korea and even the Philippines." Bebe put the top on her empty salad bowl and shoved it into her bag.

"Then when did it come to the States?" Emma asked, her mind thinking of other fermented things like vinegar and kimchi. She wasn't a fan of those, but she did like sourdough bread.

"Oh, that was the Dutch East India Company. They brought barrels of the stuff from Japan. Wait, it went to the Netherlands first, then on to Hawaii in the early 1900s. The first commercial brand of it was made in Hawaii by the La Choy company in the 1930s."

Emma grinned and licked fruit nectar from her spoon. "That is way cool. I can't believe you know all this stuff."

Bebe seemed embarrassed by the compliment. "Well. You've probably figured out I read a lot."

"Um-hmm. I figured. Do they really add mold and yeasts to it?"

"'Fraid so." She opened a packet of crackers. "Traditional soy sauces take months to make, but they're filtered at the end to get all the particulates out."

"Still. I dunno."

Bebe popped a cracker into her mouth and comically tried to talk around it. She laughed, covering her mouth with her hand.

"Yes?" Emma inquired teasingly.

Bebe lowered the hand a moment later, cheeks crimson still. "I was just going to say, you have these delicious amino acids so you may never need soy sauce again."

"Yes, and now that I know you like them as well, we'll keep this bottle here at the office."

Bebe's eyes deepened. "Do you have more at home?"

"Oh, heck yeah. I buy it by the gallon. And I even have another spray bottle," she answered, rolling her eyes.

Bebe laughed and snatched up the spray bottle, holding it close to her chest as though to protect it from marauding hordes. "Yes, let's do that," she whispered loudly.

CHAPTER SIXTEEN

The Spring Fling

Friday night was considerably cooler than the morning had been, and Bebe was glad she'd brought her blazer. She shrugged into it as she exited her car and handed her valet key to the blue-clad attendant outside the downtown Albuquerque hotel.

Bebe had always loved this historic hotel, even though she seldom stayed there. Events there were fun, though, and the staff was always attentive and pleasant. She stepped back and stared up admiringly at the tall brick tower before stepping back under the portico area. She knew Thomas had reserved the smaller meeting room, which also provided access to the covered garden areas. It was her particular favorite of all the meeting area options, and she was grateful that TWEI's current employee roster still fit in it. If the company continued to grow as it had, they'd soon have to rent one of the bigger meeting rooms. Bebe sighed. She wanted Thomas to be successful, but she truly cherished the small family feel of the upstart company.

"Hey, girl!" Sheila Grant came across to greet Bebe and gave her a one-armed hug. "You guys have outdone yourselves tonight."

"Hey, I had nothing to do with it. I attended one setup meeting and then Ada and Cathy had at it."

"Connie helped, too, and tried to rope me in. I just had too much going on. I told you they downsized at the community college and Nina lost her job, right?" At Bebe's nod, she continued, "Well, she's been talking my ear off. She's so depressed."

"Is she here tonight?"

"Oh, I insisted. She's gonna have a good time if it kills me." She laughed, and Bebe joined in.

They had been walking steadily through the expansive main lobby and toward the meeting area. When they entered the room, Bebe let loose a low whistle. "Oh, man!"

Sheila shared a victorious grin. "Didn't I tell you?"

In holding with the spring fling theme, Ada and the others had decorated the entire room with a riot of spring colors. Using flowers, real and artificial, they had decorated every available surface with bright white, grass green, Barbie pink, robin's egg blue, and a beautiful pale tangerine color. Even the real flowers had been dyed in those colors, and matching ribbons swept gracefully with the slightest breeze or movement nearby. Looking up, Bebe was amazed to see long ribbons and crepe paper streamers tied to banners proclaiming spring well-wishes. The gals had outdone themselves.

"Doesn't it smell heavenly?" Nina said, approaching the two. "All those flowers!"

Bebe leaned and hugged Nina carefully. Nina was a tiny woman, five feet tall and ninety pounds sopping wet. Every time Bebe held her, she was worried she'd break her. Her size seemed an odd pairing with her wife, Sheila, who had a larger, lankier frame. "How goes the job hunt, sweetie? Any luck?"

Nina frowned and rolled her eyes. "What is with this town? I figured I was a shoo-in at least at one of the colleges, but there's no empty slots anywhere."

"How would you feel about teaching at a private girls' school? High school maybe? I know it would be a step down from being a college prof, but history is history, right?"

Nina's eyes widened. "That would be so great. Do you know of any openings?"

Bebe frowned and spread her hands wide. "I'm not one hundred percent sure but I'll check with a friend of mine. She might have something."

Sheila grabbed Bebe's hand and squeezed it tight. "Oh, thank you so much, B. That would be way cool. I think my girl is going absolutely stir-crazy with nobody to teach stuff to."

"So, where's our new girl?" said a soft, deep voice behind Bebe. She turned to see Dam and his beautiful wife, Stevie.

"Stevie!" she exclaimed, throwing her arms about the stout Native woman. "I haven't seen you in so long. How are you?"

Stevie grinned, flashing a bright golden incisor. "I'm doing well. It's good to see you again."

Bebe loved the way Stevie spoke. Though curt and to the point, it was almost musical. If she had been gay and single, Bebe might have moved on her because she was just so beautiful. Her pale brown face was smooth and round and it was dominated by snapping, intelligent brown eyes. Her calm, no-nonsense demeanor also drew Bebe in.

"So, Emma?" Dam asked. He was looking particularly fine, dressed in khaki chinos and a patterned button-down shirt. His usual sandals had even been replaced by soft-looking penny loafers.

Bebe glanced around the room. "I don't know, Dam. I do know she was coming tonight but I haven't spied her yet."

"No worries," Dam said with a shrug. "I just wanted Stevie to meet her."

"I'll send her to you if I see her," Bebe promised.

Dam and Stevie walked away, and to her surprise, Thomas approached her, slowly working his way through his friendly, welcoming employees.

"When did you get back in town?" Bebe said, studying his face for signs of distress.

Thomas was a handsome man, though he grew his thick dark hair too long for Bebe's tastes. He often pulled it back into a ponytail with shorter pieces loosening to frame his face. He was thin and was wearing long board shorts and a bright orange Myrtle Beach T-shirt.

"Nice you dressed up," she teased, pointing a forefinger to his clothing. "Aren't you going to speak to the employees?"

He shook his head. "No can do. I have a seven o'clock presser fundraiser at Spence's."

"Please tell me you'll change your clothes."

He snorted. "Of course. I'll even put on the penguin suit. Listen, if you feel it's appropriate, will you say a few words? I'd ask Ralph or one of the other managers, but...well, you know."

Bebe nodded. "Sure. What should I say?"

"Oh, just the usual, thanks for being with us, trusting us. Here's to another great year."

"Be glad to, if the opportunity presents itself."

Thomas shrugged. "Yeah, informal is good, too, so don't belabor it. See you later."

Bebe blinked her eyes and the introverted software genius was gone, slipping out a side door.

CHAPTER SEVENTEEN

Spring

Bebe was sitting at a round table talking to Stewart Kent, one of the software engineers, when she saw her. She still pretended interest in what the shy, older gentleman was saying but her mind danced the Charleston in appreciation of the vision before her.

Emma had unbound her hair, and the wavy curls created a gleaming backdrop for her freckled face and green eyes made luminous by the hotel chandeliers. She was wearing a gauzy, sleeveless summer dress that fell to midcalf, and the dark blue color of it popped when set against her coppery hair. Though she wore summery sandals, she carried a black sweater over one forearm, obviously in case the weather cooled.

She was breathtaking.

"Stewart," Bebe said when there was a break in conversation. "I hope you'll excuse me. I need to welcome our newest employee and help her feel comfortable here. You remember how daunting that was, don't you?"

Stewart ran one hand across his short beard and grinned. "I do, indeed, even though it was almost twenty years ago. Go,

go on and welcome her. Bring her over so we can meet her."
He made a shooing motion and Bebe patted the hand he had
resting on the table before walking away.

"Well, aren't you pretty?" Bebe said after Emma had freed
herself from talking with Laretta.

Emma frowned. "Oh, don't you start, too. I've had just about
all the compliments I can stand, thanks to Ralph corralling me
as soon as I walked in."

Bebe groaned. "Oh no, just ignore him like the rest of us do.
Come sit at our table, it's where all the cool cats hang out."

Emma lifted one eyebrow but allowed Bebe to guide her
across the room.

"Emma!" called Pol Donald as they approached. "You're
late!"

Emma sat in the chair Bebe pulled out for her. "I know, I
apologize. The bus schedules run loose and wild in this city and
there was a delay on Central."

"Oh man, you shoulda give us a call. We woulda come get
you." This was said by a beautiful, dark-eyed woman sitting next
to Pol. She was wearing an attractive forest-green wraparound
dress that dipped low in the front, exposing her glorious pale
cleavage. Her long dark hair, pulled back on one side, fell across
her shoulders.

"Oh, Emma," Pol said, leaning forward. "This is my
girlfriend, Gwen. I forgot you haven't met her yet."

Emma reached across the table and took Gwen's hand. "It's
so nice to meet you and I sincerely thank you for the offer. I'll
try to remember it if I ever get in this situation again."

Pol smiled and sat back in her chair, adjusting her vest,
preening because Emma obviously liked her girl.

"Hello, Emma, good to see you again," Stan Ramey, Edie's
assistant, said, bobbing his head at her. He'd come alone this
evening but Bebe knew he'd always been a close friend to Pol
and Gwen.

"Emma, I don't think you've met Stewart yet," Bebe said.
"He's one of our earliest employees, beginning with us as a
crackerjack proofreader. He now works down with Dam, and
he and his wife, Dorothea, have been married for forty years."

"Yes, and it's amazing he's been able to put up with me that long," Dorothea said, extending her hand to Emma. She was studying the new girl with overt curiosity as her free hand moved to check the lay of her short ivory hair.

"Now, hon," Stewart protested good-naturedly. "I think we need to flip that right around." He reached and patted the hand that she had returned to the tabletop.

"Wow," Emma exclaimed. "Forty years. I can't even imagine that. My parents are coming up on thirty-eight years together and I thought that was a long time."

Bebe sat back and watched as Emma easily engaged in conversation with their coworkers. She was a natural socializer and Bebe felt a shard of jealousy, or maybe loss for what could have been in her life. She did well when working, but her social skills away from work were somewhat lacking. By choice, actually, but still...

"There she is," Dam said, pausing on his way past the table. He had a full plate of food in one hand but beckoned Emma to follow him with the other. "You have to come meet my Stevie. She says we can't leave the party until she meets you."

Emma stood obediently. "Well, excuse me, guys. I'll be right back."

"Why does she want to meet me?" she asked, gazing up at Dam.

Dam laughed and wrapped an arm about Emma's shoulders, leading her away. "Oh, you think I haven't been singing your praises at home? Get real, girl."

Pol was watching Bebe. "Well, she's a bit of something, isn't she?" she said finally.

Bebe turned and met the intense, almost knowing gazes of Pol, Gwen, and Stan. She glanced at Stewart, but he was focused on the DJ, who was setting up her station. Dorothea had left the table a few minutes earlier, saying she was checking out the food offerings.

Bebe blushed but tried to keep her voice even. "She's a good worker. Dam says she's helped him so much in setting up new modules."

"Mm-hmm," Pol said, a smirk brightening her face.

"Look—" Bebe began but was interrupted by Gwen.

"She's really beautiful, isn't she?"

Stan cleared his throat. "Not classically, of course, because of the freckles and the pale skin that goes with it."

"But that hair," Gwen said. "It lights up the room."

Stan nodded. He returned his gaze to Bebe. "How is it working with her? I've always heard that redheads have vicious tempers."

Bebe blinked her eyes. "No! I mean, I think that's an old wives' tale. She's never been anything but pleasant since she's been here."

"I hear you two have lunch every day," Pol said, watching for Bebe's reaction. "What do you guys talk about?"

Bebe gathered calm about herself like a precious shawl. "What don't we talk about?" she replied. She stood. "I think I'll get something to eat."

She could hear Pol and Gwen chuckling as she left the table, but she was determined not to let it bother her. She got in line behind Edie.

"Are you having a good time?" she asked the science floor manager. Edie was dressed in pink leggings topped by a bright pink and green floral shirt. "You look so pretty in that top."

Edie grinned, laugh lines extending upward along the sides of her scalp. "Well, aren't you sweet? I like to dress a bit more feminine when I'm away from work."

"Did Louie come with you tonight?"

"He did. Who do you think I got these stuffed mushrooms for?" She glanced at her plate with disgust and shuddered. "I can't stand mushrooms. Slimy little fungus."

Bebe laughed. She was surprised that Louie, a fifty-year-old vegan hippie, would even eat anything that was fried. "Well, I hope you'll get something else for yourself."

Edie squinted at Bebe. "Of course. Have you ever seen me pass up free food?"

Bebe smiled and shook her head as Edie moved away.

"I like her," Emma said, approaching on the right side. "She makes bald a fashion statement, you know?"

"That she does," Bebe agreed. "She's been at TWEI almost as long as I have, so we've known one another a long time. She's always been super confident."

"Speaking of that, someone said you'd been at TWEI for, like, fifteen years?" Emma lifted a plate and placed a heaping spoon of potato salad on it.

"Yep, right out of college."

"Did you study publishing? Is that why you came here?" She bypassed the huge serving dish of pork barbeque and went for the baked beans.

"No, English mostly. I came back to Albuquerque because I have family here and, when I heard about the company, I thought I'd give it a try. I liked it, so I stayed on." Bebe compared their plates and smiled. They were loaded with the same vegetarian foods.

"It seems like a good place to work," Emma mused as she eyed a flower-themed charcuterie board. She lifted her eyes to Bebe until Bebe met her gaze. "I really like working here."

Bebe's gaze lingered on Emma's, and for a brief moment, she forgot where she was.

CHAPTER EIGHTEEN

Emma Eyes Acceptance

The hotel the company had chosen for the spring fling was amazing—a big, beautiful brick and adobe structure. The interior lobby featured beautiful rustic Saltillo tile and was filled with worn but comfortable-looking leather sofas fronted with heavy wooden coffee tables. Majestic earth-toned armchairs, with substantial wooden end tables, had been positioned to create several cozy conversation areas in the expansive room.

During her brief time in Albuquerque, Emma had never had the opportunity to visit this part of town. Upon viewing it from the bus, she had liked the way the area had undergone an obvious urban renewal but still maintained its historic Western atmosphere.

An atmosphere that was, luckily, very evident in this hotel.

Once inside, she had followed the signs and eventually emerged into the room designated as the TWEI Spring Fling. The pastel floral and ribbon decorations for their company party were superb, transforming the old, Spanish-style hotel section into a flower-bedecked, magical wonderland.

Emma was overwhelmed by seeing the thirty-plus employees of TWEI all in one place. They were a motley group, as were their significant others. Ages ranged from about twenty all the way up to some, like Stewart, who appeared to be in their late seventies. Oddly enough, there seemed to be a good portion of alternative lifestyles, mainly gay and goth. When she'd met Pol with Gwen, she'd experienced an aha moment. Of course, Pol—a small, typical baby butch who'd immediately set off Emma's gaydar—would have a beautiful femme girlfriend. She felt comforted by the fact that if she *did* find a new girlfriend, the relationship would be welcomed by the workgroup.

She returned her attention to Ada, Laretta, and their plus-ones, a group who had welcomed her and Bebe to their table when their old seats had been filled by newcomers.

"I never would have thought that medical and scientific publishing would have boomed for as long as it has," Ada's husband, Paul, was saying. "I mean, Thomas and the others took a hell of a risk."

Bebe nodded as she took a bite of green pea salad. "They did. But I guess they saw an easier way to get the scientific method out there."

"I hear about that method all the time," Ada said. "What does that mean, exactly?"

Paul nodded in agreement and watched Bebe expectantly.

"Hmm." She placed her fork next to her plate. "The method of explaining an idea actually goes all the way back to Aristotle, but it didn't come into common usage until Francis Bacon started using it in the sixteenth century."

"But how does it work? The idea?" Craig asked. He was Laretta's date for the evening and was a handsome Black man who carried himself regally. He was a banker, a loan officer, and Laretta had met him while applying for a loan to build a gazebo on her front lawn.

"Oh, right. The scientific method is to observe something, then define it and question it. Then you gather your data together and hypothesize why what you observed is happening. Then you test that hypothesis and predict why it will happen again."

She noted several blank looks around the table and decided to provide an example. "One, you define the problem—let's say people in London are dying from cholera. Two, you gather background information. Where is it occurring? What links the people who are sick? You find out there is one specific place that the cholera seems to be concentrated in. Then you form a hypothesis. Maybe the community well located in that central location is what's making people sick. Cholera is a waterborne illness, after all. Then you observe what happens when you close down that well, testing your hypothesis. The final step is drawing conclusions. That well must be infected with cholera because once people stopped getting their water from that particular well, the cases of illness dropped dramatically."

"And in a scientific paper," Laretta added. "You have your abstract, which explains the paper, then your introduction, which explains what you will try to prove. Then you enter the methods you will use and the results you get. The final part is the discussion, which reinforces the introduction, and then the references. Graphs, tables, and photos can be used as well."

Ada nodded. "I've looked in several of the journals. There's always so much information in there."

"I'd hazard a guess and say that most of the progress humankind has made has come about due to scientific publishing," Emma added. "And scientists being able to reproduce the results and improve on them."

"And it covers so many areas," Bebe said. "There's advances in medicine, from illness all the way to nutrition. Then there's science, from space to microbes, plus we also do journals on certain sports, like skateboarding, for example, and other special interests. There's no end to them."

"I bet Thomas is rolling in the dough," Paul mused.

Bebe and Laretta laughed. "You'd never know it, the way he dresses," Bebe said.

"True. He's got the college frat boy down to a science, don't you think? You should have seen him earlier, wearing shorts and flip-flops," Laretta said.

Emma's mouth flew open. Had she missed meeting Thomas again? "He was here?"

Bebe smiled at her. "Only for a minute. He had some other event he had to go to."

"Probably a party at Lintey Beach," Laretta said, then guffawed at her own joke.

Emma screwed her nose up. The name sounded vaguely familiar but she knew there were no beaches in Albuquerque. "Lintey Beach? Where's that?"

Bebe laid a palm on her forearm and Emma felt suffused with warmth. "It's just a little sandpile down on the river. Laretta was just being a smart-ass."

Laretta grinned and took a sip of her cocktail.

Emma found her gaze wandering across the room and she marveled at how welcoming everyone had been. Then she sighed sadly, remembering her circumstances. How welcoming would they be if they knew how she was lying to them on a daily basis?

CHAPTER NINETEEN

Bebe at Emma's Place

Later that evening, when the music had died down to easy listening tunes, Bebe insisted that she be allowed to give Emma a lift home.

"I know my city, even if you think you'll be perfectly safe," she asserted. "You just don't take chances here. Too many drug problems that lead to a lot of crime."

Emma had agreed, and soon she was ensconced in Bebe's spacious Subaru. The night had indeed turned chilly, and Bebe was glad Emma had donned her sweater.

They made some small talk but also enjoyed a good bit of comfortable silence as they passed through the brightly lit city streets. Soon—too soon in Bebe's mind—they reached Emma's apartment complex and Emma guided her to the proper entrance.

"So. You'll come up for a cuppa? I have some nice black that my mam imports from Ireland." Emma peered in at Bebe from the open passenger door.

Bebe glanced across at Emma, realizing anew how much she craved getting to know this enigmatic redhead. It was uncharacteristic for her, and she felt inundated with trepidation. Yet she persevered, helpless against her own curiosity and attraction.

"Sure. Wait here for me while I park."

Emma closed the car door and Bebe pulled into one of the empty slots outside the building.

Though nervous, Bebe felt reassured by Emma's bright welcoming smile as she approached on foot.

"It's this way," Emma said.

They walked side by side in silence along the sidewalk and then through a heavy side door into a small vestibule with a wide, metal stairway stretching to the upper floors.

The apartment building, though old by modern standards, was scrupulously clean and appeared well cared for. "This is a nice place," Bebe murmured, grasping one of the sturdy handrails and studying the grates that made up the metal steps.

Emma laughed. "Maybe, but no elevator. After a few months of carrying groceries up two flights, two floors, this place loses a little of its charm."

"Oh, I bet," Bebe agreed. She shrugged. "At least you'll keep in good shape." She made her voice as positive as possible.

Emma rolled her eyes and led the way upstairs. "I've sure gotten used to it during the past five months. I guess you get what you pay for."

"So, the rent's cheaper? Than what?" Bebe was disturbed by how entranced she was by the curve of Emma's calves as she mounted the steps ahead of Bebe. Her light summer dress swirled with each step, and the occasional glimpse of the soft, alabaster skin behind Emma's knees made Bebe's heart stutter in her chest. She found herself deliberately slowing her ascent just so she could savor the view.

"Than most of the others I looked at. It took forever to find one I could afford. Prices are crazy in this city," Emma replied.

Two floors later, they paused in front of a door bearing a large, beautifully crafted grapevine wreath.

"This is me," Emma said as she unlocked the door.

The first thing Bebe noticed was the lingering smell of incense. And not some plastic substitute, like those sold in department stores. This was the real deal temple incense, and it was made from a powdered resin that Bebe particularly liked. The second thing Bebe noticed was the smallness. The kitchen was little more than a galley, and the combined dining and living area wasn't much more than ten-foot square. Two doors off to the left obviously led to a bathroom and bedroom, probably equally as small. It was almost claustrophobic to Bebe, but Emma seemed to have made the most of the space, not over-filling it with furniture or sentimental clutter.

Bebe realized that Emma was nervously standing in the center of the room, awaiting her approval. Bebe answered truthfully.

"This is the cutest apartment I think I've ever seen. How did you end up finding it? Apartments in Albuquerque can be really scarce."

"Here, sit while I put the kettle on." She indicated a worn but comfortable-looking love seat.

Bebe settled herself and noted that, unlike her own parents' home, there was a decided lack of artwork on the walls. Not many knickknacks either. There was a coffee table with a stack of books and a laptop on it, and a small dining table in a corner of the kitchen area that held a monitor and computer tower. Bebe knew about minimalism, but this was the first time she'd actually seen it in person.

"Well," Emma answered, taking a seat across from Bebe in a pocked, woven recliner. "My friend Alice knows someone at that real estate firm on San Mateo." She frowned and pressed an index finger to her plump bottom lip. "Can't seem to remember the name, now. Anyway, she did the research and, pricewise, we winnowed it down to this place."

"And you've been here five months? How do you like it?"

Emma rose when the kettle clicked and brought back two mugs. "I can get you milk and sugar if you need it, but I want you to experience this tea first. I think it's just the best ever." She handed a steaming mug to Bebe. "Don't worry about coasters. You can just set it anywhere."

She regained her seat and continued as if there hadn't been a break in the conversation. "It's not the Taj Mahal, that's for sure, but, well, it kind of suits my needs at present."

"Man, this is delicious," Bebe said after taking a cautious sip from her mug. "I don't think I need anything else in it at all. You said your mother gets it from Ireland?"

Emma grinned and nodded. "She does. She has relatives there still and they stockpile the stuff for her and then ship it across the pond every six months or so. And, bless her heart, she shares with us children."

"She sounds nice. All I ever get from my mom are the occasional fancy lunch and token gifts for special occasions. Certainly nothing that helps promote our British roots."

"Ahh, British." Emma smiled at Bebe from across the mug held to her lips. "We're sworn enemies then."

Bebe scoffed at the statement. "We're both UK so we have to have a certain amount of détente. Wait. North or South Ireland?"

Emma placed her cup on the coffee table then leaned back. "We're the Republic, but my mam passed from the Catholic ages ago. She now tends to follow the old ways, you know, May Day and the other harvest or fertility festivals. I was brought up that way. I did have the choice to go to a Catholic school but I chose not to. I like her ways better. But, if you think about it, the old Irish rituals seem to mirror the Catholic rites."

Bebe was fascinated and heartily grateful that Emma wasn't a Jesus fanatic.

"What religion do you follow?" Emma asked curiously, tilting her head in that adorable way she had when she was listening.

"I don't want to tell you, as it may cause a rift," Bebe replied slowly.

"You know you can tell me anything and I won't judge you. I hope you realize that. Judging others isn't what friendship is about." Emma was frowning now, and it made Bebe feel regretful.

"It's just, I was raised in an atheist household. We read the Bible but only as an academic pursuit. We also studied just about every other religion out there but found them all lacking in some fundamental way." She watched Emma closely, seeking a reaction.

"Lots of folks believe God and Jesus are just composites created by man and that the Bible isn't necessarily a holy book. It's like that old Native American saying, which is close to what my family holds true as well. Loosely remembered, it says that if you put a Christian Bible out in the wind and the rain, it will eventually be destroyed. Their Bible *is* the wind and the rain."

"Wow, that's powerful," Bebe remarked quietly.

CHAPTER TWENTY

Saying Good Night

They had talked nonstop for more than four hours. And consumed half a box of black tea. The evening spent with just the two of them once more proved without question how easy they were together.

Emma was amazed yet again by the wealth of knowledge Bebe possessed. It almost made her speechless. How could one human brain hold that much knowledge? Who knew that Western Taipan snakes in Australia were the most venomous snakes in the world? Who knew that octopuses in the ocean had otherworldly DNA that probably came in on a meteor? And that they were highly intelligent, able to open jars and use tools? Who knew these things? That was so Bebe, just sharing her esoteric knowledge, always gently guiding Emma onto a new absorbing, unexpected topic. It was one of the things she cherished the most about their friendship.

Cherish. Emma had begun to realize that she cherished having Bebe in her life. She simply could not imagine a day in which Bebe didn't share a new node of knowledge with her. Or didn't look at her with those stormy yet admiring eyes. Eyes that were naturally dark fringed, with sweeping black eyelashes that would make anyone jealous.

She moved to the window and sighed. She couldn't see from this angle where Bebe had parked, but she knew—felt—that Bebe had already headed to her home, an apartment in Uptown Albuquerque. Emma tried to imagine what living in such a posh location would be like. She tried to imagine what Bebe's apartment would be like. Full of books, no doubt.

She turned away from the darkness outside and walked into the kitchen area. She ran a quick glance across her meager apartment, hoping that Bebe hadn't been too put off by it. She had seemed comfortable enough and had lingered, not rushing away.

Emma reached into the sink and touched a forefinger to the rim of the mug Bebe had used. She thought of those lips closing on that mug and knew she was in trouble. She was falling for her coworker in a big way. What was she supposed to do with that?

After almost a year of dealing with Donna, spending time with Bebe was a truly refreshing, almost healing life choice. Could she choose Bebe? Maybe she already had. Should she choose Bebe? Probably not.

She left the mug in the sink and turned off the kitchen light. She checked the door locks and, satisfied, turned off the lamp in her living room.

The bedroom was dark save a glow from the streetlight outside. Emma entered the bathroom instead, bathing the room in bright, sterile white light. She looked at herself in the mirror, seeing her dear mother's visage. What would lovely Foxy Dakota do in this situation?

"Mam? What now, Mama?" she whispered to the mirror. "I...I think I might be falling in love. For real this time. What should I do?"

The reflection offered no answers, so Emma slowly brushed her teeth, then her hair, and prepared for bed.

Their goodbyes that early morning hour had been tense. Had Bebe wanted to kiss her? Emma certainly would have welcomed it. Shyness seemed to have put both of them off it, though. There had been a hug of farewell, however, and Emma remembered the deep, Oriental scent of Bebe's perfume. She remembered the press of their bodies together. Bebe seemed so slim in appearance, but pressed against Emma, there had been an unexpected plushness to her that pulled Emma in.

Emma switched off the bathroom light and stared out into her darkened apartment, waiting for her eyes to adjust. She made her way cautiously to the bedroom and the bedside, then switched on the small lamp there. She still didn't know whether Bebe was a lesbian. They had both discussed veiled relationship issues, establishing that they were both single. Emma guessed that was something, at least.

She pulled back the coverlet and slid beneath it. Her pillow was soft and welcoming and she thought again of Bebe's softness. Pushing the thought away, she turned on her side and lifted the paperback from the nightstand. Many years ago it had been her favorite romance, and the dog-eared softcover proved it. It was a heterosexual romance, a historical one, and sometimes she felt a bit guilty for loving it so very much. Though well-read in romantic fiction, she'd yet to come across a lesbian romance that thrilled her as this one did.

She knew she needed to sleep and she knew it was the tea talking to her, but tomorrow was Saturday and she had no plans. So, she'd sleep as late as she dared, but tonight…tonight she would read. Tonight, the heroine in her book would be her beautiful Bebe, and Emma, a bit less masculine, would be the hero who pretended not to love Bebe but secretly knew she could not exist without her.

CHAPTER TWENTY-ONE

Donna Finds Emma

Emma's phone vibrated noisily on her wooden desktop and she snatched it up, glancing apologetically at Bebe. Checking the screen, she saw that the call was from an unfamiliar number. She was wary these days about answering unknown numbers. Just in case.

She frowned at her fear. This insanity had to stop. She was not going to live the rest of her life expecting shadow monsters. She pressed the answer button and immediately regretted the action. She gasped when the hated, sexy voice of Donna sounded in her ear.

"Hello, sweetheart—" Donna began but Emma cut her off with a harsh whisper.

"I am not your sweetheart and how did you get this number?" Emma muttered urgently.

"You really think I don't care enough to seek you out? You're my life, sweetheart. We belong together."

"Okay, I'm hanging up. And changing this number."

"Doesn't matter. We share an account now." There was an infuriating smug satisfaction in her tone.

"But…how?" Emma growled in frustration. "Don, so help me God—"

"Oh, don't give me any of that God crap. We both know that doesn't mean shit to you." The real Donna shone through.

"Go to hell, you. I'm hanging up now."

She disconnected the call then blocked the number. Aggravation and despair swamped her. Now she had to once again get a new number. And it sounded like she needed a new cell phone service provider. This time she couldn't cut corners and use a cheaper service. Obviously, if Donna could squirrel her way into Emma's account, Emma couldn't get by with saving a few bucks each month. You got what you paid for. Still, she was amazed that Donna had been able to sign onto Emma's account. She'd probably sweet-talked some witless girl at the second-rate phone company.

She breathed in a sudden gasp of panic. This meant that Donna knew her new name. How had she figured it out? What loophole had Emma missed?

This was a disaster. It meant that Donna quite possibly could turn up at TWEI at any time. She lifted her gaze and fixed it on the busily typing Bebe. Her new…love, her Bebe would find out all about her. Unbearable.

With a deep sigh, she turned back to her own monitor. She had so liked working here. She had hoped she might leap the hurdles and foster a real relationship. A tickle on her cheek let her know that a tear had escaped. She brushed it away along with her fear about Donna. Maybe if she did a really good job here, the management would overlook her lowbrow dyke drama. Maybe Bebe would understand what she'd been through.

But then everyone here would discover that she'd been in a relationship with not just a woman, but an abusive one. She sighed again and let fatalism come to the forefront. It was out of her hands now. At least she had only used a first initial with her new last name. Maybe that would help keep Donna confused for a while. Slow down her pursuit.

Though it was hard, she immersed herself in work until Bebe interrupted. "Are you ready for lunch? My stomach has been growling for the past fifteen minutes and I'm surrendering to it."

"Um, sure, sure," Emma said, her mind unfocused and still in panic mode. "Lemme make a quick call and I'll be right up."

Bebe smiled nervously at Emma. "Okay. Want me to get you an iced tea?"

Emma forced a smile. "Oh, that would be great. Thank you."

"No worries," Bebe replied, lifting her reader from her desk and tucking it under her arm. "See you in a bit."

Emma sighed and closed her hand onto the hated cell phone on her desk. "Damn! Damn, damn," she muttered as she pressed a button.

A sleepy greeting met her ear and she replied in a harsh whisper. "The bitch found me."

"No!" Alice's voice sharpened in dismay. "No, Pony, no! Don't tell me this shit first thing in the morning."

"I'm serious," Emma whispered, glancing around the office and to the door to make sure no one could hear.

"What did she do?"

Emma could picture Alice raising up in her big bed, short blond hair tousled, last night's makeup smeared around her bright blue eyes.

Emma took a deep breath. "She conned someone in the phone company. Put herself on my account. Got my number."

"She *called* you?" Alice's voice rang incredulously.

"She did," Emma wailed quietly.

"Oh, hun, we gotta get you somewhere else, somewhere safe. I don't know why you won't come and live here with me."

Emma, even in her fear, could sense Alice's mind clicking through possibilities. The love of her dear friend percolated through her being and she felt the beginnings of a sense of peace.

She'd met Alice Shumaker at the practical college while she was working there in the software development department. Alice had been a student, studying yoga, of all things. She said studying yoga helped her be a better exotic dancer. As if the men at The Studio Club noticed how good her dance moves were.

They only cared about how much flesh she could reveal before the obscenity police descended on the establishment. Emma had to smile but it quickly faded.

"I am so tired of running, Al. I don't want to do it anymore. The worry is just too much for me."

"You can't go back there. There, with her." Alice's tone was sharp.

"No. No." Emma's voice was a tortured whisper. "I hate to do it, but I think I need to leave Albuquerque."

Alice yawned loudly. "You'll never escape her that way. We need to stand up to her. Fight fire with fire."

Emma shook her head in the negative, even though Alice couldn't see her. "You know what happened last time I tried that. My chest was so bruised, it hurt to breathe."

"That's when you should have turned her in. The cops needed to know, needed to lock her up then."

It was an old argument, so Emma didn't feel the need to rehash the impossible situation she'd been in. Was still in, obviously.

Alice sighed. "So, what do we need to do? Let's brainstorm."

They fell silent as both pondered possibilities.

"I know, I'm adding you to my phone service. Just cancel yours. We'll go tonight and get you a new phone."

"Al, great idea but I can't afford it just yet. I will cancel, though, and we'll simply have to email for a while instead of texting."

"I'll pick you up at five. Going back to sleep. Love you. Be safe."

The line disconnected and Emma shook her head as she pocketed the phone. Alice always had been incorrigible. She was like a tornado that revisited Emma's life on a regular basis. Thank goodness.

Emma grabbed her lunch from her desk drawer and headed to the elevator.

CHAPTER TWENTY-TWO

The Angry Lunch

"Let's talk casseroles today," Bebe said as Emma took a seat across from her.

"Hmm, what's that you have there?" Emma inquired. "Is it a casserole?"

Bebe nodded and slid it closer to Emma so she could see what it was. "It is the oldest casserole. A macaroni and cheese casserole recipe first made its appearance just before the 1200s."

Emma smiled, pushing away her fear and doubts. "So, is this casserole *that* old?"

"Hardy har," Bebe said as she took a bite.

"Okay, so tell me," Emma said as she busily pulled out her hummus and cucumber sandwich.

"Well, let's go back to our old friend of the spaghetti, Tommy Jefferson. After he visited Italy, he brought home a pasta machine. His daughter, Mary, dutifully learned how to make pasta and began baking it in a dish with cheeses and spices layered in between. She enhanced it, and soon casseroles were being served in the Jefferson White House when he was president in early 1800. She even added them to her published cookbook."

Emma chewed thoughtfully, her mind reviewing Bebe's words, but she was also thinking about how Bebe and Donna were polar opposites of one another. Donna never discussed, just commanded. "It seems Mr. Jefferson changed a lot of things in the days of early America."

"Ah, he was brilliant. Did I tell you that I went to his school? And was damned lucky to get in as I wasn't a Virginia resident."

Emma blinked slowly in response.

Bebe grinned. "Yep, good old University of Virginia."

"Wait. Why is it his school?" Emma frowned, not sure her current panicked state of mind could follow Bebe's wave of information.

Bebe looked confused. "Well, he founded it, like in the early 1800s. He was big on expanding knowledge, deeming it one of the most important endeavors of humankind."

"I am really beginning to like this guy," Emma said thoughtfully. She studied Bebe's square, pensive face. "I had a second cousin who went there but he's an old guy now. I remember he said they call it 'the grounds' instead of a campus."

Bebe nodded and twirled her fork in her pasta and cheese dish. "Yeah, a throwback to the old days. I used to love going into the rooms on the lawn, that long, grassy stretch behind the rotunda. Usually only tenured profs and exceptional students live there. I think there's like ten or twelve little apartments but they are all so cool and furnished in traditional colonial style. It truly brings history to life."

"So, you didn't live on campus, I mean on the grounds?"

"I had an apartment near Rugby, but my girlfriend was a Lawnie. I stayed there with her a lot. Now, back to casseroles." She gestured toward her mostly empty bowl.

Emma grinned, but inside she wondered about the use of the term girlfriend. Had Bebe just come out to her? "Okay. Tell me about casseroles."

Bebe blushed but continued, "In ancient Greece they had a word for little cup that sounded somewhat like casserole. That word eventually morphed via the romance languages into a word meaning pan, *casse*. Eventually this came to describe mixed dishes that were cooked via an oven. They were filling but easy and became important during the Depression, mainly 'cause you could throw in whatever you had on hand."

"That makes sense," Emma added. "If they had an oven. Many were practically homeless."

Bebe rested her chin on her propped-up palm. "Too many really *were* homeless. Sad time. In the fifties, something called the hotdish added canned veggies to the meat and pasta, or rice, and it became a good way to feed a family."

"We've come such a long way, but casseroles seem here to stay," Emma said. "I think it's so cool that you are interested in history."

Bebe grinned, seeming to fall more at ease. "I seem to be interested in almost everything," she admitted.

"Uh-oh," Emma said. She had spotted Ralph entering the lunchroom. He spied them and lifted one hand in greeting before hurrying toward their table.

"Hello, you two," he said, before pulling a chair from a nearby table and joining them.

Emma watched as Bebe stiffened right before her eyes and she realized that she was just as wary of Ralph as she was.

"Glad to finally find you here. You were telling the truth, y'all do eat at different times every day."

"Now, why would we lie about that?" Bebe said in a slow drawl.

"I see you have mac and cheese," he said, eyeing Bebe's bowl.

As though suddenly losing her appetite, Bebe covered her bowl and pushed it into her lunch bag. "Yep, it was good," she said, lips tight against her teeth.

"My mama makes the best mac and cheese. We had it at Easter and it was so good." He turned his attention to Emma. "What's that on your sandwich? Doesn't look like anything I've ever seen before." He brushed his brown hair off his forehead and leaned to peer at her food.

Emma sighed, heartily wishing he would go away. "It's just hummus and cucumbers."

He frowned, narrowing his gaze. "Hummus?"

"Chickpeas, mashed with some lemon and sesame seeds. Some olive oil. It's made into like a paste to spread on bread."

"Well, doesn't that sound interesting. Do you make it yourself? Or do you buy it?"

Emma watched Ralph's lips move but her tolerance level was way low today. Why was he even making conversation with her? She'd had enough.

"Oh, you can get it most anywhere. I think I got this at Whole Foods but Sprouts carries it as well." She stuffed her sandwich into her lunch bag. "Now, if you'll excuse me, I promised my mam I would give her a call on my lunch break."

She saw the shocked look on Bebe's face but was helpless in the storm of her chaotic emotions. "So sorry, but you know how mothers are."

She stood and strode from the cafeteria.

CHAPTER TWENTY-THREE

Bebe Home Alone

A bright yellow Volkswagen car was idling alongside the sidewalk next to the TWEI back exit to the west parking lot when Bebe left work that evening. She had to do a double take when she realized the big headlights were framed by whimsical black eyelashes. Her eyes lifted curiously to the driver, and she saw a beautiful blond woman behind the wheel. Big brown sunglasses hid her eyes, but her bright smile found Bebe and left her somewhat breathless.

Emma came out through the back door, spotted Bebe regarding the car, and paused in midstep. She waved briefly in acknowledgment then quickly stepped into the waiting yellow Beetle. Bebe turned away and walked to her Subaru Crosstrek and opened the door to let the day's hot air bleed out a bit as she tossed her briefcase and blazer onto the passenger seat. Her gaze rose and she watched the retreating Volkswagen pull out onto Nautilus Avenue, the main street in this industrial park. She sighed. Her life was beginning to seem a bit weird these days and she wasn't sure how to feel about it. Her best move was avoidance, and she knew she'd figure out a way to continue on that familiar path. Still, she couldn't shake the feeling that change was coming. And a change that probably wasn't for the best, if her current state of tension was any indicator.

Seeing Emma rush from the lunchroom earlier had set off alarm bells in her mind. Had Ralph done something inappropriate to Emma? Had he said something? Emma had certainly not been her usual bubbly self that afternoon. In fact, she'd been downright sullen and even impatient with one of the software engineers who'd stopped by with a question. It had been a weird, weird afternoon.

Lost in perplexing thoughts, Bebe nevertheless made it home safely. The heavily gated apartment complex she lived in was one of the best in downtown Albuquerque and she paid a good price for it. Security was important for any woman who lived on her own, an edict battered into her by an overprotective father. She absently used the remote to open the gate, and as she waited her thoughts flew, as they so often did these days, to Emma. Who was the beautiful woman who had picked her up from work? A part of her hoped it was a lover but then another part of her balked. Community was one thing, but the jealousy that reared up was unexpected. Shaking her head in frustration, she pulled into the resident parking lot and into her assigned slot.

A cool silence greeted Bebe when she stepped into her apartment. Persistent sunlight warmed through large south-facing windows but was quickly lost in the spacious two-bedroom residence. Sometimes it felt too big for just one person, but examining her motives, she realized that perhaps she did harbor hope for a new relationship one day.

Placing her briefcase on the table, she strode slowly into the bedroom, blazer trailing from one hand. She thought again of Emma and sadness filled her. She probably wasn't a child of Sappho after all, as evidenced by the phone call Bebe'd overheard that morning. It seemed as though she was having trouble with a fellow named Don.

"Comfy, are you?" She turned after hanging up her blazer and watched Peabody respond to her question with an indulgent yawn. He was in his usual place, tucked part of the way into the crevice between her two bed pillows, and, as she watched, he rose and performed a lovely feline stretch for her, offering a dismissive back paw shake against a corner of one pillow as finale.

"Let me get changed and I'll see to your supper, darling boy. You wouldn't believe my day. Tilda forgot about the changes I needed on the Phillips manuscript and Sheila had so many questions, all about a new manuscript that came in. Sheesh."

She pulled on sweatpants and her favorite Miami Beach T-shirt. "And then there's Emma," she said pensively. "Always Emma."

Peabody watched her from the counterpane, his dark gray form resting in a sphinxlike posture, big golden eyes blinking slowly as he took in this information. Bebe knew he'd been hearing the name Emma steadily for some weeks now, and she fancied that he'd come to recognize it.

"Yes, her." How Bebe wanted to be with her right now. She remembered her adorable freckles glowing in the candlelight at the party and how she had so wanted to kiss her. She paused before Peabody, one hand on her hip, the other pulling thoughtfully at her bottom lip. Her thoughts flew to Sappho. The Greek poet. The isle of Lesbos. She sighed.

"Okay, Pea-boy, let's get some food in you."

Peabody performed one more majestic feline stretch before leaping to the carpet and following Bebe into the kitchen.

Sappho was married to a man and had at least one child, according to most historical records. Bebe had, for some time, failed to acquaint a sixth-century Greek woman—a wealthy, married Greek woman—with her own personal sexuality, preferring women instead of men. In fact, Sappho's supposed lesbianism had long been a subject of debate with no real resolution.

Peabody bumped against her calves, bringing her back to the present. She finished pulling open a can of cat food and dumped it into his bowl. He eyed her with a disapproving glance as she placed it on the floor so he could dig in.

Bebe slid an e-reader from an end table and curled up into her favorite corner of the sofa. She didn't open the reader right away, though, simply resting her open palm atop it.

All that had been discovered of Sappho's supposedly lesbian-based poetry were just a few disparate fragments. And of the approximately six hundred fifty fragments, only a few were about love, and several of those were directed to beautiful young men. Most were political or about her family and some served as anthems of instruction for how women could become better wives and lovers. Tales of her supposedly rampant homosexual encounters were documented only in bawdy, comedic parodies of Sappho and her tribe of women singers. Were they based in fact? Bebe wondered. Even Sappho's death by suicide was supposed to be due to unrequited love for a young man.

If honest with herself, Bebe felt embarrassed that her so-called lesbianism, her desire to have a sexual and emotional connection with a woman, had been so mislabeled and misdirected. Sappho the poet and musical artist may well have fallen into the obscurity of history if not for a feminist uprising in the early nineteenth century. Somehow, during this time, Sappho had become a never-denied feminist and lesbian icon.

She sighed. If not lesbian or sapphic, what would one call her love of women? She hated the term "women loving women" because as much as she loved her mother, she had no desire to go to bed with her. Maybe the term should just be loving. Or just human.

Brushing the disheartening thoughts aside, she opened her reader and lost herself in a new book of trivia she'd bought on Saturday. Speeding past some facts that she already knew, she paused on some new information. The book listed the ingredients for a healthy relationship which included honesty, trust, respect, and open communication between partners. Bebe thought about her ex, Caroline, and realized anew why the relationship had fallen apart. A healthy relationship also included effort and compromise from both people. Partners needed to respect one another's independence yet share important decisions.

Neither of them had lived by any of these rules.

Oh, Bebe had told herself that Caroline also wanted a quiet life staying at home. She should have seen the red flags when they'd dated. Caroline was always eager to meet friends for an impromptu lunch or supper and insisted on dragging Bebe along. Then, when Bebe fell into her characteristic silences, Caroline would get angry and later rage at Bebe for being antisocial. So, Bebe made a resentful effort but then only felt secure when she was imparting some poorly received arcane knowledge to their friends, which also angered Caroline. Bebe just couldn't win. The honeymoon ended after just a couple years. Bebe finally stayed home alone and Caroline went out alone, eventually finding a new lover who liked people better than books.

Bebe, as she so often did, pushed those thoughts aside and lost herself in the forest of e-book trivia. Peabody, tummy full and bath finished, leapt onto the sofa and curled into the warmth of his companion's lap.

CHAPTER TWENTY-FOUR

Emma Tries to Heal

"I have no idea how she discovered my new name. And I'm super glad I used a postal box for the address, otherwise she'd be at my door. She'll still no doubt show up one day when I go to the postal center to pick up my mail. You have to give phone companies an address."

Alice shook her head as she switched lanes. "This so sucks. It's like you can't escape some stalkerish asshat no matter how hard you try."

Emma fell silent. Was she doomed to deal with Donna for the rest of her life? How did people escape abusive, controlling partners?

"I want you to get a new number, too. We'll even trade your phone in, if that's okay. You bought an old-style cheapie one. We need to upgrade you. You're a 'puter nerd for chrissakes, flash that!"

Emma blew a raspberry at her friend. "I'm paying for it, though, now that I'm gainfully employed."

Alice shook her head and slotted the Volkswagen into a parking space outside the phone store. "Only if you use cash.

I don't want a paper trail with your name on it. Obviously this devil has mad skills of some kind to get added onto your phone account. Everything has to be in my name, which may also be risky as she knows who I am. I think we can keep her confused, though."

Emma nodded. "And she doesn't know we've stayed connected." She bit her bottom lip. "At least I hope not." She looked around nervously as they exited the car.

"Well, at least she doesn't know about my new job. And this new, cute little car," Alice said, caressing the hood of the Volkswagen.

Emma rolled her eyes and grimaced comically as Alice chuckled.

Getting the new phone and new number was easier than she'd expected, although the time waiting their turn for service took a good while. Emma traded in her old phone for decent credit, as it was new, then chose a much fancier smartphone. Alice added Emma to her account, shielding her in a family plan, then set up the payments for the phone as part of her own monthly payment. She shrugged nonchalantly at Emma's promises to pay them.

"I know where you live," she responded with a mock evil laugh. "So, buy me some supper. Where should we go?"

They chose a favorite diner close by and were soon sitting across from one another. Emma sighed deeply. "I can't thank you enough, Al," she said. "You're an amazing friend."

Alice sipped her water and set her menu aside. "Look, I hate what you are going through. It so sucks. Why can't she just leave you the fuck alone?"

Emma dropped her head. "I don't know and I hate that I didn't see the signs. I never imagined I could be so stupid."

The server came and they placed their orders, a Reuben sandwich for Alice and a grilled cheese for Emma, fries and sodas all around.

"You're not stupid," Alice said once the server walked away. "You were busy with classes and excited. Your job was new and you were doing a lot of creative stuff. And she's sly." Alice sat back and folded her arms across her chest. "Oh, man, is she sly."

Emma nodded in agreement. "I can't believe how easily she distanced me from all my friends." She lifted her eyes. "I cherished my friends."

Alice leaned forward and patted Emma's hand. "I know, babe. She's just evil and wanted complete domination. I saw Katrina on campus and she told me that the whole crew was watching you back then because Donna told them you were having a nervous breakdown. That's just wrong, you know? She had them believing they were *helping* you."

"Oh, I know. I know," Emma said softly. She lifted her gaze to her friend. "Thank you for being persistent. Without you, I would never have been able to go through with this plan. You are such a lifesaver."

Alice frowned. "I'm not so sure now. I can't believe she didn't just hightail it off to find a new victim. We made it as difficult as we possibly could."

"And it's risky, to boot. I could totally lose my job, maybe my career, if TWEI ever discovers I've lied about stuff."

Alice sighed. "I know. At least the credentials are real and the DBA." She stuck a tendril of escaping blond hair behind her right ear. She grinned. "Just the names have been changed to protect the innocent."

The server returned with their food and they fell into a comfortable conversation, Emma catching up on old friends from the IT department at the college.

Finally, quiet fell, and leaning back, Emma changed the subject. "So. I think I'm, like, attracted to this woman at work." Her gaze lifted to gauge Alice's response. She needn't have worried.

"Oh. My. Gosh!" Alice exclaimed loudly. "Tell me more. All about her. Is she sweet? Pretty? Of course, she's sweet or you wouldn't waste your time. Pretty, too, I bet." She glared at Emma. "Right?"

Emma hastened to reassure her. "Right. And we talked all night, you know, after that work party I told you about? She's so interesting. Amazing, really. And I don't think she has an abusive bone in her body. She's just not that way. She does start off as maybe a little intimidating and she does get riled up about work stuff, but..." She paused and shrugged. "She's a lot of fun when you get to know her, and those eyes—"

"What color are they?" Alice was leaning toward Emma, arms folded on the tabletop.

Emma knew her grin was goofy but couldn't seem to help it. "That's just it. They're like this gray color, you know, stormy. But they change when she's laughing or going off on another coworker. Sometimes they are kinda pale when she's thinking. Oh, and she's a big, big reader, reading every chance she gets."

"Well, that's right up your alley. I never saw you without a book or a reader at college. Do you still read as much?" she asked, head tilted curiously.

"I do, but I spend a lot of time gaming these days, you know, with Crosshairs? But I've had this mad desire to start reading some torrid romances again." She grinned shyly at her friend.

Alice laughed. "Ah, Crosshairs. How is he? I miss those evenings hanging out with him."

"Doesn't he come by the club? He used to."

"Yeah, not since I moved to the new one. The Studio Club is farther from his house on campus and, between you and me, I think that thing with Donna showing up the way she did has him a little spooked, too, worrying she might show up again."

Emma nodded sadly, painfully remembering how Donna had caused a ruckus at the club where Alice used to work. Bless Alice, she hadn't told her where Emma was living but had threatened to call the police, effectively chasing her away. "I know, that's why we game and chat online instead of hanging out like we used to. In answer to your question, he's doing great. He's dating a new guy, Chad, and is in the throes of new love. They're even talking about being in a throuple relationship with a gal named Heloise."

"No shit? Heloise?" Alice shrugged. "So, this woman at work. Does she like you?"

Emma sighed deeply and pinched one corner of her paper napkin. "I don't know, Alice. I just don't know."

"And you're afraid, for so many reasons, to let her know how you feel." Alice pointed a french fry at her friend.

Emma nodded, and a heavy silence fell as they both mulled this truth.

"I want to tell her. I want to be with her. Like I said, we went to that party dance thing at work and she was so much fun. Then back to my place for tea and we stayed up all night talking. It was everything I could do not to grab her into my arms and tell her about it."

Alice leaned forward and pushed her disheveled plate to the side. "Pone, honey. Please don't let that bitch Donna put you off having a good relationship. That's just not fair to you. What she did was not your fault. Tell me you know this." She watched Emma expectantly.

"I do, but—" Emma began.

"Tell me that what she did was not your fault." Alice's voice was firm and demanding.

Emma sighed. "What she did was not my fault. She's an abuser."

Alice sat back and smiled. "Now, tell me more about this intriguing coworker. Describe her for me."

CHAPTER TWENTY-FIVE

Emma and Bernie

After Alice dropped her off at her apartment complex on the far end of Montgomery Boulevard, Emma found her head swiveling as she examined her surroundings before hurrying inside. This was a new behavior, but after the morning's phone call she realized she needed to be ever more vigilant. Donna was not going to just go away, even though she had pointedly been told that she had no place in Emma's life.

Her apartment felt strangely empty. Maybe because Bebe wasn't there.

Emma still missed the two dogs that she had left with Donna. After much hand-wringing, she had realized that Donna could easily trace her through their vet and she did know that Donna was a good dog-mom. So, she'd given them a tearful farewell before sneaking away, hoping that, as they had been Donna's pets originally, they wouldn't miss her too much—as long as they still had Don.

She stepped into the dining area and laid her backpack onto one of the two kitchen chairs. The small table was a bit of a mess, remnants from last night's pizza debauchery lingering. Emma sighed wearily and set about cleaning up. She noted that the waste bin was overflowing and paused to discern whether it was close to trash pickup day. It wasn't, so she had a few days before the dumpsters were filled to the brim. She crammed the pizza box into the bag and checked her smaller wastepaper baskets. Soon, she had a full bag and carried it down two flights to the dumpsters out back after casing the surroundings carefully.

On the way back upstairs, she pondered what to do to fill her evening. She usually played with her gaming buddy Crosshairs, but her heart just wasn't in it tonight.

Standing by her one recliner, she unfastened her trousers and let them fall to the floor. Stepping from them, she lifted her laptop from the coffee table and settled onto the love seat, her mind caressing the thought that Bebe had once sat there. The laptop was warm from resting on the wooden table, so the bottom surface felt good on her bare thighs as she sat tailor style. She should have left it at the small computer station she'd set up next to the living area windows to keep it cooler, but the after-pizza coma had distracted her yesterday evening.

She sighed as she opened the laptop. She just wasn't sure she was up for being cheery with Crosshairs, plus she feared she would be too distracted due to the day's crazy events. Her sense of security had fled with that call from Don, and she needed some time to decompress. And not think of Donna. Even the memories of their year together had become painfully uncomfortable. Her twenty-twenty hindsight always seemed to expose the alarming behaviors she had missed. Lately, she'd made it a point to study abusers, which Donna certainly was, and she'd learned that their charm always won their victims back. This, even after bones were broken and possible death pending. Emma did not want to be one of these victims, those who defended their abusers. It was bad enough just realizing that the mistreatment was happening to her. There was just no way she could defend it.

Tapping the computer screen to wake it, she saw that her cousin Bernie had messaged her. She smiled. She loved her family so much and Bernie was one whom she could trust completely and confide in with no worries.

Heya, Bern. I just got home. What's up?

Bernie had replied by the time Emma had checked her email accounts.

I saw Sissy yesterday. Bridget had to get her braces adjusted again, the poor kid. She is living on over the counter pain meds, these days.

Poor kid, Emma echoed.

She'd never required braces, so she could only imagine the pain her brother Bear's oldest was going through. Her cousin Roddy had suffered through braces when he was in middle school, and it seemed he had a busted lip every other week. Of course, Roddy was big into sports whereas Bridget was more of a television junkie.

That so sucks, she added.

For sure, Bernie responded. *Glad you and me are old ladies.*

Emma laughed. *Doesn't matter. Look at Cher. She was like almost like forty years old when she had hers straightened.*

A big mistake in my book. She was attractive with her crooked teeth. If mine were crooked and I was thirty, I'd just say never mind. Especially after seeing what Bridge is going through.

Well, remember that it's not just for looks. Keeps the teeth healthier, or so I've been told, Emma pointed out.

Yeah, I guess. So, how's work? Is that Bebe person still treating you well?

Emma nodded even though no one could see her. *She is. She's so smart, Bern. I wish you could visit with her one day, just to hear her go on about the coolest info. Lunch with her kind of makes my day.*

Hmm, she sounds interesting and you seem to be a might interested in her.

Emma felt her cheeks pinken. *Well, she is pretty special. But that workplace thing, you know…never a good thing.*

True but it would be nice to see you with someone who was good to you.

There was a pause and Emma briefly held her head in her hands.

Donna found me, she wrote finally. *She called me.*

Oh fuck.

Yep.

So, what do you do now? Come on home. Please? We can look after you, protect you.

Emma frowned, loath to admit that she had been thinking the very same thing.

I know, I know. Worry that it might put all you guys in danger. She always had a gun. A pistol and a rifle. If she found me there… well, it could be horrible. So many could be hurt.

And also be witness to your abuse, Bernie wrote. *They would understand. We know what those people are like. Especially here in the back country. There's lots of abuse in small towns. Frustration makes people mean. We'll take her on as a family.*

I'll think about it, I promise.

You best had. Are you safe for now?

Yes, she only called, didn't come around.

Good. Thank goodness for small miracles.

There was a lengthy pause. *Well, listen, Bran brought me a beer and he wants me to go sit out back with him. You be careful, though. Really careful, okay? Text me right away if she comes anywhere near you, all right? I got that Albuquerque police station number right here in my phone.*

Emma smiled. She had such an amazing family.

Wait. I had to get a new phone so I have a new number. I'll text it to you right now, so save it.

Will do. Love you.

Love you back. Hi to Bran and the kids.

Emma stared at a far wall, wondering if she should, indeed, give up and retreat back into the fold of the family. But maybe, just maybe, with Alice's help, she was now in the clear.

CHAPTER TWENTY-SIX

The Past Returns

That Friday morning, Emma sensed Ralph before she saw him. He was standing in the office doorway staring at her. He seemed unusually pale, and she was worried he might have taken ill.

Bebe was studying him as well, frowning. "Ralph? Are you okay," she asked, glancing at Emma.

Ralph pointed at Emma. "You. Come with me." His tone was low and harsh.

Emma shrugged at Bebe but hurried to follow Ralph from the office. He was walking too fast, and she had to racewalk to keep up with him. They crossed the spacious conference area and he ushered her into his big corner office toward the front of the building. He pointed to a chair as he took a power position behind the desk. He stared at her a long moment, and Emma clasped her hands together.

Surely what she had been fearing on a daily basis wasn't about to come true. "Ralph, I—"

"Don't waste your breath talking to me. Obviously everything you say is a lie, *Ms. Dakota*." He watched her with brown eyes gone steely.

She'd been found out. And it was way worse than she'd expected. "No, now, I only—"

"I received an anonymous call early this morning." He turned in his chair and stared out at the blue sky peppered with plump white clouds. "And would you like me to tell you what the caller said?"

He turned back to her, spreading his hands dramatically. "I was told that my recent hire has been lying to me from the beginning. *Lying* to me!"

"Ralph, really. Let me explain." She laid her hands on his desk, palms up, hoping he would hear her.

"I looked you up, you know. You're quite impressive. Magazine stories. Patents. Honorary degrees. Pony Dakota, creator of the famous Gallop Software System." He used his right index finger to make a spiral. "Whoop-de-doo."

"See?" Emma offered. "I only changed my name. Everything else I told you was true." She knew her cheeks had to be crimson, but she wouldn't cry. No, she wouldn't cry. Not in front of this ogre of a man. The ogre who was essentially her boss.

He sighed and turned his chair so he was once more facing the window. "I just don't know how you got this by the comptroller. Or Amy in HR."

Emma leaned forward. "There, see? It's a DBA, I'm doing business as E. Vernon, so it's not a lie. Not really."

"Is that how you sleep at night?" he asked, his voice low, almost a growl. "Is that how you deal with being a liar, a deceiver? The people here trusted you and you have made a mockery of that trust. How can we be sure you won't deceive us again?"

Emma was deflated but felt anger stir. "Don't you even want to know why I lied? I assure you I had a good reason—"

"I'm sure you did. Now, I have to decide what to do with you. Once Thomas finds out…" He shook his head. "I just don't know how he'll take it."

Emma flailed under this new onslaught. Thomas would know everything, as would Bebe and the other editors. As well as all the software engineers downstairs. Forcing herself to be calm, she stubbornly set her jaw. "Look, Ralph, I do a good job. I've had no complaints. And my credentials are real. A simple name change should not make a difference to my duties here. I think you're being a little unfair—"

He turned and gazed at her with a superior air. "Unfair? Seriously? Do you even know what a pickle you are in, missy? We've got breach of contract, all sorts of legal trouble for you."

"Breach of—" Emma stared at him, her mouth hanging open.

He leaned forward, folding his hands atop the desk. "Now, as you are an accomplished employee, with credentials that appear to be true—"

"Appear!" Emma's anger hit a new level.

He continued as if she hadn't spoken. "I won't fire you. At least not right away. I do plan to keep very close tabs on you, however. Very close. I mean, you could be an industrial spy. I want to make sure there are no more lies, no additional subterfuge. You'll report to me every morning and at the end of every day, and I will make sure your duties are carried out in a transparent, above-board way."

"You don't think—"

"And I won't say anything to Dam and the others yet, as long as you do as I say. I also had better not discover that you are stealing proprietary information. I'll be checking your station each day, I can assure you of that." He held up a palm and closed his eyes. "I know there will be many late nights, just the two of us going over your day, but it can't be helped. If you want to keep your job here at TWEI, then you will have to go the extra mile to prove to me that you can be trusted."

He watched her but Emma would not give him the satisfaction of seeing how upset his veiled innuendos and threats had made her. She knew what he was up to, recognized his seduction of her via blackmail, and it made her hate him even more. She lowered her eyes and forced herself to speak in an even tone. "Yes, Ralph."

"Good. You can go back to work."

"And my name?" Emma kept her eyes on her shoes so he wouldn't see the extent of her anger.

"Well, everyone here knows you as Emma. We'll let that be for now. I can certainly see why you changed it. What sort of weird name is Pony Dakota? Emma Vernon is much prettier."

Pony Dakota turned and left the room, and it took all the willpower she could muster not to slam the door.

CHAPTER TWENTY-SEVEN

Pony Reveals All

Bebe jumped when Emma stormed into the office. She watched as Emma woke her computer monitor and began angrily pressing buttons on the keyboard.

"Emma? What's wrong? What did he say to you?" She rose and approached Emma slowly. "Emma?"

Emma turned and looked at her, and she saw the explosive anguish in Emma's red-rimmed eyes. Bebe took her by the shoulders. "What? Emma, please talk to me."

Emma's lips moved but no sound came out beyond a deep sigh.

Bebe moved to the door and gently shut it so they could be alone. She wheeled her chair to Emma's desk, sat, then turned Emma so she could take her hands.

"What's happened? Please tell me." She held Emma's hands tightly as though she could take away the pain the other was feeling.

Emma took a deep breath. "I have to leave. Leave Albuquerque and go back to Virginia."

Bebe felt her heart sink. Was she going to lose the woman she'd begun to care for so deeply? "Why? What on Earth would make you leave? Did Ralph do something? You have to tell me."

Emma dropped her gaze. "It's my fault. I lied." She lifted sorrowful eyes. "My name isn't Emma, not Emma Vernon."

Bebe was perplexed. "What do you mean? Who are you?"

"My name is Pony, Pony Dakota. Not Emma." She hung her head.

Silence fell as Bebe tried to digest this new information. "I don't understand."

"It was to escape Donna. She's my ex. My abusive, controlling ex. I knew if she found me she'd never leave me alone. I…I had to disappear completely. I guess I should have left Albuquerque right away but I…I like it here and—" She lifted her gaze to Bebe. "Oh God, please don't hate me, Bebe. Please. I'm not a bad person."

"But wait." A niggle of anger churned in Bebe's belly along with the confusion. Emma, this Pony Dakota, had lied to her, to all of them at TWEI. "How did—"

Pony chewed her bottom lip. "I just lied. I changed the name on my documentation, my résumé."

Bebe shook her head. "But that's not possible. You couldn't—"

Pony sighed and hung her head. "It was easier than you might think. If you have the skills."

"What about the school and employment records? Did you actually get all those degrees you listed? Or were they lies, too?" Bebe knew her seething anger was rising to the surface. She hated a liar.

Pony lifted an incredulous gaze. "Of course, I did!" she spat. "I only changed my name on them, the credentials are absolutely real. And I just kept everything on the web in my real name but made it so it couldn't be traced to me here and now. It was like Pony disappeared abruptly. I even added a brunette stock photo for this name! And that was so if she did any searching, I, the real me, wouldn't come up anywhere. The computer field is a big one, and I was hoping she wouldn't be able to figure out that the online E. Vernon was me."

Bebe reared back, dropping Emma's…er, Pony's hands.

"Then how did she find you?"

Pony shook her head. "It was stupid. I used a cheap phone provider to save money and she was able to sweet-talk someone there into giving her information about me, including my name. She probably used some strange timeline there to track my new name down. Like when I got the new service."

Bebe thoughtfully pressed four fingers to her chin. "She was the one who called you the other day."

"She did."

Pony looked at Bebe with her beautiful green eyes. "I meant no harm, Bebe. Please understand. But it was the only way to get out from under her thumb. I was hoping her rudimentary computer skills would serve me well. I never saw this happening."

Bebe could tell that the other woman was beyond distressed, and a slice of regret pushed through her.

"I don't know quite what to feel about this," Bebe murmured.

"Betrayed, to begin with. Lied to. Distrusting," Pony stated quietly. "I'd understand if you never wanted to talk to me again. I can only hope that you will eventually, in your own time, come to understand about this."

"But why leave town? What's changed?"

Pony inhaled a deep, shaky breath. "Donna must have found out where I worked. She…she called Ralph and told him. Now Ralph wants me to…well, he wants to stay very close to me, in case I lie again, and as long as I allow that, he won't tell anyone. I can't do that. I just can't." Her voice had fallen to a bitter whisper. "That's why I'm leaving you. Even though I don't want to."

Bebe stiffened and she felt fire suffuse her. That scheming, blackmailing Ralph. Like quicksilver, her anger switched from Emma's…Pony's subterfuge to Ralph's hideous blackmail plot. "That scheming bastard," she muttered.

"I won't be…" Pony whispered again. "I'm a lesbian and he makes me sick."

Bebe nodded agreement. "Yes, I thought so."

Just the idea of him and Pony together made Bebe's stomach clench. "Look, we'll figure this out. Somehow. Will Donna show up here? Do you think that's a possibility?"

Pony thought about it. "I guess she could. I mean, she got Ralph's number, or at least TWEI's, so she knows where this place is."

Panic twisted her features and Bebe understood how frightened she was of this woman. She took Pony's hands in hers again, trying to comfort her. "Look, we'll just have to make sure you're protected. This is a secure building. She can't get in."

Pony nodded. "That may be why she just called. Anonymously, of course."

"So, she's a coward and a snake. But that cowardice just might keep her from showing up and making a scene. At some point I want to hear the full story, but for now let's just get you safe. Keep you safe."

Pony just shook her head sadly. "I'm beginning to think that just can't happen anymore."

Bebe rubbed a palm along Pony's forearm and tried to smile reassuringly. "Hey, it's not like you to lose faith. We'll work it out. Together."

Pony lifted her gaze to Bebe and Bebe saw the tiniest glimmer of hope. She so hoped she'd be able to keep her anger tamped down long enough to help Emma—no, *Pony*—be safe. She didn't know if she could rekindle the feelings that had begun to grow for her coworker, but that decision would have to wait. She would deal with that later. When she had to.

CHAPTER TWENTY-EIGHT

Planning an Escape

Pony studied the shift as Bebe's demeanor went from anger to calculation.

"Okay, we'll talk more about this later. Why don't you go home? I'll cover for you with HR. I'll call later and we'll see what we can figure out, okay? Let's not make any rash decisions just yet."

Pony knew her eyes were brimming with tears. "You mean you don't hate me?" Could it be that Bebe understood why she had risked everything just to get some semblance of her life back?

She grasped Bebe's hand tightly, but Bebe slowly extricated that hand. Sorrow swamped Pony. She may very well have lost her.

"Later. You need to leave now."

Pony took a deep breath. "Let me get my stuff off the server and I'll go." She quickly closed out her files, then the computer, and cleaned out her desk, praying that Ralph wouldn't show up before she left. Finished, she stood at the door, backpack hugged close to her body. She still glanced around, hoping that Ralph had already gone to lunch.

"Well, goodbye, then," she said, her voice choking on the words.

Bebe, who'd been silently staring at the floor, looked up at her. "Okay. I'll…I'll be in touch. You be careful, okay? Out there amongst the English."

Tears brimmed in Pony's eyes, but she was determined not to let them fall. She nodded, heart thudding painfully as she realized that sharing that movie with Bebe was just one more thing she'd lost.

Making it safely outside the back door, Pony paused and let her gaze scan the parking lot. It was clear—no Donna, thankfully—and she sighed, realizing she would never feel safe again until she got back to Virginia. On the bus, on the way home, she made a mental list of things she needed to do. It was overwhelming, so she pulled out her phone and called Alice, telling her what had happened.

"Oh, Pone, no," Alice wailed. "Don't go, please? We'll figure something out. We'll go to the law again. We'll insist they protect you."

"A restraining order? Seriously. No, I'll just go back to Hillside Gap. There's jobs there. I may have to drive a bit, but that's okay. At least my family is there."

"What if she comes there? What are you gonna do then?"

"I have to believe she won't. She's at best a coward and might not want to go that far out of her way."

Pony could hear rustling on the other end of the line. "What are you doing?"

"I'm getting dressed. Where are you?"

"I'm on the bus, heading back to my apartment to pack. Will you sell my furniture for me? There's not too many things and you can keep whatever you want."

Alice blew a huge raspberry. "Shit, Pone. I'm on my way. I'll see you there."

The phone call died and Pony stowed the phone in her backpack. She stared out the window, feeling a strange numbness creeping across her. She truly hoped Alice wouldn't beg her to stay. Her mind was made up and she knew, even through the spreading numbness, that she needed to be home. Home with her family. They would help her, they would heal her pain and her loss—the loss of her life in Albuquerque and the loss of a possible new love. And right now, she needed that more than anything.

Alice was waiting for her at the bus stop when she disembarked near her apartment complex. "Wow, you got here fast," Pony said.

Alice engulfed Pony in a perfumed embrace and Pony felt tears rise yet again. She had to remain strong, though. She had a lot to do.

Letting her go, Alice took Pony's hand and they walked along the sidewalk the short distance to Pony's apartment complex. "Can we have some of that tea your mama sent? We'll need to talk this out," Alice said as they entered the vestibule of Pony's building.

"Of course," Pony replied. "But you can't change my mind. There's no way I can stay here."

Winded by emotion, Pony paused on the first landing and bent forward, trying to catch her breath.

"Are you okay?" Alice asked, laying a palm on Pony's back.

"Yeah." She straightened with sheer determination. "I'll be okay."

Once in her apartment, Pony studied the rooms with new eyes, making mental lists of what needed to be taken care of. She placed her backpack on the floor next to the love seat as Alice stepped into the kitchen and filled the kettle.

"I wish my cousin Bernie was here. She'd have all this stuff taken care of in a heartbeat," Pony muttered.

"Well, you got me, at least," Alice said. She cleaned mail off the small table and placed the sugar bowl in the center. "You have any cookies?" she asked, opening the small pantry.

Pony sat at the table. "Top shelf. The blue box."

Soon they were both seated at the table, comforting cuppas in front of each of them, a plate of untouched cookies between them. They looked at one another, faces grim.

Alice sighed. "I'll help you in any way I can. You know that."

Pony nodded. "I know. You've always been a good friend."

Silence fell again. Pony took a sip of her tea. "I may have to be here a few days. Plane tickets are so expensive when you try to fly right away."

"I can help. I've got some money squirreled away. So, did you turn in your notice?"

Pony shrugged. "Not exactly, though Bebe said she'd square it with human resources. At this point, I don't much care. They'll probably blacklist me anyway and make it so I won't be able to get anything in my field again."

"Oh, Pone, don't say that. You love what you do," Alice said sadly.

"I'll probably work my way back to it. Virginia is a long way from New Mexico, and maybe after some time passes, I'll find something."

"I hate that this is happening to you," Alice said. She had closed her bright blue eyes and was rubbing the warmth of her tea mug along her cheek. "I hate Donna and what she's done to you. And I can't believe you have to leave the good things you found here, like me, like Bebe."

"She hates me now."

"Why? Because you changed your name? How shallow is she? Did you tell her why?"

Pony nodded. "Not that it did much good."

"Oh. So, it went like that, did it?" Alice frowned.

"Pretty much." Pony took a deep breath. "So, let's talk logistics. I will pack up all my stuff into a couple suitcases. Then I can check the bags at the airport to get everything home. You'll take care of the furniture?"

At Alice's nod, she continued, "Good, thank you. I'll get online this afternoon and set up my flight so we'll have a timeline to work in."

"You're gonna be breaking your lease," Alice informed her.

"Shoot. I hadn't thought that far ahead. That'll cost a fortune."

Alice nodded. "It will. You should finish out this month, though, so maybe it'll be a little less."

"I've already paid next month's, too. I usually do two months at a time in case I run short. Maybe the company will put that toward paying off the break-lease fee."

"They might. It's worth a try. Maybe fib and tell them you have a sick relative you have to go take care of. Maybe they'll cut you some slack."

Pony shook her head. "Nope. Done with lying. No good ever comes from it. Not even in the short term." She dropped her gaze and pressed her warm cup to her forehead. "How did this happen?"

A firm knock sounded at the apartment door, and they looked at one another in terror.

"What if it's her?" Alice asked in a harsh whisper. "Donna?"

"What if it is?" Pony said dully. "I'm not afraid of her anymore. As far as I'm concerned, that bitch can just bring it on. I have ab-so-lutely had enough."

CHAPTER TWENTY-NINE

The Plan Manifests

Bebe once again found herself in Emma's small, uncluttered apartment. Not Emma, no. *Pony.* Pony had opened the door quickly, angrily, but her mouth had fallen open in surprise upon seeing Bebe in the doorway. Nevertheless, she, with a weak form of resignation, had ushered Bebe inside.

"Well, I guess you are the famous Bebe that Pone keeps talking about." A beautiful blonde, curvy but slim, rose from her seat at the table and moved toward Bebe, hand outstretched.

Bebe took it automatically, shaking it. "Yes, Bebe Simmons. Nice to meet you." She stared into beautiful, merry blue eyes, surrounded by laugh lines that crinkled adorably. Her golden hair was cut into a short bob with gleeful, irregular bangs.

"And I'm Alice, Alice Shumaker. I've been friends with Pony since she moved to Albuquerque."

"Sit," Pony ordered. She was in the kitchen heating the kettle and preparing tea. Bebe obeyed, her eyes never leaving Alice, who'd reseated herself across from Bebe.

"I'm just here for moral support," Alice said, spreading her hands wide. "I can't believe she has to leave. It's just not fair. People should be allowed to live wherever they want."

Bebe nodded. "I agree. Have you guys sought any legal help? Like, against her, I mean."

"Oh, yeah, many times. It seems like there are so many reservations and restrictions to legal recourse. By the time they'd be able to take any action, she'd be hurt again, or worse." Alice shrugged and lifted her cup. "But they'd jump right in to help if she was murdered, right?"

Pony approached with a tray bearing the fat-bellied kettle of hot water and a decorative jar of tea bags, and Bebe experienced a sudden déjà vu moment that warmed her inside. Not that her anger toward Pony had completely dissipated, but the drive home and then to Pony's apartment had calmed her somewhat. At least enough to approach Pony's rescue with some amount of reason.

Pony pushed the cookie plate aside, centering the tray on the table. She lifted a cup and placed it in front of Bebe, then filled it with hot water and a tea bag. She pulled the chair from her desk area toward the table and perched on it as Alice helped herself to more hot water and a fresh tea bag.

"So, Bebe," Pony asked in a nervous, wavering voice. "Why are you here? Is something wrong? Do I need to go back to the office before I leave?"

Bebe sat back, wondering how best to present the idea she wanted to broach.

"Do you need me to go?" Alice asked Pony. "Do you guys need to work something out?"

"No, stay please," Pony said with a deep sigh. "I hope you'll stay."

"Look," Bebe said haltingly. "This situation is just a little bit crazy—"

"Little bit, ha!" Alice retorted.

Bebe shrugged and nodded. "I truly believe we just need a little time to decompress. To come up with some solutions."

"I agree," Alice said. "But she can't stay here looking over her shoulder all the time. What kind of life is that? Don't get me wrong, I want her to stay here, I do, but not at the expense of her mental well-being."

Bebe sipped her tea then held up her hands. "Right. I'm not arguing that point. I'm just saying that Emma has special talents that are invaluable at TWEI. We don't want to lose her. None of us want to lose her."

"Pony," Pony said dully. "My name is Pony."

Bebe closed her eyes for a long moment. "I know. I'm sorry, but it's going to take me a little more time—"

"I'm not going back there to be Ralph's little plaything and I can't believe you are asking that of me." Pony's voice was angry and her green eyes snapped with ire.

Bebe reared back. "Of course not!"

"Well, then, what?" Alice asked.

Bebe felt Alice's critical, questioning gaze on her. "I think… well, I think she should leave town for a while. Let the dust settle. Thomas and TWEI have made a few friends on the city council. He may be able to get her some workable protection. As long as she is still working for him."

Pony scoffed. "He won't. Not after Ralph tells him I lied. He'll fire me immediately."

"So that's a moot point," Alice muttered.

Bebe's anger flared again. "Why can't you just trust me? Surely you realize I am trying to help you get past this." She took a deep, calming breath. "So, I have a plan."

Pony opened her mouth to speak again but Bebe held up a hand to stop her. "Will you just *try* to trust me?"

Pony nodded but lowered her gaze to her hands.

"My plan is this. That you don't make any final decisions just yet. You'll leave town, go back to Virginia for a week or two, and when we come back, we'll see what has transpired in our absence."

Alice stared at Bebe, her gaze curious. "We? We who?"

Bebe sighed again, feeling like she was being too dramatic. "Me. I thought I'd go with her. To make sure she's safe."

Pony's head shot up and she studied Alice with wide eyes, as though imparting a message of disbelief.

"I have a ton of vacation time and though you don't, we'll address that later. Amy in HR said this type of situation—don't worry, I just told her you were being stalked by someone—could probably qualify under family medical leave. You know, emotional trauma."

Pony turned her gaze toward Bebe, and Bebe noticed that her spring-green eyes had lightened somewhat. "You'd do that? I mean, go with me?"

Bebe shrugged. "Why not?"

Pony stood and began pacing across the small living room, using her spread fingers to tick off reasons Bebe shouldn't go. "There's the plane tickets—way, way expensive. Time off work, I know how important your job is to you. You won't want to fall behind. Then there's the people in the office. What will they say if, probably when, they find out we went on a trip together?" She paused and studied Bebe. "Well?"

"Well. None of that matters. What matters is your safety. All of that can be dealt with when we get back." Bebe stared as good as she got.

"I think it's a hella good idea, Pone," Alice said quietly. "I mean, she's willing to deal with all that you said just now. That's pretty frickin' nice in my book."

Bebe looked away and swallowed the last of her tea. "Just say thank you and let's get on with it."

"Thank you," Pony whispered as Bebe stood and slid the chair neatly under the tabletop.

"You're welcome. I'll go on home and pack a bag, then run my cat to the kitty hotel." She checked her watch. "We'll go in my car, of course. I had it serviced last week, and I'll stop to fill up on my way back here. Can you be ready to go in, say, an hour and a half?"

Pony's face looked as though someone had slammed it with an iron skillet. "Um, hour and a half? Sure, sure. But c-car? You mean to get to the airport, right?"

Bebe touched Alice's arm. "It was so great to finally meet you, and I love your little Beetle, by the way. So cute with those eyelashes."

Alice seemed gobsmacked as well. "Aw, thanks. It was nice to meet you, too."

Bebe turned her attention back to Pony. "I just thought a road trip might be more fun. It's only about seventeen hundred miles to Virginia, about two days. Plus, Donna doesn't know we'll be traveling by car. She'll probably be checking flights. Okay, I'm going now but I'll be back soon."

It had gone better than expected, Bebe thought as she closed the apartment door and jogged down the two flights to the vestibule. Sure, it was a crazy idea, but Bebe had never been more certain of anything in her entire life. Thank goodness Emma…Pony…had sort of agreed.

CHAPTER THIRTY

Saying Goodbye

"So that was Bebe," Alice said. She blew out a heavy breath. "Wow. She's something."

Pony silently stared into space and chewed on a thumbnail.

"Are you okay? What are you thinking?" Alice rose and cleared the table, putting the tea things away. She watched Pony closely as she washed the few mugs and the plate.

Pony rose slowly and moved toward the bedroom. "I guess I need to pack."

Alice dried her hands and followed her friend. Pony was lifting her suitcase from the high closet shelf when Alice started pulling jeans and shorts from the square cloth drawers in Pony's cube-type bureau. "So, I guess you need clothes for, like, fourteen days?"

Pony placed the case on the bed and looked at Alice. The comical look on her face must have set Alice off because Alice broke down into helpless laughter. She even plopped flat on the bed, holding her sides. Pony tried to resist. She did. But soon she was laughing helplessly as well.

They quieted sometime later.

"I guess we have to laugh about it," Pony said, staring at the ceiling from her supine pose on the bed. "Thinking I'm leaving for good."

"I guess. I don't think it could get any crazier, but you *are* coming back. Are you scared?" Alice turned her head to look at Pony, who was sprawled next to her.

"Of course. Of Donna. But also about being alone with Bebe for two days. You know, until today, I had never seen her in jeans and a casual shirt. Only business suits, even at the party. Kinda weird."

"Hmm." Alice returned her gaze to the ceiling. "She sure looked good. I had no idea she was so classically beautiful. Even though her face is kinda square and her mouth wider than, say, most pout-mouth models you see. And that long, thick hair."

"It's so expressive, too. Her face. Did you check out those gray eyes? I mean, who has gray eyes? I've never met anyone who had them."

"I did, once. My humanities prof. He had them. One time I asked him about how unusual they were and he told me only three percent of the world's population have gray eyes."

"Whoa and I thought my green eyes were weird." Pony pulled herself into a sitting position and gently slapped Alice's lean belly. "I gotta get ready."

Alice rose to her feet. "Yeah, better. Please, let's not piss her off. She's really being nice about this."

Pony lifted the suitcase from where it had bounced from the bed to the floor. "I know. She really is. I so thought she'd absolutely hate me. I mean, she's kind of straight-laced in some ways. And honest. Surely lying has to be a real sin in her eyes."

Alice handed Pony a small stack of T-shirts. "I dunno, Pone. She seems…well, savvy. You know what I mean?"

Pony frowned and shrugged, then busied herself with deciding what to take. A quarter hour later, she fetched her simple toiletries from the bathroom.

Alice had curled up on the love seat and was leafing through a technology magazine. "I don't know how you read this gobbledygook," she called to Pony.

Pony stuck her head through the bathroom doorway. "What?"

"These magazines." Alice shuddered. "Hey, what do you need me to do while you are gone?"

Pony sighed and brought her small travel bag out to place on top of her suitcase. "Nothing I can think of. I don't even have any plants anymore. I wish I knew what was going on at the office."

"Can't help you there, sweetie. Want me to drive by on my way to work each afternoon, just to see if I see Donna lurking around?"

Pony lifted a forefinger to her bottom lip, thinking about the suggestion. "That might be a good idea. And let me know if you see her at the club or anywhere else. It's a good idea to know where she is."

"She won't go after you guys, will she?"

"To Virginia?" Pony sat on the edge of the recliner. "Lordy. I sure hope not. I want to think she's a coward, but the way she's been acting…no, I don't think so. Who's going to tell her where I went? And besides, she probably realizes my family would make mincemeat of her if she showed up there."

"Does she even know where it is? Has she been there?"

"No, we never made it there during our time together. But she may know the name of the town, if she remembers it. I mentioned it only in passing, though, and never dwelt on it."

"I'm surprised you talked at all, especially after she cut you off from your friends and started controlling everything."

Pony nodded. "True. Hostility doesn't necessarily lead to good conversation."

"Well, I'm gonna go so you can get ready to lock up," Alice said, rising. "I still have my key, so let me know if I need to check on anything."

Pony stood and pulled Alice into a lengthy, warm embrace. "You are the very best friend," she muttered against Alice's shoulder.

They moved apart and Alice touched Pony's nose with a forefinger. "I'm just glad you aren't leaving for good. Be sure and thank Bebe for me, you know, for being so smart."

Pony smiled even though she knew her eyes were worried. "You got it."

After Alice left, Pony sat next to her luggage and wondered if she was doing the right thing. Truthfully, she just wanted to escape. Escape to the welcoming, understanding bosom of her large family. The past months had been fraught with worry, fear even, and she just wanted it to stop.

Her mind shifted and she thought about spending two days in a car with Bebe. And two nights. It was terrifying but exhilarating. She wondered about Bebe's reasoning. Could this horrible situation actually be reversed? Pony didn't think so, and she had gone into it fully understanding what the ramifications could be if lying about her name were discovered. She and Alice had discussed her means of escape from Donna at length. Changing her name, plus seeking out new living and employment options had been the only thing that they thought might work. And it had. At least until now.

CHAPTER THIRTY-ONE

The Journey Begins

Pony seemed to be a little uncomfortable as they sped along Interstate 40 heading east and Bebe was worried. Was she doing the right thing? Doubt nibbled at her but she felt propelled by instinct to get Pony to her family where she could find some measure of peace.

Bebe and her mother had once volunteered to help with donations at a women's shelter just outside the city. The abuse she had witnessed peripherally during that month of volunteer work had scarred her psyche. The hardest thing had been seeing many of the women repeatedly go back to the one who had abused them. And there was a tree outside the county courthouse with purple ribbons tied to the branches. Seeing it so often broke Bebe's heart and ended her volunteer work. It was too painful because each ribbon signified a woman who had died at the hands of someone who claimed to love them.

They passed into Texas and Bebe glanced at Pony, whose head was turned away watching the changing scenery. Bebe could not allow Pony to become a statistic. Pony could not become a purple ribbon on a tree branch.

"Did you know the price of gas dropped? I was surprised," she said, her tone light.

Pony turned, and those green eyes glowed in the late afternoon sunlight. "I saw that on the news. I also pass gas stations on the bus. I've been watching the prices come down."

"I need to read about how all that oil pricing works. It's never interested me too much, but now America is trying to break the Middle East control by digging for our own oil. As you can see out the window, Texas is just peppered with oil rigs and even refineries farther south. I can't decide whether that's a good thing or not."

Pony shook her head. "Not good. For the environment or for the people who drink water nearby. And don't even get me started on the harm fracking is doing to this country."

"Fracking. That's like using explosives or something?" Bebe set the cruise control on her steering wheel. I-40 was an easy straight shot almost all the way to the East Coast.

"Well, water pressure, mostly. They use it to break, fracture, the bedrock so they can get more oil with each drilling. I, personally, think it's so bad for the environment, no matter how safe they say it is."

"Sounds brutal," Bebe agreed.

A comfortable silence fell and Bebe relaxed somewhat. She felt like some of the distress that had entrapped Pony had abated, and this boded well for the decisions Bebe had made.

"So, back to talking about gas. Do you even realize what a misnomer that is?"

Pony frowned at her. "What do you mean?"

"Okay, gas is short for gasoline, right? And then there's natural gas, which totally is a gas. Gasoline is actually a liquid."

"That does seem weird."

"I read that the word gasoline came from the trade name Cazeline invented by John Cassel in the 1800s. When Cazeline went generic, common usage changed it to gasoline."

"So, why gas? Just to shorten it?" Pony was doing that adorable head tilt and Bebe melted just a little.

"Yep. It's also said that it came about because the vapors from gasoline are so flammable. Distillers wanted to remind people of that by saying gas."

Pony shrugged. "I guess that's smart."

"I guess. But it's weird to call a liquid *gas*. And a bit of trivia, it was first discovered as crude oil by this fellow who dug up petroleum in Pennsylvania in the late 1800s. Just like that Clampett guy on that *Beverly Hillbillies* show." She grinned at Pony. "But what *he* found, he distilled down to kerosene and used it in his oil lamps. And although his distillation also produced gasoline as well, he had no use for it and dumped it. Though many used it topically, believe it or not, as a treatment for head lice."

"Yuck," Pony said. "I bet that smelled great."

"Everything I read said it worked great. They didn't mention the smell. Or the fact that the fumes could ignite." She paused thoughtfully. "I wonder how many people had their hair catch on fire."

Pony looked at Bebe with wide eyes. "Oh, don't say that! That's horrible."

Bebe slowed to change lanes behind an eighteen-wheeler, then reset the cruise control. "Yeah, that would be bad. It's interesting how many things are made from petroleum. Those nasty, smelly oil rigs provide us with petroleum jelly, kerosene, asphalt, and diesel fuel, of course. Plus heating oil, wax, lubricants, and some solvents. Even stuff like makeup and shampoo. I guess we'd lose a lot if we did away with all of them."

Pony snorted and turned back to the window.

"Do you drive?" Bebe asked. She hadn't thought of that before. About why Pony took the bus.

Pony turned a curious gaze on Bebe. "Oh, of course."

Bebe sighed. "So, by not driving, you are helping the planet?"

Pony chewed on a thumbnail. "Well, I guess it does, but I actually like taking the bus. When I left...the west side of the city, I didn't have access to a car anymore. And that was okay with me."

"The west side. Is that where you and Donna lived?" Bebe glanced across, hoping she wasn't stirring up more grief.

Pony didn't appear overly troubled by the question. "We did. I was working at the college, in sysadmin, living in an apartment near campus. I met her there, at the college. She was a student but already had a house on that side. I think her parents arranged it for her. Or maybe her grandmother. Anyway, after a month of dating, she invited me to move in. I thought it was a good way to save a little money. I also thought I was in love."

Bebe thought about her time with Caroline. Not abusive certainly but still a failure due to poor choosing. "It's amazing how blinded we can be by the hope for love and intimacy. How we depend so much on other people for that."

Pony tilted her head again. "But you don't seem to. I mean, you seem pretty okay being by yourself."

Bebe frowned. "It's that obvious, huh?"

"Oh, no criticism implied." Pony reached across and laid her hand on Bebe's thigh, then quickly removed it. "I sort of admire that, you know, not being so dependent on others. Sometimes I think my backbone has disappeared and I'm just a marshmallow. Look how I depend on my family. I write one of my cousins just about every day and my parents and siblings at least once a week."

Bebe considered her own parents. Her mother Imogene Frances had been born into the wealthy Thomasly family, who still had interests in one of the main legal firms in Albuquerque. She was charitable and certainly duty-bound, but her relationship with her only daughter was cool—genial, but not necessarily intimate. She fostered the idea that a woman had to be powerful and independent. Bebe's father, Sherman, was a busy administrator of the city's public schools and so Bebe's relationship with him was only somewhat cordial as well. She couldn't imagine speaking to them as often as Pony spoke to hers.

"There's nothing wrong with that. Family should be important." She wasn't sure she meant it, but she felt it was the right thing to say.

CHAPTER THIRTY-TWO

Supping and Sharing

They stopped for drive-through veggie burgers and kept moving. This was A-okay with Pony as she really wanted her family. Seeking the warmth and understanding of them had become an act of faith, a religion that she fervently believed in. Not that being with Bebe was a stoic exercise, but Pony wasn't sure enough about how Bebe felt about her. It was a confusing issue, and she just didn't have the emotional stamina at the moment to deal with that.

Pony's confusion about Bebe's feelings had begun to gnaw at her. She had come to appreciate Bebe's steadfastness, intelligence, and especially her honesty. Living a life that was a lie had to put Bebe off. What Bebe had done for her, though, rescuing her from a job pandering to Ralph…well, it was something special.

Darkness had fallen, and the huge white wind turbines of northern Texas appeared to be shimmering ghosts. Pony had counted their red lights for a while but soon tired of trying to remember the previous number.

"Hey, Bebe. Do you believe in astrology?" This was as good an opportunity as any to get to know her coworker.

"Hmm, I think so." She shifted in her seat, straightening her back. "It's just astronomy, and that's about as ancient to humankind as it can get. It's like the foundation for everything."

"I know." Pony turned in her seat so she could face Bebe. "Ancient kings even used diviners when their babies were born to predict their future, based on their birth date. And then there's all the monoliths, like Stonehenge."

"What sign are you?" Bebe asked, glancing across.

Pony grinned, teeth flashing in the light from the dashboard screen. "You first."

"No fair! I'm a boring old Sagittarius."

"Ah, a truth seeker. An adventurer."

"Hmm, maybe. My life is pretty boring, though."

"Yeah. Mine, too. I'm a Taurus, May eighth. Child of the nineties."

"November twenty-third. Child of the nineties, as well. Though actually, I'm a little older, so some of the eighties, too."

Pony's voice held her grin. "Don't worry, I won't ask."

"Hmm, thanks. Taurus is a good sign. Oh, wait, you just had a birthday? I'm so sorry I missed it."

"No worries. I celebrated with Alice. Very low-key, though, just drinks and Italian food." She fell silent for a long moment. "You know, Taurus is a sign known for stubbornness and—"

"Some certainly good things, too, like earthiness and sensuality. Don't forget those traits."

Pony laughed, the sweet sound brightening the car's interior. "Oh, yeah. I'm in a real sensual mood after all the crap that's happened today."

Bebe chuckled. "Yeah, you've had quite the day today. And I want you to know how sorry I am about all this."

Pony squinted across the seats, trying to discern Bebe's meaning. "Seriously? What do you have to be sorry for? I'm the one who put my job in jeopardy by lying about who I am."

"True, but I feel some responsibility about not speaking out about Ralph earlier. Even before you came along. I had suspicions, doubts, but nothing concrete. I should have been more on top of that."

"It's not your responsibility to police the whole editorial office. Adults work there and we should know how to handle a creep like him."

"I know, but it bugs me."

"Has he ever really done anything to anyone? You know, really sexually harassed them?"

Bebe sighed and stretched her arms toward the windshield. "Not that we're aware of. He's flirted with others but never took it to another level until you came along." She glanced at Pony and smiled. "It must be the red hair. He certainly talked enough about it."

Pony looked out the window. "Hmm. And how do you feel about redheads? We're a pretty spicy bunch. Hot-tempered and again, stubborn."

"You don't scare me, Miss Hot Temper. I've never seen you lose your temper once in, what, three months of working together? I will agree with the stubborn part, though. I've seen a bit of that."

Pony laughed, still watching the shadowed passing scenery.

Bebe sighed loudly. "By the way, Pony? Pony Dakota? What sort of name is that?"

"Just…it's just family stuff, okay?"

"But then…why Emma Vernon?" Bebe seemed confused.

"I just kind of made it up. It's pretty run-of-the-mill. I was trying not to draw attention to myself."

"Okay. Back up. You have, what? Five degrees in various computer sciences and managements. A regular college degree, specializing in communication technologies. Plus a patent for software? Come on, you really think no one would, like, notice?"

Pony couldn't help the grin that spread across her face. She was proud of her accomplishments and having to fly low, because of Donna, rankled. "Yeah, I worried about that."

"Before I left the office, I scanned all the articles, the ones about the software you developed, the awards you've won. You are very talented with computers and how they operate. I stand in awe of that."

Pony turned her gaze back to Bebe. The barely perceptible lights from the dash hid details but the warmth of Bebe's respect and admiration flowed across to her.

"Thank you for saying that. This has been a rough year, since trying to escape Donna's unwelcome efforts to control my life. Sometimes I even doubted my skill and accomplishments. After all, how could a smart woman fall for Donna's manipulation? Shouldn't I have seen it? Dealt with it better? Stood up to her more?"

"Look, you knew enough to lay low and not anger her. From what Alice said, she can be pretty violent."

"Shouldn't I have spied some clue about that? Shouldn't I have noticed her violent tendencies?"

"Not necessarily. What was the first indication of her temper?"

Pony pulled in a deep breath. "It was in the early days. I'd been living with her almost a month. She was asleep one Saturday morning and I wanted to make breakfast for us. I grabbed up her keys from the table by the door and drove to the local market to pick up a few things. When I got back, she met me at the door. Her face was so angry. She took one of the bags from me and…and she carried it to the kitchen and slammed it on the kitchen counter, breaking some of the eggs, I discovered later. I sat my bag down and she grabbed me by the chin—well, she shoved me around pretty good."

"Just because you drove her car?" Bebe frowned in the dimness.

"Right. I'd driven it before, but with her in the car and that had been okay. I didn't see what difference it made but obviously I was wrong."

"How did you react, after that?"

"I brushed it off, at first, trying to believe it was just a fluke. Then I came home one day a few months later and she'd bought me some new clothes, baggy clothes, certainly not my style. My regular clothes steadily disappeared until the stuff she'd bought was almost all I had. She insisted I wear my hair the same way every day, too, braiding it for me every morning. Whether I wanted it braided or not."

"So, she was controlling as well as violent." Bebe looked questioningly at Pony.

"Yes. It was so easy for her. She could charm anyone, make excuses for her behavior," Pony whispered, averting her gaze. "I am so ashamed that I, like many others, fell for it."

Bebe sighed deeply. "Did she become more abusive?" she asked quietly.

"She did. Oh, not so much in the early days. In the beginning, to win me over, I guess, she was so sweet."

"They always are," Bebe agreed. "Those abusers."

"And I should have been prepared for it. Should have expected it would worsen. I can't believe I let myself be so blindsided."

Bebe shook her head. "You can't blame yourself. It just is, and what matters now is what you do with it."

Pony lowered her head. "I should have done more, legally. A restraining order. I didn't want her to know anything about me, though. About where I am now. I just wanted to escape."

"But…" Bebe thought a moment. "I understand," she said finally. "It would be good to have some legal recourse, but I feel that it's sometimes ineffective in cases like this. Do you think she'll leave you alone now?"

Pony fixed her gaze out the window again. "God, I hope so," she whispered.

CHAPTER THIRTY-THREE

Two Beds

"You paid for the petrol and the food. I pay for the lodging. It's only fair," Pony said.

Bebe hesitated but finally shoved her credit card back into her wallet and the wallet into the back pocket of her jeans. "If you say so."

She studied Pony as she paid, wondering how she could still look so fresh and together. Bebe was exhausted and knew she must look rough. She'd driven for more than eight hours, more than five hundred miles, ending up in east Oklahoma. They were both overdue for a rest.

"Is it okay if we share a room?" Pony asked, putting her room card into her wallet. She handed the other card to Bebe.

Bebe nodded. "Of course. Silly not to."

"Yeah, thought so."

"Have you thought about food?"

Pony tilted her head while thinking. "I'm always up for pizza."

"Ah, yes, I forgot." Bebe grinned at her.

"Let's order in so we don't have to go back out. You've driven enough for one day."

"Good idea." They made their way to the elevator, dragging their bags behind them. "You know, I actually like driving. I often take road trips."

"Alone?" Pony was watching her with a curious gaze. "I'd be terrified to do that." She pressed the elevator button for the third floor.

Bebe shrugged, feeling oddly defensive. "I've always done it."

"And you're never afraid? Suppose you broke down?"

They stepped out onto the third floor and Bebe checked the room number. She checked her card cover against the directional placard on the wall. "It's this way."

"I have triple A, and thus far, it's never been an issue," Bebe continued as they strode along the carpeted hallway. "I guess it's not necessarily safe. I mean, the world we live in…" She paused at their room door.

Pony placed a hand on her arm before she could insert the card key. She studied Bebe's face with a worried gaze. "Take me next time. Please? I would travel with you."

Bebe felt something inside her essence fracture as she met Pony's gaze. She let go of her bag and placed her hand atop Pony's. "Of course. I would like that. It would be fun."

Pony's smile was radiant, and Bebe had a hard time letting go of her hand so she could turn away to open the door.

The room was neat, clean, and typical of most hotel rooms, it smelled of powerful air freshener. It had two queen beds, a desk, and two chairs around a small round table. Bebe peeked into the bathroom and saw it had been modernized with a walk-in shower surrounded by glass.

"This is nice," Pony said, sinking onto one of the chairs. "Which bed do you want?"

"Doesn't matter. I'm too tired to care." Bebe studied Pony's slumped form. "Veggie pizza okay?" She moved her bag to the foot of the bed closest to the door and searched on her phone for a local pizza parlor that delivered. She placed the order then sat across from Pony.

"So, you'd really go on a road trip with me?" She was trying to engage Pony as it seemed she'd drifted away, lost in her own thoughts.

Pony turned an unfocused gaze on Bebe. "Yes, although we may never have that opportunity with me in Virginia."

Alarming thoughts gamboled in Bebe's head. "Don't say that," she said quietly. "You still belong in Albuquerque."

Pony shook her head. "She'll never let me live in peace. We both know that. I should have left New Mexico right away."

Bebe was panicked by the hopelessness that had infiltrated Pony's voice. She reached out instinctively and pulled Pony's hands into hers.

"Hey. Hey. Let's not make this worse than it is. Come on, no negative thoughts." She sighed heavily. "My grandma died when I was young, but she always used to tell me that time is the best thing to cure all ills that come into this life. You and I are betting on that now, aren't we?"

She was surprised to see tears well in Pony's eyes, and her heart hurt.

"We. I like the way you say that," she whispered. "It makes me feel…like there's some light at the end of my tunnel." She smiled and a tear broke loose and raced with frantic haste along her cheek. Bebe reached up and used a thumb to smooth it away.

"Thank you for driving me home," Pony added, her voice breaking. "I can't tell you how much it means to me."

Bebe fought back her own tears and hoped her smile seemed sincere. "You just did, Pony. You just did."

A knock at the door broke the tender moment, and later, full of pizza, they sprawled on their individual beds watching a true-crime documentary. "The neighbor did it," Bebe said during a commercial.

Pony looked curiously across at Bebe. "How could you possibly know that?"

"You don't see it?" Bebe realized that Pony had obviously not been paying attention to the program.

Pony rolled on her stomach, propped herself on her elbows, and studied Bebe. "What are you on about?"

Bebe turned onto her side so she could see Pony better. "Didn't you notice how helpful he was during the investigation?"

"And that's bad?" Pony rolled her eyes.

"Look, guilty people have certain mannerisms. One, they're too helpful. I mean, he kept inserting himself into the search for her. Two, they avoid eye contact—he always looked away when confronted or spoken to directly. Three, they project their guilt on others. He was blaming her best friend for the crime."

"And that means he did it?"

"Absolutely. Also, these types of programs have patterns, too. For example, did you notice that there have been no real interviews with him, you know, by the news guy? That means he's in jail."

Pony watched her and then blinked slowly, one time. "Omigosh. You're right. I never paid attention to that before."

Bebe rolled onto her back. "So, let's see if I'm right."

Pony gave a short laugh and fluffed her pillows, settling in for the final quarter of the show.

Watching her, Bebe suddenly didn't care if she was right or not. It didn't matter. What settled in her thoughts and shocked her into immobility was the fact that soon she would be sleeping, semi-dressed, next to Pony. Not in the same bed, true, but that didn't stop the uncharacteristic fantasies that now, unbidden, rolled through her mind. She turned away and tried to focus on the program, finding it difficult when the image of Pony's beautiful eyes, darkened with passion, appeared and persisted in her mind's eye.

CHAPTER THIRTY-FOUR

The Final Leg

"What do you mean, how can I do that? You have to talk to people. We all live on the same planet, right?" Pony studied Bebe with rampant curiosity.

Bebe had just commented on how easy it was for Pony to socialize. This after Pony had struck up a somewhat meaningful conversation with a woman in line at the coffee shop where they'd picked up a hurried breakfast.

"But they're boring," Bebe whispered, as though imparting a great secret. She scooted lower in the passenger seat and dropped her chin to her chest.

"Hmm." Pony blinked slowly, deliberately. "But the characters in your fiction books aren't?"

Bebe was startled by the statement. "Well, no, not really. I mean, they do exciting things, meaningful things. The everyday people we know, well, they live in mundaneness. Their lives plod along, day after day, and they find some joy in…" She paused to take a deep breath and gather her thoughts. "For example, they get so excited if their kid graduates from high school, or their daughter has an already expected baby. Or their dog goes to the groomer. Aren't these things normal things? Events that are supposed to happen? I mean, what makes these things so special? It makes me sad that people live such dull lives that they are forced to celebrate the most mundane happenings."

Pony slowed and changed lanes. "Mundane." Her voice was thoughtful yet melodic.

"Well, you know what I mean. I have a hard time listening to people drone on about the minor happenings in their lives, I—"

Pony held up a staying palm. "No. No. Don't go there. Look, I fully realize how intelligent you are, what an egghead you obviously always have been, but you fail to see the most important issue."

Bebe lifted her chin and stared at Pony. "And that is?"

Pony blew a raspberry at the windshield. "It all comes down to compassion," she said calmly. "Use that magnificent brain of yours and think about it."

"Okay, think about what?"

"That those mundane happenings are all that these people have. Unlike you, and maybe even me, who have a constant stream of stimulating input from books and computers, most people only have what they can get from their daily, yes, their mundane lives. The input they have comes from friends and family, television, church socials. That's pretty much it. Some may not even read for pleasure because they never developed the habit of doing so."

"I'm not sure I know what you mean." Bebe was frowning.

Pony lifted her gaze heavenward in frustration. "Oh, for Pete's sake. Let's talk specifics. Take Cory, who works downstairs with Dam and his bunch."

"The surfer boy with the blond hair that never looks combed?"

Pony nodded. "Yep, that's him. Somehow he became a programmer, mainly because he learned well in school. I swear the kid has a photographic memory. Now, upon speaking with him, I discover he's never actually read a book for fun, a fiction book, especially. But he is crazy about getting together with his friends and cosplaying, mostly *Star Trek* characters."

Bebe looked confused when Pony glanced across. "Cosplaying?"

"Yes, people who cosplay get together socially and wear costumes to represent characters in, I dunno, TV shows, Japanese anime, favorite movies. The field is endless. They, most of the time, cobble costumes together by themselves instead of buying ready-made pieces. He and I have spent gobs of time talking about this. Usually on Mondays, when he has some new fun thing that he did during the weekend to share with me. Or he'll tell me that someone was so cutesy in such and such costume. Honestly, I don't care about it. I'm too old for cosplay, it just doesn't appeal to me. But I listen. I listen because this is important to Cory and I care about him as a coworker."

"But aren't you bored?" Bebe studied Pony as she awaited an answer.

"Well, define bored." Pony shifted in her seat and took a sip of her coffee. "I guess I'm not necessarily bored because I feed on his excitement, his joy. I actually like how engaged he is."

Bebe sighed and turned to study the passing scenery. Things had greened up considerably as they approached Tennessee, and Pony wondered if Bebe liked the plethora of green trees alongside the road or if she missed the tan rocks and wide vistas of her desert home.

"Do you ever feel excited when people share themselves with you?"

"I don't know," Bebe answered, looking down again. "I think maybe I get impatient. My mind always drifts away, usually back to the latest book I'm reading. I just want to be there reading instead of listening to people go on and on."

"That explains a lot," Pony muttered. "But I have to admit I'm amazed at how well you get along with everybody at work with that attitude. And how you took me under your wing. You didn't have to be nice to me."

Sunlight coming in the side window slanted off Bebe's face, making her look younger, more tender than normal. She lifted her chin and studied Pony before answering. "You're special. I knew right away that we had some kind of bond."

Warmth filled Pony, and she smiled. "Really? Right away?"

Bebe shrugged. "It was like I...well, I knew you. And I was grateful that you were a bit older. Not some twenty-something slacker as I had envisioned."

Pony forced a frown but felt a grin creep through. "Seriously? Is that what you think of us software engineers? That we're all Gen Z lazybones?"

Bebe had the grace to look embarrassed. "When you put it that way, it doesn't sound so charitable, does it?"

Pony shook her head, raising her eyebrows as she glanced at Bebe. "I was happy you were older, too. I hate always being the elder in the room."

"See? My programmer stereotype wasn't so far off now, was it?" Bebe grinned in a self-satisfied way.

"Yeah, yeah," Pony said, waving a hand nonchalantly.

A companionable silence fell as they traveled through Tennessee. They'd made good time with light traffic and higher interstate speeds. The closer they came to Virginia, the more at peace Pony felt. Her future was still a muddled mess, but she felt like the indecision and despair was no longer going to choke the life from her. She glanced at Bebe, who was sitting sideways and had gone all dozy from the engine noise and the warm sunshine. Those beautiful gray eyes were closed and her pale cheek was made peach fuzzy by the harsh light. She was beautiful.

"You'd better keep those eyes on the road," Bebe said in a low, drowsy voice.

Pony turned her eyes forward quickly, as though she'd been pinched. "How did you know I was looking at you?" she choked out. She knew her cheeks were flaming crimson.

"Mmm," Bebe said. "I'd know those green lasers anywhere. Wanna stop for lunch? I'm hungry."

Pony sighed loudly, dramatically. "I guess I'm in for a lonely afternoon. If you get some food in you, you'll probably go out like a light."

Bebe yawned, covering her mouth politely with one hand. "I'll need some good sleep if I'm going to drive through the night."

"You mean we'll drive through?" Pony couldn't hide her surprise. She'd just assumed another hotel was in their future.

Bebe sat up and stared around as if trying to place her surroundings. "I thought since we're so close to Virginia. You said it was in the southwest part of the state, right?"

Pony nodded. "Yes. Just across the border. You take seventy-five north, like going to Kentucky, but you get off on side roads."

Bebe smiled, gray eyes amused. "So, you're telling me that when I get to seventy-five north, make sure you're awake."

Pony shrugged. "Umm, yep, that *would* be best. I can't imagine you getting lost in rural, truly rural, Virginia."

"Is it really that bad?" Bebe looked skeptical.

"Oh, you have no idea," Pony warned.

CHAPTER THIRTY-FIVE

Hillside Gap Township, Virginia

A small pack of dogs surrounded the car when the long dirt driveway finally emptied out onto a pleasant homestead site. A wooden post-and-rail fence defined the huge yard lot of a two-story American Foursquare with pale blue weatherboard siding. A wide, deep porch adorned the front of the house and the well-maintained wood of it gleamed bright white in the midday sun.

"Oh, my gosh!" Pony cried as she flung the passenger door wide. "Buster!"

"Wait!" Bebe cautioned but was roundly ignored as two dogs plowed onto the front passenger seat that Pony had vacated. A large golden retriever smiled inches from Bebe's face, his pale tongue lolling comically from one side of his muzzle. The tongue came to life then and licked Bebe's chin, the resulting moisture of the lick's path up her cheek making the escaping tendrils of her dark hair seem to project outward from her head. A smaller dog, maybe a terrier mix, pushed his way under the retriever and stepped into Bebe's lap, tail wagging the dog as he whimpered an expectant welcome.

"Carney! Salem! Get off her!" Pony scolded, one arm wrapped around a huge brown Labrador mix.

The two dogs welcoming Bebe immediately turned and scampered away to Pony's side, and Bebe breathed in a huge doggy-scented breath.

Squeals from the direction of the house drew Bebe's attention and her heart, still on alert from the doggy welcome, raced anew. She suddenly remembered it was Sunday and people would be home. Two children emerged from the front portal, racing across the grassy yard toward the wooden gate and reaching it even before the screen door slammed shut behind them.

"It's Pony, it's Pony," a young, dark-haired girl cried out.

"Pony! Pony! You're here!" shouted a chubby, red-haired youth.

The two children gathered around Pony, and Bebe's mouth fell open as she witnessed the chaotic scene unfolding just outside the car. She knew she needed to get out of the car, but she just wasn't up to it yet. As she watched, another child, a barefooted toddler wearing just a disposable diaper and a T-shirt, slowly descended the porch steps and waddled toward the gate. He was followed by a curvy woman, a blonde whose eyes grew large when she spied the car. She quickly ducked back inside and the house immediately ejected a geyser of people, all shouting and milling about as they tried to see who was visiting.

Pony shook off the children and dogs and stood, one hand shielding her eyes from the bright sun as she looked toward the house.

The mob of humanity moved forward quickly, the speed causing Bebe to hold her breath with something akin to terror. Then, at the fence, it stopped with uncanny abruptness, parting like the biblical Red Sea. A figure stepped into the void. The first thing Bebe noticed was that the woman moved like a queen, like royalty. Then Bebe was struck by the glorious riot of deeply colored hair that frothed loosely across the woman's shoulders. That hair! It was the color and texture of rich red paprika. Paprika that had been massaged in places to a heavy bright ginger.

The hair dwarfed the small body of the woman who bore it. Her thin, bare arms were pale against the dark blue of her sleeveless shirt, but as the woman approached, Bebe saw that they were just as freckled as the woman's pale cheeks and nose. This had to be Pony's mother. The resemblance was too keen. Maturity seemed to be the only dividing factor. That and the crystal blue of the mother's eyes, different from the spring green of Pony's.

The mother paused at the gate then slowly opened it as Pony smiled and moved toward her. Framed by the wooden picket gate and the fence on either side, the two embraced for a long moment. When they separated, Bebe was struck by the tenderness of their commingled gazes. Words were exchanged but so softly that Bebe couldn't make them out.

Their loving juxtaposition reminded Bebe of a painting by Emile Munier, a French portraitist from the 1800s. She had seen the actual work once while attending a conference in Washington DC and touring several art galleries while there. She had been deeply touched by the rich colors highlighting the lovely affectionate exchange between a mother and daughter. Created in 1888, the oil painting, one of his final works, had been hailed as a true masterpiece of his career and it was one Bebe would never forget.

Nervously, she quietly freed the door latch and stepped from the car. She was immediately pinned by a couple dozen sets of curious eyes.

A noise drew her attention, and her gaze flew from the crowd to the doorway of the home. A man stepped through it, allowing a screen door to slap shut. He studied the scene with remarkable calm as he slowly fastened a button-down flannel-looking shirt over his lean waist and chest. His smile appeared abruptly and, even from the twenty yards separating them, Bebe saw his unabashed joy at seeing Pony. He descended the porch steps and approached the gate.

"Da!" Pony cried out as she threw herself into his arms.

"*Ma wean! Ma wean!*" the man said as he whirled Pony about, her splayed sandalled feet barely missing the heads and faces of those who were still crowded around them. Pony laughed and, to Bebe's view, she was transformed into a ten-year-old child in her father's arms. The sight warmed Bebe's heart.

"Da! Come meet Bebe," Pony said as she extricated herself from his grasp. She nudged the gathered dogs aside and pulled him around the car by their clasped hands.

Bebe, seeing their approach, nervously pressed her entire back hard against the closed car door, as though the metal of the vehicle would protect her from the burden of socializing. And the dogs. She needn't have worried.

"Bebe, this is my da, Steve. Steve Dakota. Da, this is my friend, Bebe." Pony watched them both closely and Bebe could tell that this was an important moment for Pony.

Bebe extended her hand, ready for a polite greeting, but Steve, with boisterous good humor, pulled her away from the car and wrapped her in wiry arms, lifting her bodily from the ground. He spun them both once as the dogs sounded their joy, then he gently placed her back on her feet.

"'S grand to meet you, Bebe. Welcome to our humble home. Have you ever visited the wilds of Virginia before?" He squinted at her as he waited for her to regain her composure.

Bebe was taken aback by his obvious brogue and the delightful lilt to the words engendered by it. It took her several seconds to respond. "Y-yes. I mean no. I've never been to this part of Virginia before, only Charlottesville and up north nearer the DC area."

"Ahh, the money lands. Up there with all the rich politicians," he said, scoffing.

"Now, Da, don't go on so—" Pony began but she was interrupted by her mother.

"So, is this the Bebe you've been telling us about then?" she said as she approached them.

She extended one pale, slender hand. "I'm Foxy, Pony's mum. It's so good to finally meet you."

"Back, back you beasts!" the curvy woman said to the dogs. "I'm cousin Bernie. Welcome." She had sidled next to them, and she grasped Bebe's freed hand and shook it with firm force.

"Pony's been telling us all about you but she never said you were such a skinny little drink of water."

Bebe was confused. Her mind flew to the term "tall drink of water." It was an old Scottish reference for someone tall and attractive, so that was good. Yet in the vaudeville acts of the early twenties it had a derogatory meaning, portraying someone as lanky and scarecrow-ish. She agonized about which meaning Bernie intended. She could only hope it was meant in a positive way.

"Well," she prevaricated, even as her cheeks flamed crimson.

"You've embarrassed the poor lass, now, Bernie. Let's get them both inside with a cuppa so they can pull body and soul together. Traveling so just takes it out of you," Foxy said. She took Bebe's arm in the crook of her elbow, and they strode toward the house together, two dozen interested family members and three bouncing dogs following along behind.

CHAPTER THIRTY-SIX

Home, Where the Heart Lives First

Fey, it was good to be home! Pony stepped into the oh-so-familiar sitting room of her parents' cozy home. The scents from the dried herbs hanging along the rafter in the kitchen wafted through and teased at her nose, as did the ash from the fireplace behind her. She took in a deep, nurturing breath, feeling the stress from the past six months slough off her shoulders. There was a certain release when a person returned to their childhood home, a sense of being looked after, no matter their age or status in life.

"I'll put the kettle on," Pony's mother said as she slipped past, one hand briefly laid along her daughter's back. "You few just sit comfy now." Salem and Buster followed her, no doubt seeking a treat. Carney, the little terrier, stood by the door as though making sure everything was in its right place.

Ollie, Pony's favorite of the four farm cats, slept atop a bookcase in a sunbeam. He sneezed and looked at her with sleepy eyes. She moved close and scratched his head.

Pony smiled at Bebe, who stood as though shell-shocked in the middle of the oval woven rug bearing colors that pulled the room together. Her hair was still mussed in the front by the dogs but she was adorable in her jeans, trainers, and Oxford shirt.

"Welcome to my home, Bebe," Pony said softly. She reached out and took Bebe's hand, pulling her to a favorite well-loved sofa. They sank together into the deep, feather-stuffed cushions. Bebe's obvious bewilderment and fear stung a bit and Pony caught her bottom lip with her teeth. She had a lot of explaining to do about her huge and hugely eccentric family. She wished she'd given Bebe a bit more warning while they'd been on the road. It never occurred to her as they had so many other topics to discuss.

"I guess you're wondering—ooof." Colm Coo, Bernie's youngest son, just eleven months old, launched himself onto Pony's lap. He was followed closely by Bernie's older boy, Penn, and his cousin, Cinna, who was Pony's uncle Pierce's only child. They stood close, Penn leaning his upper body on the sofa arm.

"Bone," Colm Coo said as he settled himself into Pony's lap.

Pony sought clarification from Cinna, who shrugged.

"I think he's tryin' ta say your name?" she explained.

"Ahh, that makes sense," Pony agreed. She caught a glimpse of Bebe's horrified face and had to laugh.

"Can you say Bebe?" she asked, turning the toddler so he could face her. "Bebe?"

She handed the child to Bebe and he immediately wrapped his chubby fist into her long ponytail that had fallen forward across her shoulder. "Baby," he said, reaching up with his free hand to twiddle his fingers under her chin. Bebe's eyes grew wide and her mouth pursed as she stared at the child.

Steve passed in front of the sofa and scooped up the baby, carefully disengaging Bebe's hair. "C'mon, CC, me boyo. There's a biscuit with your name on it." He grinned at Bebe and winked.

Pony laughed. "Da to the rescue, as usual."

Cinna had wandered off and, with Carney in her lap, was watching her cousin Roddy play a video game on the large-screen TV. Penn disappeared into the kitchen with Steve.

"So, kettle's heatin'," Foxy said, coming into the room and perching on the edge of her favorite armchair. "Tell me what's goin' on out west these days. Are you still likin' the new position?"

Pony leaned forward. "I am. The hardware there is state-of-the-art. And the owner even hires women programmers, so there's that."

"Sounds like a perfect place for you. So, Bebe, Pony tells me you're an editor?"

"Yes, ma'am," Bebe replied after clearing her throat. "Of medical journals. I've been there at TWEI, I guess, more than fifteen years now."

"So, you're tellin' me that you're likin' what you do?" Foxy watched her with a teasing gaze.

Bebe smiled finally and Pony's heart stuttered in relief. "I must. Not sure I'd be able to do much else."

Foxy narrowed her eyes and watched Bebe suspiciously. "You're a bookworm, you are. Aren't you?"

Bebe leaned back as though startled. "You...how do you know that?"

"It's the sight she has," Pony explained. "We never got away with anything when we were younger. She always knew what we'd been up to."

"Oh." Bebe's face bore an incredulous expression and Pony had a sudden worry about how open-minded her new friend actually was.

"Reading is important," Foxy continued. "There's naught wrong with the flights of fancy writers create. I've always said it's the best way to make a productive nest in this life we're given. You take what you need and let go what you don't."

The toddler Colm Coo made a sudden return to the room, this time in the arms of his mother, Bernie. Buster followed and collapsed onto the woven rug in the front door area.

"All changed," she announced as she planted the two of them heavily into an armchair. "Fresh as a daisy."

She handed the child a cookie and turned her gaze to Bebe and Pony. "Pony, we've missed you. I don't know why you had to stay with that evil one out in the wild, wild west. Won't you come home now? Where you belong?"

Pony shook her head sadly. "It's not so bad out there. I used to get lonely now that I've moved out on my own, but it's gotten much better." She reached for Bebe's hand and patted it gently. She decided not to say that she might be coming back for good. That was a discussion best left for another time.

Bernie screwed up her mouth. "Well, doesn't change the fact that we miss you. If I didn't have to pay for the boys, I'd visit more. Have you seen the prices of the plane tickets these days? Highway robbery it is."

"You should make Bran take some time off one summer and y'all drive out there. There's so much to see and do. It'd be educational for Penn, learning about the Native tribes and where they live."

Bernie nodded and helped Colm Coo climb out of her lap. He raced to Roddy and fastened cookie-coated hands on the game controller. Roddy just shrugged him off and tried to ignore him, but Carney was only too happy to clean the cookie off Colm Coo's hands.

"That's a good plan," Bernie agreed. "I've never been away from this part of the country so it would do me good as well."

A loud click sounded and Foxy rose. "Tea comin' all around," she said. "Bernie, set the coffee table up, love, so we can have a proper table for tea."

Pony studied Bebe, trying to gauge how the introvert was taking the chaos that had spawned Pony and her siblings. She seemed incredulous but was maintaining well. Pony sensed a rampant curiosity seething in her and that was okay.

The heavy wooden door to the parlor creaked open and the familiar squeak of her grandmother's chair rebounded in the room. Pony couldn't help the squeal that escaped her as she leapt from the sofa. The sound set Carney to barking but she didn't care. Moments later, she was sprawled across her grandma's lap, her slight weight not even hindering the laborious process of the wheelchair entering the sitting room. Her cousin Sara Vern Dakota, who was pushing the chair, sighed loudly, dramatically, acting as though Pony was making the chore unattainable because she had added the extra weight.

"You just gotta cause trouble no sooner than you get here," Sara Vern said loudly. She turned the chair with expert ease and positioned it between two of the easy chairs. Pony didn't move. She was wrapped in the delicate arms of her paternal grandmother, inundated with her familiar Heavensent perfume. Life was good.

CHAPTER THIRTY-SEVEN

The Family Defends

Bebe was trying to make rational sense of the hierarchy of Pony's family. There were just so many of them! She easily pegged Pony's parents and maybe the grandmother—paternal, she thought—but there was a wealth of cousins and kids and... she could only shake her head.

"Did you call Cou and Bear?" Steve asked Foxy as they all sat around the centered coffee table sipping delicious, familiar black tea from a battered, pot-bellied ceramic teapot twice the size of any Bebe had ever seen. Foxy had spread delicious fresh cookies and small frosted cakes around the tray. Bebe was heartily glad to see that there were lemon wedges alongside the mounds of small cakes and the milk pitcher. Bebe had never liked milk in her tea, a preference that her mother considered barbaric at best.

The younger folk and the dogs had taken up positions on the floor around the coffee table and they were eagerly consuming the wealth of goodies Foxy had provided. Colm Coo even had his own sippy cup of tea.

"Yes, yes, they're bringing the chicken from Brawn's so Bernie and Cinna and I will start on the potato salad after tea," Foxy replied.

"I'll do the coleslaw, but I need to get the fixins," Steve said, popping a frosted petit four into his mouth. He chewed then turned to the teen who was still playing video games. "Roddy, will you fetch the coolers out the shed and spray 'em out? I'll get ice while I'm out so's we can chill the beers and the sodie."

Roddy nodded, his attention still fastened on the game.

"Mayhap I'll go, too," Foxy said. "I need a few things. You'll start the potatoes, won't you, Bern? The twenty-five pounds is at the back of the pantry. There's another twenty out back should you need it."

Bernie nodded. "Of course. Nah worries."

"Your name's not Bebe," the matriarch said abruptly. She leaned forward and fastened the gaze from keen blue eyes on Bebe.

Everything stilled. It was almost as though all had stopped breathing. The only sound was the soft musical chimes from Roddy's game. Bebe felt redness rise in her cheeks and neck.

"Um, no, ma'am," Bebe said. "My given name is Barbara. My little brother had a hard time saying it so he called me Bebe. I guess it just sort of stuck."

"Barbara. Yes," the elderly lady said, leaning back in her wheelchair. "I can see Barbara in you."

"This is my da's mam, Mrs. Astrid Dakota," Pony said into the respectful silence. "Sorry I forgot to introduce you earlier."

"I'm very pleased to meet you, Mrs. Dakota," Bebe said, trying to regain some semblance of dignity.

"Call me Astrid. It's good that you're here, Barbara. You make my Pony very happy."

Bebe glanced at Pony and was surprised by the sweet, embarrassed smile she wore.

"Better than that snake she met in Albuquerque," Bernie said. "That Donna made her life a misery, and that's no lie."

"She'd better not darken this door, I'll tell you," Foxy said sharply.

"Now, all, she's in the past and it's best not to speak her name lest she find me," Pony said calmly.

"Did she tell you about that snake?" Bernie asked Bebe.

"Bern!" Pony admonished. "I've not told her all of it, no." She smiled impishly. "No need to scare the poor girl off just as we're gettin' to know one another."

"Now, Pony, 'twasn't your doin' and you know it," Foxy declared as she placed her empty teacup on the table. She stood and gathered the empties onto a tray. Bernie and Steve rose to help. Within minutes, the coffee table was cleared, the dogs let outside, and almost everyone dispersed. Only Cinna, Penn, Colm Coo, and the matriarch remained with Pony and Bebe.

Bebe looked at Pony. "You never did explain the names to me."

Pony sighed. "Blame my da. He wanted us all to be named like my mother. You know, fox, Foxy. My older sister is Cougar and my baby brother is Bear. Weird, yes, but it works for us."

"Not even mentioning how like a wild unbroken pony you were. Even as a babe," Astrid said.

Pony laughed. "And how like a cougar and bear my siblings are, wouldn' you say?"

"Indeed," Astrid responded, nodding.

"But then...why Emma Vernon?" Bebe was confused but she did note how Pony's accent had become way more Irish than before.

"'Twas me who suggested it." Astrid said quietly. "The snake never met Sara Vern and never knew her name as such."

"That's true, I juggled her name a bit. I became Emma, or E. Vernon on paper so Donna wouldn't find me."

Astrid was eyeing Bebe with some anger snapping in her pale blue eyes. "That divvel probably figured Pony'd come runnin' home here with her tail between her legs. Staying on in Albuquerque and getting' a new job and place to live was the best move, all around. We said as much."

Sara Vern returned from her break, inadvertently slicing through the tension in the room. "All right, Miss Astrid. You're gonna have to rest up a little if you expect to go to the barbecue."

Astrid grunted once and nodded at Bebe as Sara Vern guided her chair to the doorway that led into the formal parlor.

"See you all in a little while," Sara Vern said cheerfully as she wheeled the grandmother from the room. "Glad to see you back home, Pone."

"Good to be here," Pony said in a low voice.

"We put a hospital bed in there after my granda Erdal died. Sara Vern is paid by the county to look after Grandma, and Mam likes having her around, believe it or not. Most wives hate their in-laws, but Mam and Grandma have always got along like a house afire."

Getting along like a house on fire. Bebe had heard the term before and knew it meant that the two women got along very well, maybe even fondly as they *were* family. She pondered the phrase and finally remembered that the saying was first coined in the mid-1700s. By a writer, if she remembered correctly.

Bernie stuck her head around the door of the kitchen. "Um, I know ya'll might be thinkin' you're company and all, but there's lots of potatoes that need peelin'…"

Pony rose with a smile and pulled Bebe to her feet. Her gaze met Bebe's and a silent communication of comfort passed between them. "We'd be happy to help, won't we?"

Bebe nodded and smiled nervously, hoping she knew how to peel potatoes.

CHAPTER THIRTY-EIGHT

Barbecue and Little Bears

When the Dakotas said barbecue, they meant it. A powerfully built, redheaded fellow had stopped in that town called Hillside Gap and brought home something that looked to watching Bebe like two wooden caskets that had been cut in two lengthwise. Struggling together, Steve, Roddy, and the large man immediately unloaded the crates from a lime-green truck and placed them atop a nearby picnic table. Donning what looked like surgical gloves, they unpacked the crates, avoiding the excited dogs, and loaded several dozens of chicken halves onto the grate of a cooker that looked a bit like an airplane fuselage. It was the same size and shape. The grill had been cut lengthwise as well and had a huge lid that could be shut down over the bird carcasses. The smoke that billowed out, especially when the lid was lifted, was majestic, and the emanation captured Bebe's attention for many long minutes. The rich scent of woodsmoke surprised Bebe with its acceptability. At least from a distance. She was sure that had she been standing above the heated grill as it was opened, it wouldn't be quite so pleasing.

"You Barbara?" The question was posed by a round, friendly face that appeared abruptly in front of her. Gazing from his friendly face to a second sweet countenance just behind him, she answered.

"I'm Bebe, actually. Everyone just calls me Bebe."

He extended his hand and Bebe absently took it. His heavy woodsmoke smell clued her in that he was the big ruddy fellow who'd brought the chicken to the barbecue. "Grandma pointed you out and she never did hold with anyone havin' a nickname. Nice to meet you, Miss Bebe."

"And you are?"

His mouth opened but the woman behind him pushed him aside and moved forward. "Boy's got no manners," she said, extending her hand. "Heya, Bebe. I'm Sissy, and this here's my husband, Bear."

A light bulb flashed brightly in Bebe's brain. "Oh, of course. Em…er, Pony's brother. I should have seen the resemblance."

There was a striking similarity between the two, even though Bear's size dwarfed Pony's. Both had a surplus of red hair and freckles, but Bear's eyes were a brownish-hazel color, very different from Pony's meadow-green eyes. He also wore a reddish scruff of curly beard along his cheeks and chin.

Bear lifted thick red eyebrows as he grinned even wider. "Yeah, the hair is a dead giveaway if you're a Dakota. Everyone sees us comin', that's for sure."

"Must be strong genes," Sissy added. "See them kids over there?" She pointed at a group of children gathered at the volleyball nets. "That taller redheaded gal is our Bridget." She cupped her palms around her eyes. "Hard to see who's who with all that Dakota hair out there. The one in that striped T-shirt, that's our Delaney. He'll be ten next month. The little one next to him is Jamie. He's eight but little for his age. The doc says not to worry about it, that he'll be hitting a growth spurt real soon."

Bebe nodded appreciatively as she studied the vigorous-looking trio of redheads. "And Bridget? How old is she?"

"Oh, Lord. Twelve going on thirty."

"She's an old soul, we say," Bear chimed in. "Grandma Astrid says so too, and she would know."

"She has top grades, though, so she's smart as a whip," Sissy added.

"Comes from your side of the family," Bear said distractedly. He was watching closely as his father, two other men, and Roddy worked with tongs to reposition the cooking chicken halves under the open lid of the large grill.

"With *your* parents? You gotta be kidding," Sissy said, scoffing. "And have you even met your siblings?" She grinned at her playful rebuke.

Bear rubbed Sissy's back lovingly and strode purposefully toward the men he'd been watching.

Bebe felt her throat clench in terror. It had been socially scary enough with Bear present, but now it was just she and Sissy. Alone. Whatever would they talk about? She took a deep, fortifying breath.

"So, Sissy, what do you like to do besides take care of these beautiful children?"

"Oh, I work full time, too," she said. "I work at the bank. Hillside Finance. I'm a teller."

"Do you, well, your bank, stay pretty busy?"

"Lordy, no." She grimaced and laughed. "There's less than nine hundred people spread way out through this whole township. And most of them have never even seen a bank."

Bebe's eyes widened. "You're joking!"

Sissy grinned and shook her head. "No, ma'am. There's only two part-time tellers and one loan officer in the entire bank. And that's why there's only one in the Gap township."

"Well, that's just—"

"Don't get me wrong. There's a good bit of money comin' through the bank. The older families, like the Dakotas, do a lot of banking and some do borrowin' for different projects. Steve and Foxy grow corn, for example, so that's always in flux. Thank goodness Foxy works as a nurse full-time. That gives them some good stability. Another older family grows cattle, same story, with someone working full or part-time for security. These families actually do have checkbooks instead of burying their money in the backyard in a beat-up coffee tin. Keeps us afloat."

"What made you decide to go into banking? Do you really like it?" Curiosity trickled through Bebe.

Sissy fell thoughtful for several seconds. "I do like it. I mean, I think I like to celebrate the little financial victories. You know, like the small businesses that make substantial deposits each day. It kinda warms my heart seein' 'em doin' so well."

Bebe nodded, impressed by Sissy's obvious compassion for the working man. Her mind chewed on the history of banking.

It did all start with farming, which was an interesting continuum. Merchants used to give grain loans to farmers who paid them back in grain which the merchants would, in turn, sell to traders traveling from ancient city to ancient city. And this was way before the Common Era. It then took off during Medieval times, especially with some of the wealthier Italian dynasties. The Medici bank was the first true bank, dating from the 1300s.

She touched a finger to her forehead trying to remember how long banks had been in the United States. She knew it had come across with the English settlers, but she wasn't remembering who set up the first commercial endeavor.

Bebe realized that Sissy was speaking to her and maybe had been for some time. She was saved from the embarrassment of woolgathering by the appearance of Pony, a grinning Buster at her heels.

"Heya, sis, what's happening?" Pony said, cheerfully greeting her sister-in-law. "You guys doin' okay?"

Sissy's attention diverted to Pony. "Oh, we are so good. Did you hear that Bear bought his own truck?"

"I did! He texted me a photo. It sure is a beauty. Why'd he go with neon green? Seems odd. I mean, it *is* pretty."

Sissy waved a hand as if dismissing the question. "Just so he'd stand out, of course. You know how he is. Wants everyone to see him comin' and goin' and say, 'There's old Bear Dakota.'"

Pony laughed and nudged Bebe. "That's my brother," she said proudly.

Bebe turned and studied the green truck. There was an insignia on the side but from this distance and angle, she couldn't quite make it out. "Green? Really? What does he do?"

"Towing. He even has a contract with triple A," Sissy explained.

Sissy's daughter and oldest son approached them.

"Omigosh, would you look who's here," Pony said as she gathered them close in a group hug. "Where's JamJam?" she asked, peering into their smiling faces.

"Still out with the cousins," Bridget said. Her mouth was full of corrective braces and the metal caught sunlight and flashed it into Bebe's eyes. "They're tryin' to get the volleyball net up."

"What's wrong with it?" Sissy asked as she strode away, the two kids following.

Bebe looked at Pony. "Well," she said.

Pony shrugged. "Well."

CHAPTER THIRTY-NINE

Cornerstones of Food and Rest

Looking around at her beautiful, crazy, loving family, Pony felt such emotion surge through her. Being here had definitely put her troubles at bay. So what if lecherous Ralph was trying to blackmail her? So what if she had to give up her job? So what if she had to give up Bebe and the life they might have had together?

She chewed her bottom lip and stared out across the expansive lawn that accommodated several dozens of her family members. And they were still arriving. The crowded picnic table they sat at gave them an amazing view of the fenced field behind the house, where the cooker and food tables had been set up. There were several heavy plank picnic tables as well as a dozen sandbag-weighted card tables. Chairs were scattered everywhere. The old adage of many hands make light work certainly was true in her family. It seemed they could accomplish anything in record time as long as they all pitched in. And they had, children as well as adults.

"Penny for your thoughts," Bebe said, bumping their shoulders together. "This potato salad is amazing. What's different about it?"

Pony shook off her pervasive thoughts and answered. "It's mustard. And lots of dill pickles. Some people call it German style, but my mam has made it particularly Irish."

"There's no chopped eggs," Bebe said, studying the hefty pile on her plate.

"Nope, just taties and onions, pickles and sauce."

"Do you know where that came from?" Bebe asked.

"What? Potato salad?"

Bebe nodded impatiently. "Well, yes, European settlers brought it across when they came, but it only had oil and vinegar with spices, no mayo. I meant 'penny for your thoughts.'"

"Oh, okay. So, where did that phrase come from? I bet you know."

"I do. Britain, of course." Bebe chuckled. "Four hundred years ago, a British writer named Thomas More included the phrase in a book he wrote."

"And it became that entrenched in our language?" Pony knew her eyes were wide.

Bebe nodded and swallowed a bite of salad. "There are so many little innocuous things that have crept into our language and just settled there." She reached out and caressed the tip end of Pony's ruddy ponytail where it was resting on her chest. "Like crowning glory, for example."

Pony felt heat rise up and her lips parted in a gentle pant. Why did Bebe's nearness affect her so much? She was definitely falling for the dark-haired seductress. Seductress, ha! Bebe was as civil as civil could be. Yet, there was an underlying steaminess just below the surface of her cool exterior. Pony sensed it, and she would love the opportunity to peel that top layer back and plunge headfirst into the magma pool of the woman she was coming to love.

"Guess who?" Two hands covered Pony's eyes from behind but she would know that voice anywhere.

"It's gotta be the Easter bunny 'cause she's just full of jellybeans," Pony exclaimed as she disentangled her legs from the picnic table bench so she could stand and pull her sister into her arms. "Omigosh, it's so good to see you! Where's Willem and the kids?" She looked around expectantly.

"Him and Benty are over talking to Da. Caitlin went to Debbie's house again. They're going to get their nails done so just had no time for Auntie Pony. She said she'd stop by tomorrow. She's drivin' now, you know."

A chorus of greetings caught the woman's attention. She waved and smiled to all the relatives filling the picnic table but her gaze fastened on Bebe. "Now, Pone, who is this sophisticated-looking beauty you brought for us to meet?"

"Oh, shoot, Cou. I think I got it in my thick head that everybody already knows who she is. This is Bebe Simmons. Bebe, this is my older sister, Cougar Bennett."

Bebe had already twisted in the seat to shake hands but Cou, a soft, plush woman, descended on her like a blanket, pulling Bebe into a smothering embrace. "Oh, girl, I'm so glad to meet you. Pony told Mam that you helped our girl out when there was a scuffle at work."

"Well, I didn't—"

"So, you're good people in my book," she interrupted. "Welcome to the Gap and I thank you for bringing my sister home."

And then she had moved away. "Eat up, now, y'all eat all that good food," she called out to the group as she moved around the table.

Her husband, Willem, approached next, and Pony leapt up to hug him and help him set up the two folding canvas chairs he carried, one of which was reinforced with screwed-on two-by-twos. This was important because although Willem was tall and lanky, his hedonistic wife, Cou, was not just big in personality but also big in body. As Pony watched her take a seat in her chair, positioned at the narrow end of the picnic table next to their uncle Canl and their aunt Emmy, she noted Cou had gained some weight since she'd seen her last. Didn't seem to matter much, though, because Cou said her health was impeccable according to Doctor Limon, who'd been looking after all of them since birth.

"Okay, I've met Bear, now Cougar, who else is left? Any other sisters and brothers?" Bebe asked in a teasing tone when Pony resumed her seat. "Is there a Tiger I need to know about? A Giraffe?"

Pony laughed and waved a fly away from her plate. "No, that's all of us. I don't think Mother Earth could tolerate any more Dakota kids. Three is plenty. Hey!" Pony had just realized that Bebe was picking on their names. "Don't make fun! We got enough of that while we were in school."

Bebe laid a hand on her back. "I'm just kidding. Your family is just amazing. How do you keep them all straight in your mind?"

Pony balled up her napkin and chewed the last bite of sprouted bread her aunt Chloe had contributed to the meal. "Sheesh. Let's see. You met Grandma Astrid? Well, she married Erdal Dakota, from Scotland. She was British, just a lass, but was there because her da had business dealings there. I think banking. So, they fell mad in love and they got married as soon as Grandma was of an age. They settled in Ireland, where Granda worked as a chef in a kitchen run by his brother, Alistair. It was in this big, fancy hotel and my da always talked about how they had use of the pools, the golf greens, and the tennis courts, not to mention free range of the place. Anyway, Grandma and Granda had my da, Steve, first, then my Uncle Canl. You met him earlier, that's him at the end of the table. Then they had Uncle Pierce, who's the youngest. Pierce is da to Cinna. You met her inside. He's married to Chloe. The skinny one with the dark hair and skin?"

Bebe nodded, so Pony continued, "Uncle Canl had my cousin Bernie. She married Bran Cooper and had Penn, Dryson, and baby Colm Coo, who you also met." She noted and relished Bebe's smile. "Her brother Shane's still playing the field, though he's been dating Delia Morse for a while now."

"So, Astrid had three boys?" Bebe asked.

Pony nodded. "Lord bless her."

"And Sara Vern?" Bebe was studying her closely and Pony wanted to move even closer but made herself stay put.

"Oh, I'm so sorry. She's sister to Bernie and their brother, Shane, who's not here today. He moved near Richmond for college." Pony found herself staring intently at Bebe's luscious lips and blushed. She pulled her gaze away to find her mother and her sister watching her with knowing smiles.

CHAPTER FORTY

One Bed, No Problem

Bebe seriously considered whether or not she'd ever met happier people. The clan Dakota seemed defined by laughter and play as much as their red hair. After the meal, contingents split off to play badminton, volleyball, various throwing contests such as horseshoes or getting small bean bags into large holes. Around a hastily constructed firepit, another group led by Steve on guitar offered someone on mandolin, another with a weird handheld drum, and a pretty woman who blew on pipes fastened together. The sound was incredible, perfectly played, and Bebe listened to the lively pieces with awe. A part of her felt compelled to dance but she knew she'd never embarrass herself in such a way.

Bebe and Pony had volunteered for cleanup duty, alongside Foxy, Cou, Bernie, and Aunt Emmy. This involved dodging begging dogs and making many trips into the Dakota's spacious, well-appointed kitchen and playing Tetris with the refrigerator storage. Many hands make for light work, Bebe thought as she saw how quickly things were restored to their normal state. One small table with desserts and drinks rested next to the huge, now-slumbering cooker in case anyone became peckish, Foxy said.

Later, as she and Pony seated themselves on canvas chairs that had been placed near the musicians, she thought of that proverb about many hands, often adopted by the Shaker sect in the north. She knew it was from ancient Greece but that it had been first noted in the 1300s, then later popularized by a man named Heywood who published the phrase in a book of proverbs. Maybe in the 1500s. Wherever it originated, this family proved its validity every day, it seemed.

Pony's deep yawn drew her attention. They had both driven throughout the previous night and she knew Pony had to be as tired as she was. One of Pony's hands had drifted down and she was drowsily playing with Salem's heavy fur coat. He was passed out, no doubt exhausted by his unusually exciting day and the many treats he'd consumed. A sudden concern about their sleeping arrangements played through her mind. Nevertheless, as tired as they both were, sleeping bags on the kitchen floor would be welcome.

"Sleepy?" she asked, leaning closer to Pony.

"Of course, she is," Astrid said from Bebe's left. "I'm weary as well as the craic has been mighty. I think I'll take my leave. Good night, bairns. May the peace of sleep bring you blessed brinn."

Bebe wondered what the Irish words meant, but after the wishes for a blessed night died down and Sara Vern had wheeled Astrid toward the house, she turned her attention back to Pony.

Pony smiled at her, green eyes gleaming in the firelight. "Tired I am, true, but I don't want to sleep and miss any of this glorious time with the family."

Bebe nodded. "They are pretty great."

"You feel welcomed, then?" She was watching Bebe closely.

"I do. They couldn't be any more gracious."

"One thing about my family, they do like people. They can be a bit suspicious of newcomers, though, until they get to know 'em, but they took to you immediately. That says a lot."

Sudden movement caught their eye, and Bebe saw that Willem and Cou had risen and begun dancing a lively two-step to the music. Bebe was mesmerized by how professional their movements were. Obviously dancing was a big part of their lives. Foxy and her son, Bear, soon joined them, then Emmy and Canl. Another couple that Bebe had met briefly—Foxy's brother Davie and his cute, chubby wife, Birdie—also joined the fun.

Pony turned to Bebe. "Do you…?"

Bebe was sure her deer-in-the-headlights look gave Pony pause.

Pony just laughed and jumped into the fray, pulling Bernie with her.

The world quieted just a bit as Bebe watched Pony dance with her cousin. The lively music faded away as Pony's joy in the dance, and indeed, simply being with her family, struck a melodic chord deep within Bebe's soul. Her heart felt as though it swelled in that moment and she knew, without doubt, that her burgeoning feelings were solid. She would love this beautiful, gentle, endearing woman for the rest of her life.

Three energetic tunes later, Pony finally cried defeat and came back to her seat. She was panting and sweaty, her face flushed and her smile wide. Bebe thought her never more beautiful.

Things had changed between them with Bebe's firm realization. Now the issue had become how to let Pony know how she felt about her. And should she? Bebe knew that Pony felt an abiding friendship with her, evidenced by her comments about them traveling together, for example. But could there be more? And Bebe being who she was, did she want to inflict her dour personality on Pony, who had mad social skills? Her thoughts flew to her ex and how their lives had clashed about that very issue. Would trying to be with Pony devolve into more of the same? It was a dilemma, and Bebe finally realized she was just too tired to think about it.

"Did you have fun?" she asked.

Pony had leaned back in her chair and her eyes were barely open. "I did. Our families have always loved the dance. It's an Irish thing."

"I can tell. Bernie's still going strong." They both watched as Bernie, Colm Coo in her arms, two-stepped lightly around the other dancers. Foxy's sister Penny and her husband, Shan, had risen to the musical challenge. "Why is Irish dancing and music so fast?"

"Are you as exhausted as I am?" Pony asked finally, ignoring Bebe's question. She stifled another yawn with her hand.

Bebe sighed. "I am. Where are we going to sleep? Is there a hotel nearby?"

Pony chuckled. "Not hardly. We'll just sleep in my old room. It's just gone dusk but I dunno if I can keep my eyes open much longer. Wanna go up?"

"Um, sure. Lead the way."

When they stood to leave, they were met with a chorus of good wishes and some random begging for them to stay. Foxy held up a staying palm, though, and new music quickly silenced the naysayers.

Once in the house, they mounted a narrow staircase that led to the second floor. Walking down a short hallway, Bebe peered into two rooms alongside and saw that they had been claimed. Or at least overnight bags sat in the doorways. "Who else is staying here? Is your parents' room up here?" she asked quietly.

Pony looked back. "No, they're downstairs, off the kitchen. These are for relatives. Some of them like to drink a little and my da has a firm rule. No driving after the drink."

"Good rule," Bebe agreed.

They paused in front of a wooden door at the end of the hall. It had been painted a bright spring green. A woven woodbine wreath was the only other decoration.

Pony opened the door and ushered Bebe inside. Their bags awaited them on the floor next to what looked like a closet door. A large double bed dominated the room with a small bureau to one side as the only other furniture. There was a magnificent colorful quilt on the bed and Bebe couldn't help rushing across to touch it. "Oh my gosh," she exclaimed. "This is so beautiful. And heavy!"

"Grandma Astrid," Pony offered. "She used to be quite the quilter before her hands got so stiff."

"It's amazing workmanship."

"Sorry the room's so small," Pony said, laying one palm on the quilt. "And you'll have to share the toilet and shower that's down the hall with the rest of the upstairs. The sheets and blankets are clean, though. Bernie said she saw to that herself."

"She's such a sweetheart," Bebe said as she sat on the bed and removed her shoes.

"We've been really close since we were wee ones. I'd be lost without her to talk to."

"Are she and Alice your main friends, then?"

Pony sat on the bed next to Bebe. "And you, nowadays," she said with a cheeky grin. "How about you? Do you have any close friends?"

Bebe shook her head. "Not really, just acquaintances. People always find me a bit weird once they get inside my crazy brain. I try to just keep myself to myself."

Pony nudged Bebe with an elbow. "Well, now you've got me. I like it inside your head. I think it's an awesome place to be."

Bebe felt a warm glow spread across her. "Yes, now I have you."

Later, after washing up and dressing for bed, they faced one another across the bed.

"Sorry you have to sleep with me," Pony said. "Bernie says I don't snore, so there's that."

Bebe laughed. "Hey, we stayed together in Oklahoma, remember?"

"At least there you had your own bed." Pony pulled back the quilt and top sheet and climbed into the bed. "If I kick you in my sleep, just kick me back, okay?"

Pony was asleep within minutes, but Bebe suffered. Being so close to Pony's sandalwood scent, their bare legs mere inches apart, was torture. Bebe wanted so badly to spoon her form close and bury her nose into that thicket of soft red hair. It was almost a physical ache. Instead, she turned onto her side, facing Pony's back, and twined a forefinger into a loose curl. Thereby anchored, she drifted off to sleep.

CHAPTER FORTY-ONE

Being Held

Pony woke in Bebe's arms. She wasn't sure how it happened but sometime during the night, their bodies had come together and they were holding one another. The warmth was intense, and she found herself wrapped in the delicious vanilla lotion scent of her office mate.

Office mate. Lying there in Bebe's arms, listening to the steady breath of her slumber, Pony realized anew that Bebe had become so very much more than that. Every waking hour was either spent with Bebe or thinking about Bebe. Now they were even together in sleep. She had become an integral part of Pony's life. It was a good thing, to her way of thinking.

Now, how to untangle herself without waking Bebe? She slid backward very slowly, slipping her arm from around Bebe's waist. She used her other hand to support Bebe's arm so it wouldn't fall and wake her. Within seconds though, Bebe's breathing had changed and sleepy gray eyes found Pony.

"Good morning," Bebe said. "What time is it?"

"No clue, but it's daylight."

"We slept a long time, then."

"We were so tired," Pony pointed out.

"So how do you feel now? Rested?"

"Oh, and surely. Ready for a new day."

Bebe studied her. "Do you realize how differently you speak here than when you're in Albuquerque?"

"How d'you mean?"

Bebe poked Pony in the stomach. "You've got a bit of the brogue in you, don't you?" she said, faking an Irish accent.

"Ah, fet 'n begorra. Dat's de worst brogue I've heard in me long life."

Bebe laughed and kicked off some of the quilt. Pony noted her slim, sleek leg and was momentarily mesmerized by the sight.

"Do you know the origin of faith and Begorrah?" Bebe asked.

Pony chuckled. "No, but I bet you do."

"I do. It's an exclamation and means, roughly, 'by God,' but it's just a contraction of *By Gomorrah*. It came into popular use in the 1800s but appeared first in the 1700s. Old English. It's not used much today, though, from what I understand."

"Ah, God. He hides from the Irish. He tore our lands asunder with no mercy."

"Are you talking about the conflict between Northern and Southern Ireland?"

Pony frowned. "I am, and it was a sad thing, the Troubles."

"So, you and your family truly do believe Ireland should be a free state, separate from Britain?"

"Of course! We are a very strong, proud people. And though the Celts came from central Europe, we claimed the land of Eire and made it our own."

"Let me guess, is it because you still have family over there who send you tea? From Southern Ireland." Bebe raised an eyebrow and Pony, seeing she was being teased, calmed.

"Truer words were never spoken." Pony stretched and threw off the quilt. "The leprechauns danced all night and I'm ready for breakfast." She rose and, gathering up her overnight case, raced down the hall to the bathroom, leaving the bedroom door swaying open behind her. Carney must have been waiting just outside because he came in and began checking out their luggage.

Later, after a quick shower, she returned to the bedroom wearing a thick, plush bathrobe. Bebe was still abed, dozing with Carney next to her, so Pony roused the two of them and she and Bebe made the bed together.

"What's the leprechaun thing?" Bebe asked around a deep yawn.

"Just a family saying. You know, 'May the leprechauns dance over your bed and bring you sweet dreams.' You've never heard that?"

Bebe lifted her toiletry bag. "Nope, never. I like it though. I might have to start using it."

Pony laughed. "Ah, the Irish. We do rub off on you."

Bebe blinked slowly and without a retort, made her way down the hall.

Pony took the opportunity to choose her clothes for the day and quickly donned them. She chose shorts and one of her white Oxford shirts. An idea occurred to her, so she dug down into the bottom of her closet and pulled out her worn, incredibly comfortable hiking boots. Bebe returned as Pony was choosing a light sweater to wear over the shirt.

"Hey," she asked Bebe. "How would you feel about a little hike?"

Bebe shrugged. "Sure. I enjoy a good hike. Do you have a favorite place?"

"I do. We can go up to see Old Bono and see how he's doing."

"Bono?" Bebe watched her curiously. "Who's he?"

"You'll see. I'll introduce you."

Bebe sighed. "Okay. I hope I brought something good to hike in."

"Did you bring shorts? Trainers? It's not particularly rough but you will need a jacket of some kind. It gets cool where we'll be." She paused a moment, noting Bebe's partial state of undress. After her shower, she'd just thrown on the jeans and shirt from the day before. "I'll pop down and let you get dressed. Maybe Mam left us something for breakfast."

Downstairs she discovered her mother was still home. And she'd made pancakes for the two of them.

"Ah, Mam," she cried, hugging her mother close. Foxy was dressed for work in dark blue scrubs, and Pony was so glad she hadn't left yet.

"Grandma?"

"She's had her eggs and toast already, though she gave half to that divvel dog."

Foxy turned back to the stove, dividing the stack of pancakes onto two plates. "And where's the lady at this fine mornin'?" she asked.

Pony took a seat at the huge oval table that dominated the west side of the kitchen. "She's gettin' dressed." She noted that her mother had already set the table with coffee, syrup, and a large slab of butter. "This is lovely," she added. "Thank you."

Foxy placed a plate of pancakes in front of her youngest daughter and rested one hand on her shoulder. "It's not every day my wee one comes home for a visit. Stan even gave me most of the mornin' away from work."

"That's grand, Mam. Just grand."

Bebe entered the kitchen and her eyes widened when she spied the buttered pancakes awaiting her. "Good morning," she said to Foxy, taking the seat next to Pony.

"How's about some coffee to kick-start your day?" Foxy said.

Bebe pushed her cup forward and Foxy filled both of their cups with a deliciously fragrant brew.

"You know I'm a tea girl," Foxy explained as she sat the carafe aside. "But Sissy swears by this brand. Says she and Bear drink it every mornin'."

She took a seat on the other side of Pony and sipped from her own cup. Pony knew from the fragrance wafting to her that it was indeed Earl Grey tea.

Pony chewed and swallowed a huge bite of pancake. "I thought we'd go visit Old Bono today. Has anything changed over there?"

Foxy shrugged and smirked. "Not that I'm knowin', and seriously, how often do things change around here? It's early yet though, in the season, so I'd suggest you take something warm to wear."

"Do we have any picnic fixins?" Pony watched her mother expectantly. "In case we go overlong?"

"Just help yourself to what's in the fridge," she said. "There's food from yesterday and some simpler things, too."

Pony laid a palm atop her mother's hand. "You're a gem, you are."

She glanced at Bebe, who had yet to dig into the pancakes, although she had made a hurting on her coffee. "You'd best eat up, Miss Bebe," she said, grinning. "You'll need those calories."

Bebe nodded and took a bite of pancake. Her eyes widened with pleasure.

"Yeah, she's known for her griddle cakes. She won't tell any of us the secret, though."

Foxy shook her head. "And I never will. These and my farls will go to my grave with me."

Pony frowned at her. "No need to say such a thing."

Foxy smiled sweetly and pressed a kiss to Pony's cheek. "I'll be off then. Need to get petrol this day so need more time. You girls have a lovely time out in the sunshine. I want to hear all about it when I get home tonight." She paused. "By the by, Clancy's house caught afire late last week and we're going to the church this evening to help sort goods for her. You'll both come help, won't you?"

She waited expectantly until both nodded. "Good. Tra la then." She rounded the table and unexpectedly gave Bebe a quick peck on the cheek as well.

Bebe's eyes grew very wide. She took another bite of pancake.

Pony laughed. "Before you ask, a farl is fried bread. Delicious."

CHAPTER FORTY-TWO

Old Bono

According to Pony, the Cumberland Mountains stretched all the way through West Virginia, Kentucky, and down into Alabama. As they drove through a valley below their magnificent heights, Bebe was held spellbound by their verdant, rugged beauty.

"The mountains have greened up nicely," Pony mused as they mounted a curving road leading higher into the mountain range.

Bebe noted the huge boulders on the mountain side of the narrow, curving road and leaned to look up and through the driver's side windshield. "None of these big rocks will fall on us, will they?"

Pony chuckled. "Not likely to happen, but after a harsh winter here, they've been known to come down." She looked at Bebe, gauging her fear. "Nothing to worry about. I think we'll be fine," she reassured her.

"My da used to tell us a story that one of his workers told him," she continued. "Remember the sign we saw tellin' us to watch for falling rocks? Well, once upon a time, there was a beautiful Native maiden who was in love with a young warrior but another, older man was vyin' for her hand. Her father, the chief, come up with a plan to send both the men out huntin', and whoever brought home more game would win the hand of Little Dove. The two went out into the forest and days, then weeks passed. Finally, the older man, who Little Dove did not love, returned with a huge cache of game. The chief was happy but the maiden insisted on waitin' for the other hunter to return. She waited and waited. Months passed and she never married. Finally, she and her mother went around puttin' up signs askin' for help in finding the man she still loved, whose name was Falling Rocks. So, to this day, you can still see the signs throughout the Cumberlands."

Bebe lifted a skeptical eyebrow. "Nuh-uh. No way."

Pony laughed and shrugged. "Hey, folklore has to be shared."

"It's really beautiful here," Bebe said quietly. "Very different from home."

Pony turned a curious gaze onto her. "Do you like it here?"

Bebe nodded. "I do. It's a nice change."

"So, you'll come visit me from time to time?"

Bebe fell silent for a long beat. "We'll come visit *together*. Anytime you want."

Pony navigated a narrower part of the road, bordered by a guardrail on a cliffside. "I can't go back for good, Bebe. I'll go back to settle up my affairs there, but you know I can't go back to TWEI. Mostly because of Ralph, but also because Donna found out where I work. I mean, she could easily follow me home. Then what would I do?"

Bebe sighed, wishing Pony would choose to trust in Bebe's promise to take care of the mess left behind in New Mexico. Pony had to stay in Albuquerque, and Bebe had already bent herself backward to ensure that Pony would be safe when they returned. Now was not the time to broach the subject, though. This day was their day, and one they would enjoy together.

A prolonged silence fell in the car and lasted until Pony pulled into a large clearing that had been asphalted and was surrounded by guardrails. A path had been marked with a sign saying that the path was two point five miles to Cavenorn Ridge.

"Is that where we're going?" Bebe asked, pointing to the sign as they locked the car.

Pony shrugged into her backpack. "Sort of. We're heading off to one side, though."

"You'd better not get us lost," Bebe warned jovially. She was pretty sure Pony knew the area well and she wasn't too concerned about the hike.

"Come on, scaredy-cat," Pony said, taking Bebe's arm and pulling her along.

Scaredy-cat. Another term that had become part of their modern language. If she remembered correctly, author and socialite Dorothy Parker had included the term in one of her books during the 1930s. From there, it had found everyday usage to refer to someone who was skittish and afraid.

"You're thinking about that phrase, aren't you?" Pony said, stopping their progress to grin at her. "Let's have it, then."

Bebe laughed and shared her knowledge about scaredy-cat.

Pony just shook her head and led the way along the path. "You thoroughly amaze me, you know? I can't believe you're able to retain all this stuff."

Bebe frowned at her own weirdness then brightened as she realized that she was following Pony, who was wearing short denim shorts, along the steep hiking trail. "Just lucky, I guess," she said, smiling.

The sounds of deep forest surrounded them—strange rustlings, some bird calls, strident bird chirps as they were warned away from nests in overhead branches. The smell of pine sap was heavy on the air, and Bebe took a deep breath, relishing the scent. "Smells good here, doesn't it?"

Pony looked back over her shoulder. "It does. I just love it in the woods. This part of Virginia is a lot more humid than Albuquerque, but up here you don't really notice. I guess it's the elevation."

"I guess," Bebe agreed. She was trying to decide, once again, whether to broach the tense topic of Pony leaving Albuquerque.

And once again, she decided against bringing it up. The day was too beautiful, too serene to interrupt with talk of practicalities.

After another twenty minutes of slowly meandering along the trail, Pony veered left along a smaller trail.

"Uh-oh, where are we going?" Bebe asked. She tried to impart nervousness but truthfully, she wasn't nervous. Not one bit.

This trail was narrower, and bushes grabbed at them from both sides.

"Watch the stones on this path," Pony warned. "I wicked twisted my ankle once, and Bear and my da had to come carry me home."

"Can you get a cell phone signal up here?"

"No way, but Da always insists I carry a satellite phone in my pack. Good thing he did that day. Even then it was two hours before a usable satellite came into range."

Bebe grinned. "You mean they had sat phones way back then? Amazing. Your dad must have been cutting edge."

"Hardy har," Pony responded. "Hey, we're here."

"Here? Here where?"

The bushes parted then, and Bebe quit breathing for just a few seconds. The amazingly beautiful Cumberland Mountains surrounded them and were spread far below, imparting incredible shades of blue, green, and gray as far as the eye could see. An honest-to-goodness golden eagle flew across the vista, calling out his distinctive screech before disappearing behind a ridge.

"Omigosh," Bebe whispered. She'd seen a lot of sights in her forty-plus years, but this one made the others pale in comparison. She realized that Pony was watching her and not the mountains around them.

"Look down," Pony said gently.

Bebe complied and saw that they were standing on a huge, solid rock outcropping. It was bare stone, worn smooth by time and weather.

"Say hello to Old Bono," Pony said.

"Old Bono," Bebe repeated. "Hello."

Pony moved to one side where a fallen cedar tree trunk had been manhandled into a sort of seat. She lowered her pack then carefully waved a nearby stick around behind the log.

"What's that for?" Bebe asked curiously.

Pony spread her arms, maybe indicating that Bebe was an idiot. "Rattlesnakes. Duh." She must have seen the alarm on Bebe's face. "None there, don't worry."

She sat and patted the log next to her, inviting Bebe to sit with her. "Are you hungry?"

"Not after that breakfast," Bebe answered. "Your mom is an amazing cook, by the way. Even the stuff she made for the barbecue was delicious."

"She is. Be forewarned, though. Never expect me to cook like that. I can barely boil water for tea."

Bebe liked the idea of expectations, or the lack thereof. "You sound like we're about to become an old married couple."

Pony looked at her with that adorable head tilt. Her green eyes were sad and shadowed. "I would have thought that, liked that. Once." She turned away, her gaze scanning the amazing scenery before them. Moving her gaze down to the backpack, she pulled out a can of beer. She handed it to Bebe and took one out for herself. "Open it carefully. It's been shaken a bit."

They both held the cans away from themselves as they opened them. The coolness must have helped because they didn't spew as expected.

Bebe hated that Pony had been saddened by their situation. "Here, let's toast to a future that still could be," she said as she held out her can.

Pony reluctantly touched cans with her, and they both drank. "Best friends?" Pony said.

Bebe shook her head. "I want more."

Pony looked at her quizzically. "More? More what?"

Bebe took her free hand and held it tightly. She leaned in and placed her lips softly onto Pony's beer-scented ones. Their eyes met and sweet, honeyed emotion grew between them. They kissed again, and Bebe finally knew how Pony felt about her.

CHAPTER FORTY-THREE

Community

Pony's heart was breaking. Just as she found a love that she could believe in, she had to move more than two thousand miles from her. How could the goddess she believed in be so cruel? She looked at Bebe as they walked along the larger trail and they shared a fond, loving smile even as Pony despaired.

It was dusk already. The two of them had explored the area around the trail, then returned to sit close together atop Old Bono for hours, holding hands and watching the mountains change into their evening finery. And they had talked. Oh, how they had talked, all the while carefully avoiding the fact that they would soon be parted. Both had grown glum, though, as they had packed up their beer cans and the wrappers that had held their peanut butter and jelly sandwiches. Pony had wondered if Bebe felt the loss as keenly as she did. Not just of their magical hours together but of the now difficult long-distance relationship that was to be their future.

At the car, Bebe threw the backpack into the back seat and opened the driver's side door. "I'll drive," she said. "You navigate, okay?"

Pony nodded and slid into the passenger seat.

Bebe backed the car around and pulled onto the road that led down the mountain. "Thank you for introducing me to Old Bono," she said once they were underway.

"I've been going up there for what seems like forever. First with my da and mam, then my siblings, then later on my own. It's a great place to think things through and to get a bigger picture than just what worries you in a moment."

"You have to admit, it's a little scary up there. When you went out to the edge, my heart stopped."

Pony smiled. "I didn't mean to scare you, love. I just wanted to see if the squirrels still had their nest under that side rock."

"Shame they left the nest, but if I were a squirrel, I wouldn't want to sleep under there, risking the fall of death every time I turned in my sleep." Bebe shook her head as Pony laughed at her.

"We should probably go straight to the church," Pony said, leaning one hand on the dash as Bebe navigated a tricky turn in the road. "Mam and the others probably went there right after work."

"Will they be mad that we're late?"

"Not likely. I'm sure there's a crowd there. Will you be okay with that?"

Bebe shrugged "I guess I'll have to. I want to be wherever you are."

"You know, we need to talk about the future," Pony said nervously. "I know it's not pleasant but—"

Bebe took her hand. "Not now, okay? I want to bask in those kisses we shared. Bask in being with you. I don't want to think that far ahead. Can you do that for me? Hold off until I'm ready?"

Pony frowned but nodded. "Sure, sure, hon. I can wait. I'm sorry I'm so sad about it. I mean—"

Bebe squeezed her hand. "Shh. Not now, okay? Be happy. You're with your family. We don't want to let anything spoil that, now, do we?"

Pony caressed Bebe's forearm and smiled, pushing her disturbing thoughts away. "No, you're right. I'm so glad to be with them. I haven't asked you since yesterday. What do you think of the entire clan Dakota?"

"They're amazing. And your mother's family is just as much fun. I wish the Lowes had come earlier. I barely got to people-watch them."

Pony laughed. "My Granda Lowe is a maniac. Did you see the way he held his arm up as he wiggled then spun Grandma Deb around at the dance?"

"No offense, but aren't they a little old to be that crazy?"

Pony nodded energetically. "Yeah, right? Irish people just don't seem to age the way other people do. They just get scrawnier and tougher."

"Hm, something to look forward to," Bebe muttered. She cleared her throat. "I meant to ask you. What is with your father's family name, Dakota? Isn't that from one of the languages of the Great Sioux Nation?"

Pony grinned and nodded again. "So how did my Scots dad's family come to be called that? I forget about it sometimes. Their name, when they came across, was Donchraidh. And of course, not one person in Boston could pronounce it properly. Finally, someone, an American checking them in, said Dakota, because it sounded somewhat similar and that's how it came to be."

"Wow. Say that again."

"What? Donchraidh? You like that?"

"Yes, but I could never say it. Holy cow. I see why it was changed."

"Gaelic, especially Scots Gaelic, is a hard turn to master. Sometimes my da gets talkin' too fast and I have no idea what he's on about."

Pony directed Bebe into the town proper and they parked on the side of the main road as the expansive parking lot was full.

"See? Told you," Pony said with a deep sigh as they locked the car.

The town of Hillside Gap was small, with just about all of the businesses lining the gently curving Mountain View which served as the town's main street. Pony spied lights on two side streets but she knew they were just housing communities for many of the nine hundred residents.

It seemed as though everyone in town had gathered together at the huge clapboard church, and Pony took another deep breath, gearing herself up to socialize as they approached the front doors.

Bebe, on the other hand, seemed to have oddly little trepidation as she stared up at the beautiful metal Celtic cross that was well-lit atop the high steeple.

"Well, let's head in and see if we can help. Poor Clancy's house caught fire and she has six bairns. I hope they didn't lose everything."

Inside the church, Pony was greeted enthusiastically by the townsfolk. It took the two of them a good thirty minutes of handshakes, hugs, and introductions just to get to the area around the altar where tables of clothing, kitchen utensils, and new toiletries in ziplocked bags rested. Foxy was already there, kneeling next to a quietly talking woman.

Pony approached from the side opposite Foxy and threw her arms about Clancy, rocking her gently to and fro in her chair.

"What doesn't take us makes us stronger always," Pony said, her gaze finding Clancy's deep brown eyes, which were heavy with past tears. "You'll get through to the other side, I promise."

She asked after the children just as Maven approached. Maven, at thirty years old, had been just behind Pony at Hillside Memorial High School.

"They're all right as rain," Maven answered for her mother. "Little Alec got a burn to one arm but Dr. Limon believes there'll be nary a scar."

"Oh good. He's wee yet, so he'll have time to heal," Pony responded. "Were your little ones in the house as well?" Pony remembered that Maven had two young sons that Clancy looked after but she couldn't recall their names.

"No, thankfully, they were home with me."

Pony caught Maven staring at Bebe, who was standing to one side looking a little lost among the fray around them. Pony grabbed her hand and pulled her closer. "Mave, this is my girlfriend, Bebe, from New Mexico."

"New Mexico? I'd heard tell you were working there now. I—"One of Maven's boys ran up and grabbed her hand, muttering something about candy. Maven shrugged apologetically and let herself be pulled away.

Bebe was grinning, her gray eyes bright. "Girlfriend. I like that."

Foxy must have overhead because she got to her feet, one comforting hand still on Clancy's shoulder. Her smile rivaled the sun. "Well, well," she said, pulling Bebe close to her side. "Welcome to the family, little Barbara."

CHAPTER FORTY-FOUR

Entwined

The Hillside House of God was a huge church but, interestingly enough, had no pews. Instead, there were two long metal racks at the back of the room with hundreds of folded chairs stored in them. Bebe guessed when it was time for church, you just grabbed a chair and sat where you wanted. Odd but interesting.

After Foxy had introduced her to Clancy and they visited a while, Pony and Bebe had wandered to one side where people were sorting donated clothing by size on top of a trio of folding tables. Although she didn't know the entire Clancy family, she helped sort just by using the sizes on the labels. She was eyed with curiosity by many of the older woman but, seeing that she was with Pony and truly there to help, they welcomed her roundly.

One pile, obviously for young Alec, made her heart hurt. He was so small, just a toddler. And to have to be injured in a fire, well, it just wasn't right. She picked up a tiny pair of faded denim jeans and smoothed out the legs before folding them and adding them to his pile.

"Can you help me fold this, ma'am?"

Bebe looked down and saw a small girl, no more than four or five, looking up at her. She had straw-colored blond hair, uncombed, and wore a dress too big in the shoulders. It had slid to one side, exposing one pale, thin shoulder.

"Of course, I can," Bebe said. "Let's get you up here so we can do it properly."

She lifted the girl up and sat her on a cleared edge of one of the tables. Together they laid out the small chemise-style dress and Bebe helped her smooth it and fold it.

"What's your name," Bebe asked, trying to make conversation.

The girl smiled, her baby teeth like little white opals. "I'm Elly O'Brien. What's your name?"

"I'm Bebe. Nice to meet you." Her eyes drifted to the handwritten sign saying the donations were for the O'Brien family.

"Bebe, like a BB gun?" One forefinger wandered to her mouth as she pondered her own question.

"Exactly. You don't have a BB gun, do you?"

Elly shook her head, eyes wide. "Oh, no. But my brother Johnny has one." She leaned forward and whispered more information. "He shoots rabbits with it." She glanced at Clancy. "Don't tell Mama about it, okay?"

Bebe shook her head. "No. No, I won't. So, you had a fire at your house. I'm so sorry."

Elly released a heavy sigh. "My mama said it was a leak in the stove."

"Did it explode? Blow up?" She studied the girl's heart-shaped face.

Elly nodded. "Mama took us outside 'cause she smelled it. The baby got hit by a board though. There was fire everywhere. The grass was burning."

"Sounds horrible, but you're okay though, right?"

Elly had become distracted by a flannel shirt in the pile of clothing. "Can I have this?"

"Let's see if it fits."

Bebe helped her shrug into the flannel shirt then buttoned it for her. It was a perfect fit.

"Hey, Miss Elly. That shirt looks so good on you. See this blue here?" Pony had approached and now she indicated part of the blue-and-green plaid in the flannel shirt. "It exactly matches your eyes."

Elly grinned happily. "I think it's pretty."

"Wanna go show your mama? She needs something to cheer her up."

Elly nodded and, after Bebe lifted her down from the table, she and Pony walked off, hand in hand.

Tears welled in Bebe's eyes as she thought about what Elly and the other children had witnessed. Thank goodness Clancy had smelled the gas and kept the children outside. It could have been immeasurably worse.

A young man approached Bebe. He had a receding hairline to his dark hair, and his brown eyes studied Bebe with rampant curiosity. His clerical collar clued Bebe in to his role in the church.

"Hello, I'm Pastor Timothy. Are you new to the area?"

Bebe smiled and shook the extended hand. "Ah, no, sir. I'm just visiting. With the Dakotas. I'm a friend of Pony's. From New Mexico."

"Well, welcome to our little hamlet. Are you here long?"

Bebe smiled at his small-town nosiness. She found it oddly endearing. "No, sadly, just for one more day. I'm only on vacation and I have to get back to work."

"Ahh, the shackle of making a living," he muttered.

"So, this is your church? Your congregation? This building is so beautiful."

He smiled, one cheek dimpling in his lean face. "I thank you for that. I do a bit of carpentry work, and this actually used to be a rather rough, unfinished warehouse for the tobacco industry. Donated by one of the wealthier families."

"Really?" She glanced around at the polished wood trimmings and then down to the expertly finished wood floor. "You're very talented."

Pastor Timothy blushed. "Well, thank you. I have to admit, I felt inspired. It seems to keep the townsfolk coming to church, even just to see what new work has occurred, so that's important."

"I find the chair option interesting. You know, instead of pews."

"Ah, yes." He smiled fondly. "Pews are very expensive, and a very early congregational vote decided the issue. They liked the idea of random sitting, I think. Some of our parishioners prefer to sit alone and at the back. I have no issue with that. At least they come to the warmth of God's house regularly. That's what matters most to me."

Pastor Timothy intrigued Bebe by speaking in such absolutes, and she would have liked to discuss his ideas about God but was interrupted by an elderly woman who eyed her suspiciously.

"Pastor Timothy. The food is ready."

"Ah, good. Good. If you'll excuse me." He left with the woman and Pony came up to her.

"Hey, there," Bebe greeted her. "That Elly is a cute one, isn't she?"

Pony nodded. "She is. You were so good with her, too. She likes you." She paused and turned closer to face Bebe. "Have you ever thought about having children?" She was doing that adorable head tilt and Bebe couldn't help but grin like a fool.

"So, you think I'd be a good mother? Really? I don't know. There was a time in my life when I thought about maybe adopting, you know, as a single mother?"

"Why didn't you?"

"Work, doing it alone, my age, the messiness that babies bring. I don't know. I guess I just let the desire fade away. What about you? Have you ever thought about having children?"

"Only every day of my life," Pony exclaimed.

"Seriously? Well, why haven't you had one, or adopted? Something?"

Pony turned to face forward, seeming to avoid Bebe's gaze. "Same as you, work, doing it alone. I know, from my own family experiences, that kids are a lot of work and to do it properly takes time and patience. I do love the little imps, though."

"You'd be a fantastic mother," Bebe said softly. She moved closer so Pony could hear her clearly. "You should have children."

Bebe laid one hand on Pony's waist from behind.

Pony chuckled. "Lots and lots of them?" She covered Bebe's hand with hers. Their gazes met in a loving embrace.

"I don't know about *lots*, but one would do."

Pastor Timothy clapped his hands, drawing the crowd's attention.

"Come on, folks, let's all gather around now. Clancy and Bob, and their children, would like to have a word. After that we'll open the courtyard where food has been laid out by the Ladies Guild for all of us to enjoy."

He stepped aside and Bob, Clancy, and their group of children moved to stand at the front. Bob O'Brien was a lion of a man, with grizzled blond hair that had been corralled into a low ponytail. His face was covered with a close beard and mustache and his pot belly was his most prominent feature. Clancy, on the other hand, had a whole body that had softened into a comfortable middle-aged spread. Her long, darker hair had been braided tightly and coiled about her head into a circular crown of braided hair. Maven, holding her bandaged brother Alec stood alongside Elly, a gangly high school teen and two other boys who may have been middle-school age.

"I'd like to say, we can't thank you enough for the kindness and care you have shown us this night. God may take away but He gives more than He takes. He gave us this amazing community to look after us in our hour of need," Bob said in a gravelly voice.

Foxy approached and took Bebe's hand in hers. The touch, and the silent acceptance, brought tears to fill her eyes. She blinked them away, embarrassed.

Clancy spoke next but Bebe drifted. God. Before the Common Era, in 840, a stela bore the earliest known reference to the God, Yahweh, of the Israelites. The Germanic word, God, first appeared in a sixth-century illustrated manuscript containing part of the Christian Bible. The idea of God had been around for a long, long time, and Bebe fervently wished her academic mind would allow her to have more faith in such things. She glanced at Foxy, then at Pony, feeling some comfort in the faith that they possessed. It was enough for her.

CHAPTER FORTY-FIVE

A Brand-New Bed

Even with a full belly of church-provided food, the immediate Dakota family gathered together for a soothing cuppa before retiring for the evening. The family room was warm and cozy, and the lights of the table lamps added to the ambient peace.

Foxy filled Astrid and Sara Vern in on the events at the church with Steve regaling them with how good the food had been. He gave specific details and crowed about the various cooks who'd donated dishes.

"Some of the best cooks in the Gap work with the church guild," Astrid agreed. "And mothers are training their daughters in the skill, or so it has been going on most of my adult life." Astrid looked pointedly at Pony.

"Now, Mam," Steve said in his youngest daughter's defense. "The girls now are more career-oriented. It's just their way."

"Hmph," Astrid snorted. "Everyone has to eat, Steve, me boyo. Everyone, even the boys, need to know how to cook."

Steve shrugged and nodded in agreement. It seemed as though he knew better than to go against his mother. "I suppose so."

Pony spoke up, sharing the highlights of their hike to Old Bono, while Bebe touted the beauty of the area to appreciative ears.

"You definitely had one of the best seats in the house," Steve told them. "Was it cold still?"

"Not too bad," Pony said.

"And the Bebe was there to keep you warm, I'm thinking," Foxy teased.

Bebe turned bright red under Astrid's questioning gaze.

"Well, it's time we were all abed. The corn greets me early," Steve said.

"And the hospital calls to me as well," Foxy said.

"I'll get Miss Astrid tucked in," Sara Vern said, wheeling her away amid a chorus of farewell and wishes for good slumber.

Bebe and Pony joined in with Foxy and Steve to clear away the tea, and soon two very weary women were climbing the stairs.

"What a day," Bebe said as they approached Pony's bedroom along the quiet hallway.

"Seems weird with most everyone gone back to their normal lives," Pony muttered. She had known the entire family couldn't be with her the whole visit, but she felt a little sad and hoped she'd see most of them again before she had to make the trip back to Albuquerque. Coming back home to live here in Virginia would be a different experience at this point in her life, and Pony made a mental note that she had to have a sit down with her mother and father to plan out the rest of her year. She knew she could stay with them as long as she liked, but a thirty-four-year-old woman needed to be living her own life.

Sharing a bed that night was so different from the previous night. The intimate kisses of the day had spawned a new physical desire that seemed to be on both women's minds as they lay side by side.

"So, what now?" she said aloud, addressing this new emotion that had grown between them.

"Time. We give ourselves time," Bebe answered sleepily.

Pony held her breath as Bebe's lips brushed hers. Bebe took in a deep breath and Pony fancied that their souls met and mingled. Her heart soared as their lips met again and again and she tasted the beautiful woman she already loved.

Once settled into the cool bedclothes, Pony rested her head on Bebe's outstretched arm and buried her face into Bebe's lotion-scented shoulder, waiting. She felt no urgency for more. Just being this close, possessively loving and being possessed by Bebe's arm was enough for her. Yes, a part of her desperately craved Bebe making love to her, but she realized that there was no hurry. They could build a lifetime together if they wished.

Bebe seemed to feel the same way. "I have a confession to share," she said finally.

Pony lifted her eyes so she could see Bebe's profile in the dimness of the bedroom. "What's that?"

"I've never done this before."

"You mean…" Pony's eyebrows lifted.

Bebe chuckled, the sound resonating below Pony's cheek. "Seriously. I've never felt…comfortable enough with anyone to just do this."

Pony understood. "Ahh, you mean cuddling. You've never cuddled."

"Not really. Dolls and stuffies maybe, but never a woman. I always felt like I had to perform, like there was always something I just had to say or do."

Pony frowned and her voice was serious. "Please hear me. You have nothing to prove to me. I have no expectations, other than that you respect me. And maybe a little heartfelt emotion, some love, if you can get there."

Silence fell and Pony felt like Bebe was digesting her words. After some time, Bebe yawned and turned so she could wrap her arms tightly about Pony. "Oh, yes, I'm there," she said sleepily.

Pony smiled and let herself doze off, safe in Bebe's arms.

The trill of a cell phone woke the two of them the next morning. Pony drowsily checked her watch and saw that they'd slept away a good portion of the morning.

Bebe fumbled for the phone and peered at the caller ID.

"Hey, hey, just waking up. Hold on," she said into the phone. Pony eyed her dreamily but curiously until Bebe mimed having to go to the bathroom. She took the phone with her and Pony yawned, knowing she should rise but lacking the desire. She dozed off again.

"Okay, sleepyhead. If I'm up, you have to be up," Bebe said cheekily as she pulled the covers tight on her side of the bed.

Pony stretched, trying to wake her limbs. "I don't remember seeing that rule written anywhere," she said amiably. "Who called? Work?"

She rose and helped make the bed.

"Just my family calling to make sure a mountain man hadn't carried me off to be his baby mama."

Pony grimaced. "Oh, how gross." She shuddered at the thought.

"Yeah, well, they worry when I do anything that's not in my usual routine."

Pony stilled and realized anew how much Bebe had stepped aside in her life to help her in this situation.

"What?" Bebe said, watching her. "Are you okay?"

Pony felt moisture well in her eyes and seemed to have no control of the tears that spilled down her cheeks.

"Oh, shit, Pone, what did I do? I'm so sorry, whatever it was." Bebe rushed around the bed and pulled Pony into her arms. Pony rested her cheek against Bebe's warm, strong shoulder and felt a new contentment that she was coming to accept and desire.

"It's just us," Pony murmured, immediately realizing that it was not the answer Bebe needed. "I just want to say thank you for this trip. For being there for me. I…I just love you so much."

Bebe pulled away and used the neckline of her sleep shirt to dry Pony's face. She kissed Pony on the nose. "You're welcome, sweetness. This journey has been so…" She stopped speaking as though she had no words.

Pony smiled. "Crazy? Exasperating?"

Bebe laid a finger against Pony's lips. "Absolutely life-changing."

Pony smiled happily. "Really? You're okay with my busy, Irish clan?"

"Yes, of course," Bebe said with a snort. "But just remember one thing."

"And that is?" Pony was concerned.

"That I said I love you first. Up on Old Bono." Bebe grinned a cheeky grin.

"Oh, I'll naught forget that," she said, pressing her lips to Bebe's.

CHAPTER FORTY-SIX

The Secret is Out

They found Steve, Astrid, and Sara Vern populating the kitchen table when the two of them came downstairs. Sara Vern rose and busied herself at the counter loading bread into a large toaster as Astrid and Steve discussed the option of growing a separate, personal garden with Silver Queen corn, just for the family to eat. Carney was in his usual bed, curled in Astrid's lap.

"And a happy morning to all," Pony said as they entered the kitchen. She pulled out a chair for Bebe then seated herself. "I couldn't help but hear, Da. Did you plant the garden this spring?"

Steve pushed the teapot toward his daughter and Bebe. "I did. Moses laid out the rows an' we planted forty-five of them tomato plants an' then mounds and mounds of squash and cucumbers. The leaf lettuce is all planted as well. Under the canopy, of course."

"So, no peas? How about the green beans? I know you planted taties, and I like the corn idea. Silver Queen is my favorite."

Steve laughed. "An' well I know it," he said. "The peas and the beans were planted the week past."

He turned to Bebe. "This girl will eat her own weight in fresh veg," he said, making it sound like a warning. Bebe just laughed, once again finding his accent, though thick, endearing.

"An' where's the harm in that?" Astrid interrupted.

"Aye, none, were she home. There's nil that'll be going out to her in the west, I'm thinking."

Bebe sipped her tea and glanced toward Pony. She saw the battle going on in her face. She laid one hand on Pony's where it rested on the table. She caught her eye. "Please, don't," she said.

Pony just pulled her hand away and looked at her apologetically. She turned to her grandmother. "I may be back for a while," she said.

Sara Vern turned from the counter. "Really? You'd come back here? Why?"

Bebe swallowed nervously and averted her gaze from the others.

"My work found out I lied about my name, is all," she said in a low voice. "They let me go."

Astrid studied Pony's face. "Ah, so that was the trouble that Bernadette was talking about."

Pony nodded, her lips pressed together.

Anger flared in Bebe, and she so badly wanted Pony to trust her. Part of her understood—one's work is one's livelihood and shouldn't be left in limbo. Just that morning, though, Bebe had put the final part of her plan into place and it did not involve Pony moving back to Virginia. She spoke up.

"It's not definite. Pony's skills are badly needed in our business. She's already made some amazing innovations. We'd hate to see her go."

Astrid watched her with an astute gaze. "You mean that *you'd* hate to see her leave."

Pony was watching her as well. She cleared her throat. "Of course. I don't want her to ever leave." She lifted her gaze to meet Pony's.

Astrid was smiling as she took a bite of the thick, buttered toast Sara Vern placed in front of her. Sara Vern offered some to Steve but he motioned it away. She placed some on plates that had been stacked on the table and handed them to Bebe and Pony.

After thanking Sara Vern, Pony added jam her to toast, busily losing herself in the process.

"Seems to me," Steve said quietly, studying his tea mug. "Seems that my Pony should be the one makin' that decision."

Pony looked at him and Bebe's heart stuttered. Suppose Pony wanted to stay here, or come back here after settling her affairs? It could happen. Would Bebe be able to give up her life in Albuquerque? Where would she live? What would she do? Where was the nearest town where she could find work? These questions gamboled in her mind and she suddenly felt sick to her stomach. She leaned and topped off her cup of tea and gulped down some of the hot, heavy brew.

Pony sighed loudly. "I dunno, Da. Bebe wants me to see the lay of the land when we get back to the city. If there's any hope left, I'll stay, to be with her and the job. But if the company decides to blacklist me in the business, I can maybe come back here and find computer work in Bristol."

"Sounds like you've thought this out," Sara Vern said, taking a seat and helping herself to more tea.

"I've thought of little else," Pony admitted with a sigh. "I do love Albuquerque." She laid her hand atop Bebe's and continued, "But I can't stay where I can't work."

"But there's the college where you used to work, right?" Sara Vern offered.

Astrid tutted. "There's the divvel there still and she'd surely find our girl. That can't happen."

"That's true," Pony added. "She'd find me and make my life a living hell. And if there's a mark next to my name, the college probably wouldn't have me anyway."

Steve stood and carried his mug to the sink. He braced his back against the counter and studied the family. "You've got some decisions to make, ma wean. But remember this. You'll always have a home here. Always."

Astrid balled up her napkin and laid it on her plate. "There was a Russian author who said that the two most powerful warriors in this life, are patience and time. You need to remember that. Both of you."

She wheeled herself back from the table and headed toward the parlor. Sara Vern rose and cleaned up Astrid's place setting as well as her own. "You heading back out, Uncle Steve?"

"I am." He moved toward the back door that led outside. Salem and Buster met him eagerly when he cracked it open. "Hank and Miller need a steady hand, they do. Otherwise, I'll have corn being planted on the neighboring lands." He and Sara Vern shared a laugh, and he left the kitchen with a wave to Pony and Bebe.

After their simple breakfast of toast and tea, they cleaned the kitchen and Pony led Bebe out through the back door. Off to the right, Bebe saw the clearing where the barbecue had been held, but off to the left, across a dirt road that rounded the house, she saw a huge expanse of young corn, the small leafy plants occupying field after field of perfectly laid rows.

"I thought I heard someone, maybe Sissy, say your dad grew corn," she said. "Funny how you only see the fields from this side of the house."

Pony smiled at her. "Oh, that was a brokerage between the parents. Mam wanted the corn business not to impact the surroundings so much but, as Da only owned so much land, he had to bring the fields close to the house. So, they made a deal havin' them only on this rear vantage."

"Ah, makes sense, I suppose. How many acres does your dad have?"

Pony was leading them away from the house and down the road past the corn fields. "Only about two hundred in corn, but he has another three in horse feed."

"Horse feed? What's that?" Bebe was confused, trying to imagine what grain it would be. Oats?

Pony paused to look at her. "You know, grasses for hay, like timothy, fescue, some white clover, even Kentucky bluegrass. He makes a lot of money selling that. More than for the corn. There's lots of thoroughbred horses in the neighboring states." Pony was on the move again.

Bebe was entranced by the little leafy corn plants in their mounded dirt beds. She bent down. The swordlike leaves were dark green, with sharp edges. "Did you know that you can dry corn leaves, then grind them up to make a tasty flour?"

Pony paused. "I had no idea." She shook her head. "I can't even imagine what it's like up there in that noggin of yours."

CHAPTER FORTY-SEVEN

The Cooter

Pony got to the riverside first and she turned and waited for Bebe to catch up. "C'mon, slowpoke!" she called.

"Hey, in case you have forgotten, I am on my annual vacay here. You've no call to rush me," she protested, gaining Pony's side. "Where are we going, anyway?"

Pony grinned at Bebe, excited to show her yet another one of her favorite places. She took Bebe's hand. "You'll see. Remember, I roamed this land for the first seventeen years of my life. I have so many things to show you."

Bebe looked puzzled but seemed accepting.

Pony walked slowly along the river, making sure that Bebe was on the river side so she could appreciate the beauty of the water as it rippled, creating whitecaps across the high stones.

"It's really cool that you have a river here. Does it have a name?" Bebe asked.

"Oh, it's not officially a river, though we often call it one. It's actually just a creek, a really wide one, but it's not a river because there are no tributaries."

"Seriously? That makes the difference? I didn't realize that."

"Oh ho!" Pony crowed. "I finally know something you don't." She grinned teasingly at Bebe.

"Smarty pants," Bebe muttered. She grabbed both Pony's hands and spun them around in a circle, only connected by their hands. She did it until they were both a little dizzy and breathing hard from the exertion. They laughed as they stumbled onward.

"Well, what do you call this creek, river, whatever it is?"

Pony swallowed hard. "Don't laugh, okay? We call it the Dakota Waterway. It's even on the local maps as such."

Bebe gave an accepting nod and Pony was pleased. "Dakota Waterway. It's a little pretentious for a name, I'd say, but it's a nice name nonetheless."

Pony heard the sudden rush of water and her excitement grew. "Almost there," she called out. "D'you hear it?"

Bebe's eyes grew wide and she nodded.

Twenty yards farther and they were there. Pony stopped and took a deep breath, inhaling the negative ions engendered by the huge waterfall that divided the waterway.

"Holy cow," Bebe said, standing perfectly still next to Pony. Her mouth was open and her eyes wide.

"This is one of my special places," Pony said, speaking loudly next to Bebe's ear. "Let's go down below. I have a favorite rock."

"Will we get wet?"

"No, not too much. The falls aren't that close. Come on!"

Bebe obediently followed Pony in a slanting descent along the riverbank. Creatures large and small disappeared into the water as they descended. Pony took it in stride, but she could tell Bebe was nervous.

"Don't worry. The snakes usually stay above the falls. It's too busy down here for them."

"But what were those things that went into the water?" Bebe asked, voice raised so Pony could hear her.

"Probably just turtles. They gather here during the mating season," Pony answered.

Bebe remained suspicious, cautiously examining every step she took out onto Pony's rock. The huge boulder was one-third buried in the rushing water about five feet away from the falls. Pony held her hand tightly and they sat together on the wide, partially rounded top of the rock.

"What is it with you and rocks?" Bebe said against her ear as they settled.

Counting the one they were sitting on, there were a trio of large boulders that descended into the stillness of the pond below the waterfall. The still water part was a deep blue, fading to gray as it shoaled across a piled-up, rocky bottom.

"I used to swim here a lot, but the water level went down and it got kind of mucky on the bottom. And then there's the turtles. They'll bite sometimes if they think your toe is a worm or a crawdad."

Pony chuckled, watching Bebe pull her bare knees close to her chest and wrap her arms around them. She seemed on sensory overload, just waiting to be attacked by nature. Pony felt bad for teasing her, but she also wanted to share the beautiful rural world she'd grown up in. She pulled Bebe close, and together, shoulder to shoulder, they silently watched the waterfall cast ribbons of rainbow out into the dappled sunlight.

Sometime later, Pony pulled away and reached into the pocket of her shorts. She handed a plastic bag to Bebe. "Hold this a minute," she directed.

Leaning forward, she used a smaller rock to bang on the side of the big rock they sat upon. She waited expectantly then repeated the banging. Soon her old friend stuck his head from the water and lumbered his heavy body onto the middle flatter rock.

"Holy shit!" Bebe cried out. "What the hell is that? An alligator?"

Pony grabbed her to keep her seated. "Be still, you'll scare him. Just hold on. Old Coot won't hurt you."

"C-Coot?" Bebe looked terrified, her gaze fastened on Coot's yellow-and-black-striped, snakelike head as it bobbed back and forth.

Pony took the bag and opened it. She lifted out a large piece of bread she'd gotten from the kitchen. Coot lifted his head and peered sideways at her with his chameleon-looking eye.

"Yeah, it's me, old man. Back for a visit." She leaned forward onto her stomach, her arm just barely reaching Coot where he rested on the middle rock. She laid the buttered bread down and gently patted his large shell.

"Bebe, meet my old friend, the Eastern River Cooter." She turned her head to gauge Bebe's response.

"He's huge," Bebe said loudly. "What is he?"

"Just a freshwater turtle."

"Pony, hon, this is no turtle. This is a monster. Turtles are little things that sun themselves on logs by the riverbank, not this, this—"

"Calm down, Bebe. Yes, he's big, I know, but I've been visiting him down here since he was the size of my hand." She paused and studied Coot's new growth. His shell now had to be more than twelve or thirteen inches in length with a diameter of a good eleven inches. It had darkened with age as well, the yellow patterning more muted. He looked healthy, though. His eyes were agile and bright and his tail longer and thicker than before, meaning he was well-fed. His long, spiky claws were strong, too, and they scrabbled on the rock to better position him to beg for more food. Pony reached out to the riverbank and grabbed a handful of greenery which she slowly, lovingly fed to him.

She reached back and handed the bag to Bebe. "Here, give him a little. He'll love you forever."

"And I want his turtle love…why?" Bebe's nose scrunched in distaste and her gray eyes were guarded.

Pony just watched her, mouth tilted in demand.

"Okay," Bebe said, then sighed. She pulled a piece of bread from the bag and leaned forward, hand visibly shaking. "He won't bite me, will he?"

"Probably not. I've been feeding him a long time so he's used to it. Just slowly lay it on the rock next to him if you're scared."

Bebe eyed her disdainfully but continued to lean toward the huge reptile. As she got close to the head, which extended farther out eagerly, she did place the bread down on the stone next to him. Tilting his head sideways, he grasped it quickly and tore off a piece which he seemed to swallow whole. Bebe leaned back then scuttled farther back on the rock, still watching him as though horrified.

"Isn't he sweet?" Pony said, tickling him on the neck with a piece of long grass.

"Sweet? *Sweet?* Are you crazy? He could have you for lunch."

"Oh, stop. He's harmless." She sat up and broke the remainder of the bread into smaller pieces and then threw them onto the still water of the pond, tucking the empty bag into her pocket. Old Coot went after the bread, his huge body dropping into the water like a World War II underwater explosive. After gobbling the bread, he treaded water, his eyes watching Pony, his pug nose twitching. She knew he remembered her, even though it had been years since she'd been home.

"Goodbye, old fella. Stay healthy and have lots of babies." She stood and pulled Bebe up with her. Silently they climbed the sloping bank until they were back on the dirt road. They walked alongside the river, hand in hand.

"Did you know they can live up to forty years? The cooters. People around here call them barred terrapins."

"Barred terrapin? I guess terrapin makes sense. Although it's my understanding that the terrapin name is only used for one specific turtle these days." Bebe was watching the corn again and replied distractedly.

Pony pulled her arm to get her attention. "Don't you think that's interesting? That the same turtle can have two different names. Same turtle. Two names. Same turtle. Two names."

Bebe laughed and pulled Pony close, pressing their bodies together. "I get it, *Emma*. I get it."

CHAPTER FORTY-EIGHT

Family Hijinks

As soon as they entered the house from the back door, they heard voices coming from the family room. Pony shared a quizzical look with Bebe then led the way through into the house. The family room was full, with Astrid, Sara Vern, and two other young women that Bebe hadn't met. The television was on, showing a news program but the sound had been turned down to a low murmur.

"Oh, will you look at this?" Pony said as one of the girls rose from a recliner and approached to give her a big hug. "Look at you, all grown up!"

"Yeah, it happens when ya ain't lookin'," the girl said.

"Bebe, this is my niece Caitlin. She's Cou's girl," Pony said.

"And don't forget, the bright light of her existence," Caitlin said, rolling her eyes and making a dismissive face.

No hand was offered, so Bebe just nodded and smiled as she took in the chubby teen's appearance. Caitlin was dressed in maroon patterned flannel trousers that looked a lot like pajama pants. Above those, she wore a bright pink tank top bisected from the pants by a neon green scarf tied about her waist. She wore bright yellow plastic clogs on her feet, sans socks, and her curly red hair was bound by a bright paisley print head scarf. At least a half dozen necklaces and even more bracelets, metal and cloth, adorned her neck and wrists. She was absolutely amazing.

"I don't know if she'd see it that way," Pony said in a teasing voice. She turned to the other teen. "Debbie Mays, you sure have grown up. And you're so pretty!"

Debbie rose and moved into Pony's arms. She was a stark contrast to Caitlin, with long dark hair that framed her thin face like a set of curtains. She was thinner in body as well but wore a funky outfit similar to Caitlin's.

"Let me see your nails," Pony said, taking a good while to check out the bright acrylic fingernails both girls extended. "Who did this? She did a great job."

Bebe looked at Pony's short, neatly trimmed nails and wondered if she'd ever gone the acrylic route.

"You know Henley Sanderson? It was her daughter, Tessa. She practically runs Lila's Nail Spa now," Caitlin answered.

"She really takes her time and does a good job," Debbie added.

"I just don't understand why you girls feel a need to have those long claws," Astrid said, shifting petulantly in her chair. "We never did anything like that in my day."

"Come on, Grandma," Caitlin said. "Women in your day had to use their hands for housework a lot more than we have to, and besides, the glitter would have come off on the washboard. It's okay if you don't like them. Not everyone has good taste."

"Caitlin," Pony warned. "Watch your smart mouth."

Caitlin just rolled her eyes. "Yes, ma'am."

"But what will people think of you, flashing nails like that?" Astrid persisted.

Caitlin grinned. "Now, Grandma, don't you worry about what people think. They don't do it very often."

Bebe could no longer hold back her merriment and her chuckle sounded too loud in the shocked silence.

Caitlin seemed to appreciate the gesture, though. She moved closer to Bebe. "How in the world do you get your hair to grow that long?" She turned Bebe around bodily and ran fingers through her ponytail. "Will you let me braid it?"

At Bebe's nod, she continued, sliding off the hair tie. "Us redheads have a hard road. Mine never gets as long as I want. My curls just bind up all the length and won't let go."

"You could get it straightened," Debbie offered, watching the hair processing from a nearby armchair.

"Here, let me get a chair," Pony said. She quickly fetched a straight chair from the kitchen and pressed Bebe into it.

"I'll just comb it with my fingers," Caitlin said. "It's not that tangled. Sorry I don't carry a comb, although I always carry a knife with me. You know, in case of a cheesecake or somethin'."

The entire room guffawed but Grandmother Astrid's lip only twisted briefly. She feigned interest in the television program.

"I'm able to grow my hair a bit," Pony said when the laughter had died down. "Not as long as the Beebs here, of course, but it's past my shoulders."

"Caitlin's is, too, but she wants it to be really long," Debbie offered. She looked at Bebe. "Have you always had long hair?"

Bebe was enjoying the sensation of having someone else braid her hair. "Yep, since I was little. My mother just tied it up for the day and off I went."

Caitlin spoke up again. "So, Mam tells me you and Auntie here are an item now. That's so sweet. I tried to talk Deb here into bumpin' uglies one time, but she said she flat-out wasn't interested."

"Ew, not with you," Debbie said, wrinkling her nose. "We been friends for too long."

"Well, who then?" Caitlin asked. Her long nails periodically scraped against Bebe's scalp and it was a weird feeling.

"Well, Jodie Foster, for sure," Debbie said, ticking names off on her fingers. "And then that Gillian Anderson. She's hot. Oh, and what about that *Rizzoli & Isles* gal?"

"The dark-haired one or the blonde?" Caitlin asked.

Bebe sought out Pony's gaze and saw that her eyes were wide and her lips pressed together to hold back merriment. And maybe amazement at the subject matter.

"Oh, the dark-haired one. What's her name?" Debbie screwed up her brow, trying to remember.

"Angie Harmon," Pony offered. "I have the hots for her, too. She is so gorgeous."

Bebe searched Pony's face. There were so many things about Pony that she had yet to explore. She planned to easily dedicate her life to that task.

"Ah, this'll be why you like this one here. She's not quite as tall as the Harmon gal, but there's a wee resemblance. They both have that straight, shiny hair, too," Caitlin said, retwisting the hair tie. "All done and it's so pretty. I even braided the sides and joined it in with the rest."

"What do you think, Grandma?" she said, turning to Astrid.

Astrid, who'd been focusing on the news program, turned her head. "What's that you say?"

"Oh, lordy, Grandma," she said with a deep sigh. "People really need to start appreciating the effort I put into not bein' a serial killer. This one here." She indicated Bebe. "She's pretty, ain't she?"

"*I* think so," Sara Vern said. She'd been reading a paperback book and Bebe had assumed she wasn't listening to the conversation. "I think Pone has done quite well for herself."

Pony laughed. "Why, I thank you, cousin. I feel that way, too."

Bebe quickly thanked Caitlin and returned the chair to the kitchen, hoping she was in time to hide her flaming cheeks.

CHAPTER FORTY-NINE

Rocking Chair Interlude

After Caitlin and Debbie drove off in Willem's old brick-red pickup, saying they were in search of a fast-food lunch, Astrid found her soap operas on the TV and raised the volume. Carney crawled into her lap and was soon gently snoring as only a terrier can.

Later, when Sara Vern went to the kitchen to prepare chicken sandwiches for her and Astrid, Bebe and Pony trailed behind her. After a few moments' search, they found ready-to-eat, prepackaged rice and vegetable bowls which they warmed in the microwave. Food ready, they passed quietly back through the family room and out onto the front porch, rice bowls and iced tea in hand. Pony led them to two comfy, padded rocking chairs cradling a small table, and that's where they settled, Buster and Salem sleeping at their feet.

"So, that Caitlin," Bebe said, shaking her head.

Pony studied her as she propped her feet onto a wicker footstool. "Your hair looks nice. She did a good job."

"It felt nice. Has she always been so...awesome?"

Pony laughed, admiring Bebe's constraint. "Oh, she has. I remember her at two years old and she hasn't changed one lick. She was a smart-ass then and she's an even bigger smart-ass now. I think her purpose in this life is to serve as a cautionary tale for the young."

"Or, as she might say, she's not a hot disaster but just a spicy mess."

"That about sums it up. Hey, this isn't half bad," Pony said, stirring her rice bowl.

Bebe shrugged. "Needs some of our liquid aminos."

Pony smiled at her and leaned in for a quick kiss, happy that Bebe remembered so much about their previous conversations.

"So, tell me, what does Caitlin do?"

Pony grunted. "She's still in school. In high school. She and Debbie."

"Does she plan on college?"

"I seriously doubt it," Pony answered. "Though at one point she did want to be a teacher. Yeah, right. Cou is tryin' to get her to at least earn a two-year graphic art degree. She's a wicked artist. You know, graffiti-like stuff."

They sat back and enjoyed the quiet of the countryside. Steve's workers could be heard calling to one another far off in the distance but there was no sound of traffic at all. A gurgle from the creek could be heard from time to time, and the drone from the television intruded a bit. Pony took a deep breath of the zesty, earth-scented air and felt renewed.

"Have you noticed?" Pony asked.

Bebe looked around. The farmland around the house was quiet. She turned her expectant gaze to Pony.

"Neither you nor I have picked up our readers once. Not once since we've been here." Pony watched Bebe closely while taking another bite of rice.

Bebe's eyes grew wide and those gray orbs found Pony's. "Holy shit! I didn't even…holy moly. I haven't even missed it and I was smack-dab in the middle of a fantastic novel."

Pony nodded. "I know! Isn't it just plain weird?"

Bebe seemed lost in thought. "I wonder what we can attribute that to," she muttered thoughtfully. "I read every day, all day."

Pony took a long sip of her iced tea. "Just being here. If you want to know *my* theory, it's boredom, plain and simple. That's why you read so much."

"Boredom? No way," Bebe protested, waving her spoon imperiously.

"Hey, you were the one who told me that people bore you. That you'd rather read than be bored by the people in your life."

Bebe sighed. "I have to say, being bored is not something I'd admit to during the past four days. Even in the car, we talked our heads off."

"And there's been no shortage of activity since we've been here." Pony set her empty bowl to one side. Buster immediately grabbed it from the end table and eagerly licked the inside, growling at Salem when he tried to steal it. Bebe offered her empty bowl to Salem.

"There's nothing left in them, guys," Pony said, shaking her head at the dogs.

"I guess I'm, well, I'm *living* life here instead of reading about it."

"Truer words were never spoken." Pony watched her closely. "How do you feel about that?"

"If I thought about it long enough, I'd say I'm forever changed."

"Reading might be a bit less important in your future. Is that what I'm hearin'?"

Bebe studied her. "Will you be there? Can I count on that?"

Pony's heart clenched. She hung her head. "I want to be. I plan to be. I just can't predict what'll happen with the job."

"Pone." Bebe reached across and took Pony's hand in hers. "I'm working on the job issue. I feel good about it, feel it'll all work out to your—to our—advantage. I do."

Pony sighed. "Like Grandma said, time and patience. I'm willing to give that."

They let the peace of the countryside lull them again. After some time had passed, Pony tilted her face toward Bebe. "You're wanting to go read now, aren't you?"

Bebe laughed. "Honestly, no. I haven't even thought about it." She squeezed Pony's fingers. "Being here with you is all that I need right now. And I...I guess I like being in the country more than I ever thought I would."

Pony took a deep breath. "I do love it here. If I have to move back, will you promise to come see me?"

Bebe studied her with a steady gaze. "*We'll* come whenever we can. I promise."

They dozed off and on then, enjoying the quiet rustles in the undergrowth and the somnolent murmur of the television. A bird, a little wren, landed next to Pony and drank from the condensation on her tea glass. Pony watched enthralled. The tiny bird seemed to have no fear, from the sleeping dogs or the dozing women. After drinking his fill, he left as though eager to regain a sweetheart in the small trees around the porch railings. Bebe's eyes were still closed, and Pony felt sad that she had missed the visit. She vowed to tell her all about it once she awakened.

CHAPTER FIFTY

Family Send-off

Foxy came home about four and the younger women worked on laying out a feast as Grandma Astrid supervised from her wheelchair.

"Cou and Willem are coming, but Benty's having some trouble with homework. They may come later. Cou says he doesn't like this new teacher he has this year."

"That's a shame," Sara Vern said, slicing tomatoes and onions for the sheet pan of burgers that Foxy had just placed into the oven. "He usually likes school."

"Is Caitlin helping him?" Pony asked.

"That's what I hear. Okay, we have leftover chicken," Foxy said, washing her hands and drying them. "Hamburgers are in the oven. There's a little bit of potato salad left but lots of baked beans. We've got the mac and cheese plus the cold macaroni salad." She opened the refrigerator and peered inside. "Oh, we have Emmy's Jell-O salad left and my mam's pistachio cake. Hey, here's some peas and carrots. I forgot about those."

"Any veggies from the freezer, Mam?" Pony queried.

"Oh, right! Why don't you and Bebe get some corn on the cob and maybe some frozen broccoli out?"

"Mashed potatoes?" Astrid asked.

Pony laughed. "I guess the army is on the way. Who else is coming, Mam?"

"Well, Bernie's bunch, all of them, Chloe and Cinna but Pierce has to work. Oh, your Aunt Birdie, too. She and Cara are coming."

"Oh, awesome. It'll be good to see them. Is Grandma Lowe coming, too?"

Foxy nodded. "My da, too."

"That's grand, Mam, grand. C'mon, Bebe, let's go get the frozen stuff."

Bebe followed Pony to a detached garage on the east side of the house. At least she could ferry food even though she was helpless with cooking it. The barnlike structure was filled with farm tools, some lethal-looking to her unpracticed eye. There were several sets of industrial shelves to one side filled with neatly labeled totes.

"Wow, someone's got an organizing jones," Bebe said, reading the tote labels.

"Oh, that's Sara Vern. She has mad organizing skills. Sometimes I think she has out of control OCD, but she does a good job."

"I'll say."

There were two stark white chest-type freezers at the back, and Pony lifted the lid of the one on the left side.

Bebe moved closer so she could see the contents. It was filled to the brim with containers that had color peeking through the frost, indicating they were vegetables. "What's in the other one?" she asked.

"Usually meat as well as more veg," Pony answered absently. "I'm going to make an executive decision," she added, handing Bebe three large zipper bags full of ears of yellow corn. "We need more green, so I'm taking in some green beans as well as the broccoli."

"Wow, this is a lot of food," Bebe said, juggling the bags of corn, trying not to drop them.

Pony let the lid drop, her arms full of packages. "It's gonna be a lot of people. Man, these bags are cold!"

They hurried into the house and laid the containers on the kitchen counters. "Brr," Pony said, shaking her arms. They realized quickly that they were in the way, so they moved to the table to sit with Astrid.

Two hours later, in a kitchen redolent with the fragrance of delicious food, there was absolutely no room to move. Bebe couldn't remember how many friends and family she had been introduced to. She was getting to know some who'd been at the barbecue but there seemed to be a new cluster of people. Some even introduced themselves as friends from neighboring farms. Surely they didn't have this many people here every day.

Bebe felt a little lost even though there was always someone talking to her. There were so many repeated questions about Albuquerque, editing for medical journals, and about how Bebe liked being out of the mad city. Most of the people spoke about Albuquerque as though it was as dense and dangerous as New York City or Indianapolis, Indiana, wondering aloud how a single woman could survive there.

The faces seemed to blur together, although Pony's aunt Birdie, the wife of Pony's uncle David Lowe, stuck in Bebe's mind. She was obviously very wealthy, with perfectly coifed short hair and a judging blue-eyed gaze that surely missed nothing as she examined the room and everyone in it. She dripped with diamond jewelry and the clothes on her plump figure were designer fitted. She reminded Bebe of her own mother in so many ways.

When that judging gaze rested on her, Bebe recoiled. Obviously homophobic, Birdie had just sniffed once and turned her gaze away.

"I don't think your aunt likes me," Bebe whispered as she gained Pony's side. Pony was embroiled in a discussion, so she just held Bebe's hand until the cousin she was talking with drifted away.

"Which one?" she asked curiously. "Wait! Don't tell me. It was Birdie, wasn't it?"

Bebe nodded. "I didn't do anything to her, I swear."

Pony laughed, its sweetness drawing the attention of those nearby. "Don't you worry about that," she whispered near Bebe's ear. "She doesn't like anyone. She thinks my da's family is second class, not up to Lowe standards, and that trickles down to most of us."

"Does she know you're gay? I got definite homophobe vibes."

Pony just rolled her eyes and sighed. "Yes, but she and her snooty daughter, Cara, are the only ones who have a problem with it. Just ignore them and try to have fun. There's dancing on the back patio. Wanna give it a whirl?"

Bebe spied Birdie conversing intently with her daughter, Cara, as well as all the people surrounding them. "Nah, I don't think so. I'll watch you, though."

The party roared on until midnight, but all tired hands pitched in to put the food away and return the house to rights. There were way too many farewells as it was known that Pony and Bebe planned to leave before daybreak on Thursday.

After quietly climbing the stairs, trying not to disturb the slumbering guests along the hallway bedrooms, Pony and Bebe held one another as they fell into a deep sleep as soon as their heads hit the pillows.

CHAPTER FIFTY-ONE

Fare Thee Well, Township

On their final day in Virginia, after recuperating from the night before, Pony and Bebe left the crowded kitchen, filled with busily chatting overnight guests, and slowly drove back into the town of Hillside Gap. Spring had brought new life to the countryside, and everywhere Pony looked, trees were filled with birds dancing in their spring finery. Nests were being neatened as baby birds prepared to hatch. Spring green was a real thing, and Pony reveled in it.

"I just wanted to ride around the township and see if anything has changed," Pony said from the passenger seat.

"No sweat," Bebe said, taking Pony's hand. "I never really got to see it because it was so dark out."

They drove into the small hamlet that had once been Pony's home and a strange pain filled her heart. Nothing had changed at all except for some new signs and new parking areas. Just cosmetics to enhance the bones of her childhood.

"See that library there?" They slowed as they passed the Township Public Library. "I first started using computers there.

Mam used to bring us every Saturday to get books for the week. One time I started using one of the two computers they had, slow, absolutely clunky things, and even though I was only six years old, I knew how they worked. My mam was way confused."

She and Bebe shared a laugh about that.

"This town is really cute," Bebe said, her eyes following the many townsfolk as they went about their business. "Hey, a café featuring coffee. Wanna stop?"

Pony nodded, glad they were going into one of her favorite places. "They handmake doughnuts in there," she warned. "And they are so good!"

Bebe parked the car. "Ah, doughnuts, one of my favorite food groups."

Inside they were inundated with the scent of fresh fried bread and redolent ground coffee. Pony spied Christy Micklin behind the counter, and they had a hug fest and quick catch-up as Bebe watched with wide eyes.

"Bebe, come meet Christy. We went to school together. Christy, meet my gal, Bebe. I drug her all the way from New Mexico to here so she could get to know the crazy Dakotas."

"And look at her," Christy said. "She survived it."

"Just barely," Bebe joked.

"So how long are you guys here for?" Christy asked, wiping down the espresso machine.

"Leaving tomorrow," Pony said with a deep sigh. "I'm just taking one more looky-loo at the township before we head out."

"Well, I can tell you, nothing's changed. Time here just moves like molasses. Now, you want your regular Pone, the vanilla latte with soy milk?"

"Yes, perfect."

"Listen, I have some of that oat milk in. It's a bit creamier than the soy and I like it better. Want to try that?"

Pony's eyes widened. "Oh, I do!"

"Make that two of them," Bebe said, pulling out her wallet. "And an assortment of six doughnuts. Surprise us."

After Bebe paid, Pony led the way around the corner into a small seating area.

"Oh, hell," Pony said. With Bebe following, she stomped to a corner table where Caitlin, Debbie, and another girl, a tall blonde, sat. "And what are you girls doing out of school?" she demanded.

"Hey, Auntie Pony, guess what? I found your nose, and it was in my business."

"Smart-ass." Pony and Bebe pulled chairs up and joined the girls, deliberately crowding them.

Caitlin was actually dressed a little more circumspectly than usual. Her jeans were ragged, however, and her skull-decorated T-shirt was clearly goth, as was the dark makeup she and Debbie both wore. And there was a lot of jewelry on both. "Seriously. Why aren't you in school?"

"It's my fault, Mrs. Bennett. I had an asthma attack and they brought me here so I could get some coffee. It usually helps." She quieted and looked in confusion at the other two girls who were laughing uncontrollably.

"Polly, she's not my mam," Caitlin choked out finally. "She's mam's sister."

Bebe couldn't seem to help the grin that crawled across her face and Pony realized that Bebe actually liked Caitlin. There was something about the wild, snarky girl that appealed to her.

"Hey, I'm not that old," she told Polly. "And I'm especially not old enough to have spawned *this* mess." She indicated Caitlin.

"Yeah, yeah," Caitlin said. "Silence is golden. Duct tape is silver, you know."

"We'd better get back to study hall," Debbie said, standing and untangling herself from the chair legs. "You feeling better, Polly?"

"Yeah, I think so." She stood as well and slung her bag onto her shoulder. "I'll stop by the nurse's office and get a note for geometry. Will you guys be okay?"

Caitlin stood and gathered up her well-worn bookbag. "No one ever checks study hall, and they left Bobby Aldiss in charge. He has the hots for me, so he won't say anything."

Pony looked at Bebe and they just shook their heads.

As the trio turned to go, Caitlin turned back. "Hey, you guys are leaving tomorrow, aren't you?"

Pony felt unbidden tears swell. She just nodded and stood, indicating she needed a hug. Caitlin hugged her for a long while, then passed her on to Debbie. Caitlin and Debbie hugged Bebe as well. Polly joined in, too, and there was a sad round of farewells with promises of a new visit soon.

Christy brought their coffee and doughnuts to the table. She saw Pony's teary state and she caressed her shoulder before moving away.

Bebe took Pony's hands in hers. "It's hard to leave home sometimes," she said. "But we're not so far away. We'll come back, at least once a year."

"You don't understand, sweetheart. I'm not sad that I'm leaving, though there is some of that. A lot. But what I'm also sad about is because making a new life here will be almost impossible for me. I'm so not the same girl I was when I lived here before. I'm torn, wondering where I will go and what I will do."

"That's easy. You'll stay in Albuquerque with me. That's decided."

Pony knew her doubts showed on her face, but she tucked her chin and nodded. It was just too much to argue the point.

CHAPTER FIFTY-TWO

May the Road Always Rise Up

"It'll be good to get back," Bebe whispered to Pony as they made the bed with fresh sheets.

It was still dark outside and the two were preparing to journey back to Albuquerque. Bags had been packed the night before and goodbyes said to the immediate family after a subdued supper.

Bebe wasn't sure of Pony's mindset after the revelation of the day before, but she was determined to remain positive, hoping it would wear off on Pony.

Slowly, quietly, they descended the stairs only to find one small lamp on and Foxy standing by the front door. She opened the door for them and ushered them out into the quiet, still morning.

"I'm so going to miss the both of you. But I'll be here waitin' when you come again," Foxy said. She handed a cooler to Bebe and indicated she should put it in the car. "Just some goodies for the road," she explained.

When Bebe returned, she took their hands in hers. Her voice was like a prayer and Bebe felt gooseflesh rise as she listened to Foxy's sweet voice.

"May the road always rise up to meet you, me bairns. May the wind be always at your back. May the sun shine warm upon your faces, and may the rains fall soft upon your lives. And until we meet again, may God hold you both in the palm of His hand.

"Bebe, my darling, you take care of my wee one. And Pony, look after Bebe as only a loved one can do."

She held each of them for a long moment, then pressed kisses to their teary cheeks. "Much, so much love to you, me sweet bairns."

She waved to them until they could no longer see her in the dimness. Bebe held Pony's hand as she quietly wept.

CHAPTER FIFTY-THREE

Together

The tension that permeated the hotel room had Pony clasping her bottom lip with her teeth so hard that she felt it might bleed. Her skin tingled in the electrified air and her breathing was affected as well, the intake of breath choppy, the exhales hoarse.

They'd stopped for a late supper earlier, but Bebe had grown quieter as the evening progressed. Pony had just assumed she was tired. She sincerely hoped that Bebe wasn't escaping back into her shell of protective seclusion, and she decided not to let that happen.

Then this tension had grown, practically suffocating her. She wasn't sure the cause but imagined it could be sexual tension, or maybe a tension of long-buried, unspoken secrets hidden by the body. Secrets that might just be revealed this night.

They were ready for bed, finally, but both seemed reluctant to climb into separate beds.

She glanced at Bebe, who was sitting on the edge of one bed, face downcast, seemingly lost in thought. Just as Pony was about to speak, Bebe's face lifted and Pony saw the heady desire smoldering in her gaze, turning her eyes into dark ash that still, remarkably, burned brightly.

A phoenix, Pony thought. *It's like a phoenix.*

"Come to me, Pony," Bebe said quietly.

Pony's heart thrummed in her ears as she felt her own desire immediately flame within her. She felt herself changing forever, every molecule in her body becoming supercharged, filled with metamorphosis. For the umpteenth time she wanted to feel Bebe's body entwined with hers, craved Bebe's breath on her, her lips on her.

"Pony. Be with me," Bebe demanded gently.

"I will," Pony whispered in reply as she poured herself into Bebe's waiting arms. Doing so felt so natural, like autumn leaves wafting from sighing tree branches.

Bebe pulled them into a standing position and one hand rose to lay along Pony's cheek. Their gazes locked and new worlds opened for both of them.

"I've loved you for so long," Bebe whispered against Pony's lips. "Tried to deny—"

"But why deny?" Pony asked in a low whisper. "I'm here. I'm always here."

"Yes, waiting, waiting for me to grow a backbone, to get past my narcissistic, unrelenting fear of caring."

Pony cupped Bebe's face between her palms. "Hell, yes, waiting for you. Trying to control myself."

"Really?" Bebe's gaze was searching and steadfast.

"Kiss me, Bebe. Just kiss me now."

Bebe lowered her arms and both hands pulled Pony against her slim frame. Their gazes still commingled and so much information passed, so many promises were silently signed. Pony wasn't sure what her future held, whether she'd be with Bebe or without her, but she knew in this one moment that she had to have this woman. She had to share her body, her being, with this loving, highly intelligent walking encyclopedia. And no matter what Bebe said, Pony knew her, knew that she did indeed care. Far more than she would admit to, but Pony knew.

Their kisses deepened and reluctantly, Bebe broke away to pull the sheets and blanket loose on the bed. She placed one bent knee onto the mattress and gently tugged Pony's hand. "Lay with me? Sleep next to me?" she asked. "I need to be close to you. I'm so afraid to lose you."

"Of course," Pony replied without thinking about it. She, too, had wondered about the dreamlike nature of this new budding love. Could it be real? Was it truly their new reality?

Bebe let Pony get onto the bed first, but once Bebe had settled in Pony boldly straddled her, peering down into those fiery gray eyes. Bebe seemed surprised but pulled Pony into another deep kiss, all the while pressing herself into Pony's groin.

Pony moaned, knowing that she was already swollen and wet just by Bebe's proximity. It had been so many months since anyone had intimately touched her, and she hoped their lovemaking could last a good long while.

Bebe ran soft palms along her arms, clasping their fingers together when she reached the hands. "Will you undress for me?" she asked in a soft voice.

Pony smiled and, disengaging their hands, swept her nightshirt over her head and tossed it to the second bed.

The room grew still then as Bebe studied her in the faint light emanating from the bathroom. A forefinger came up and traced around one of her pale nipples until it stood achingly erect. "You are amazingly beautiful," she said, her voice low and laden with desire.

Pony cupped her breasts in her hands and looked down at them. "They used to be a lot firmer, but time tells all, doesn't it?"

Bebe didn't reply. She just smoothed her hands along Pony's waist and panty-covered hips as though caressing the finest silk.

Pony slid her hands under Bebe's nightshirt and gave in kind, her palms lingering in the warmth and smoothness of Bebe's abdomen. Her hands went higher and glided across Bebe's small breasts. They were hard, the nipples flexing under her fingers.

"No, not as much to offer you," Bebe whispered. "Sorry for that."

Her hands came up and cupped Pony's breasts from the sides. Her thumbs ran firmly across the nipples and Pony felt a sensation that made her feel weak. She collapsed next to Bebe, panting from her own pervasive need.

Bebe propped on one elbow and traced Pony's body with her fingers. Pony wondered if she were memorizing her body in case they had to be separated. Bebe's focus changed, though, and she tugged at the waistband of Pony's panties. Pony lifted her hips and the damp panties disappeared into the depths of the blankets at the foot of the bed.

Bebe took the opportunity to caress Pony's legs with her palm and trailing fingers. She started low on the calves then worked her way along the thighs. Her hand dipped into the separation of those thighs and her thumb briefly swept along Pony's vulva. Pony gasped and started just a little.

Bebe chuckled. Her mouth found Pony's and their kisses transported Pony away. She was carried on a tidal sea, Bebe's hand and lips drifting her from wave to wave. There was the fullness of foamy sea, then it retreated only to return seconds later.

Bebe's thigh rested across one of hers as the two came together as closely as possible. To Pony, it felt like the sleekness of a dolphin cavorting with her in the ocean waves. Fill, retreat, sway.

Bebe's lips slid away from hers and they found Pony's breast. One pull on Pony's nipple and she was done. The huge waves crashed across her with all the force of a raging ocean. Pony choked on the rising sea but managed to cry out and rise to the surface. And Bebe was there, eyes heavy with desire as she leaned to press her lips to Pony's once more.

CHAPTER FIFTY-FOUR

Home Again

The final leg of the journey was quiet but very loving. Though Bebe would have liked a repeat of the previous night, she sensed the sad, doomsday aspect of Pony's thoughts and knew they should get home as soon as possible. After each spent some time dozing in the passenger seat, they drove through the night.

Albuquerque was much as they'd left it, although traffic was lighter than usual for midday on a Saturday. Bebe looked across at Pony and realized that she had grown even more nervous during the past hour. Soon powerful decisions would be made, life-changing decisions.

Bebe cleared her throat, wondering how she could put Pony at ease. "Hey, are you hungry? We can stop and get something if you want."

Pony shook her head. "No, I'm still recovering from that french toast we had."

Bebe smiled. "Yeah, it was pretty good, wasn't it?"

"So, I guess you can drop me at my place?"

She sounded as loath to separate as Bebe felt. "We've been pretty much joined at the hip for almost a week. It'll be weird to be apart, won't it?"

Pony chewed on a thumbnail. "Yes, it'll be strange. Will you go to the office?"

Bebe thought a moment. "No, I'm heading home. Gotta unpack, start some laundry. What will you do?" She navigated off I-40 onto the Tramway exit and too soon picked up Montgomery Boulevard. She slowed her speed, wanting to have as long with Pony as possible. She reached out and took her hand. "You know that we'll be together, right?"

Pony squeezed her hand. "I know. One way or another. I guess I'll unpack as well. Catch up with Alice and let Bernie know we got here okay." She turned in her seat. "Will you know something Monday about the job?"

"I should. Tell you what, I'll make some calls. Can you come to my place tonight? We'll do dinner and talk about things. Sound good?"

Pony chuckled. "It would, if I knew where you lived."

Bebe blinked her eyes slowly as she turned into Pony's apartment complex and pulled into a parking slot near Pony's favored entrance. "Oh, man. I can't believe…Here, get out your phone."

Bebe took it and typed her address into the contacts application. She was gratified to see it brought up a map of the area around her apartment buildings. "Listen, it's by Uptown. It's those apartments that have that weird burgundy coloring by the front entrance. You've probably seen them. The place called Elysium? Come in through the front and check in at the desk, then take the elevator that's on the left. It'll let you out just down the hall from my apartment."

Pony nodded as she took her phone back. "I've seen those apartments. And it's right on the bus line, so that's cool."

"Oh, right," Bebe said with a frown. "Why don't I come and get you?"

Pony gathered up her light jacket and lifted her gaze to Bebe. "Oh, sweetheart, everything has changed and nothing has changed. The bus is fine. Hey, I'll stop in that little Chinese place I saw in Uptown and bring supper. How does that sound?"

Bebe laughed. "That sounds great. I think we could both do with a bit of Asian food after all the heavy country food we had in Virginia."

Pony leaned forward for a kiss. "So true. Now, help me get my bags out and I'll see you in a few hours."

Bebe helped unload the back of her car and watched until Pony was safely next to the building. She fished her phone out of her pocket and pressed the button for a very familiar number as she got back behind the wheel.

Then she saw her. The small, wiry woman with short, wavy black hair had to be Donna. The abuser exited a car and rushed to Pony's side, her face a grimace of rage. Pony fell back against the wall next to the entrance, her bags flying helter-skelter along the sidewalk. Donna pressed a palm into Pony's chest, pinning her to the brick wall.

"I'll call you right back," Bebe said as she ended the call and leapt from the car. She slammed the door.

"Hey!" she shouted as she stomped across the parking area. Just as she approached, her sweet, cheery Pony, using a powerful roundhouse punch, lobbed her right fist forcefully into Donna's cheek.

Donna went down on all fours, then clasped her hands to her face.

"I swear on all that's holy," Pony said loudly, chest heaving in anger and trauma. "If I ever see you near me again, there'll be hell to pay. I am not yours and I never will be."

Donna rose and Bebe saw that her face and eye were already red and swelling from the punch. "You just think again, missy. You're coming home with me." She grabbed Pony's arm as if to pull her away with her. Pony jerked the arm from her grasp so forcefully that Donna was knocked off-balance.

"Don't you touch me!" Pony cried out.

Bebe stepped closer, gaining Donna's attention, and when she spoke she knew her voice was a low growl of barely suppressed fury. "If I—if we—ever see you again, your ass will be in jail so fast your head will spin. You don't know me, but I'm *very* well connected in this city." She realized her fists were balled at her sides and she pointedly loosened them. "Don't push your luck."

Donna looked confused. She stared at Bebe, then at Pony. "Are you going to let her talk to me that way?" she asked.

Pony leveled a steely gaze at her. "Damned right," she replied. "I think you need to go and forget you ever knew me. As God is my witness, I will never let you control me again."

Donna grunted, but they both watched as she marched angrily across the parking lot and slid into her older model Pontiac.

Bebe examined Pony's right hand and found a deep purple bruise rising around the knuckles. She gently manipulated it, making sure no bones were broken. "Seems okay," she said, releasing the hand. She bent to gather together Pony's things as Pony opened the vestibule door and held it wide.

Bebe paused and studied Pony as she passed inside. "Will you be all right?" she asked.

Pony nodded as she took a deep breath. "I think so. I wonder how she knew I'd be here."

Bebe saw that the question had distracted Pony from her earlier numbness, her green eyes brightening as she pondered it.

"I bet she's been waiting off and on for you to appear," Bebe replied as she mounted the metal steps, dragging Pony's suitcase behind. "Let's get these things upstairs and see to that hand, okay?"

Pony nodded as she lifted the end of the suitcase with her left hand. Bebe looked back and was relieved to see that Pony's usual gamine grin had returned.

She'd be okay.

CHAPTER FIFTY-FIVE

Solutions

Several hours later, Pony approached Bebe's apartment, walking along an extensive carpeted hallway. It reminded her of a hotel but seemed warmer somehow, the trappings on the hall tables not so austere. The place had to be relatively new as well, because Pony could discern the lingering smell of fresh paint and new carpet. She passed the bag of Chinese food she held from her left hand to her right, then gingerly knocked on the door.

Bebe answered the knock. She had changed into fresh jeans and a pale blue Oxford shirt and had unbound her hair. She was utterly beautiful.

Bebe bent and placed a lingering kiss on her cheek. "Here, let me take that," she said, taking the bag and carrying it into an open kitchen area. Though the apartment seemed handsomely appointed, Pony couldn't tell because two men moved toward her and blocked her view.

"Pony, this is Spence. He's the lawyer for TWEI and I asked him to come discuss your case," Bebe said from the kitchen.

"My...my case?" Pony felt her heart collapse and she immediately realized anew how much trouble she had gotten herself into. She swallowed hard, even as she reached to shake his extended hand with her unbandaged left hand. She tried to smile but knew it was tremulous.

The other man extended his hand. "Hello, Pony. I'm Thomas, Bebe's brother."

Pony shook his hand, but Bebe must have seen the panic on Pony's face because she came close and guided Pony to a sofa set in a square conversation area of the living room. The men took seats in armchairs directly across. A coffee urn rested on the small table between them. Pony saw that the other three already had been served but Bebe quickly poured coffee into a fourth mug and added a sizable dollop of sugar. She handed it to Pony, urging her to drink.

Her gaze flew to Thomas, and she pondered the fact that she'd never met him before. Not in person, anyway. Now that she knew he was Bebe's brother, she could definitely see a resemblance, though his eyes were a hazel green rather than a gray. And he was, had been, her boss. He was the genius mind that had spawned TWEI. If circumstances had been different, Pony would have loved to talk software with him.

Thomas leaned forward, as though he'd read her mind. "Pony, I have to say what an honor it is to finally meet you. Your Gallop program is sheer genius. We really need to do lunch and talk about its genesis."

Pony's mouth flew open but she quickly closed it. "I would love that," she said. "Your tree hierarchy for TWEI is so perfect. I wish all companies would implement that or at least something similar. It makes life so much easier when you're trying to navigate a system."

"Okay, okay. Mutual admiration society pipe down," Spence said.

"Hey," Bebe interjected. "I'd say it's way past time for these two to meet." She turned to Pony and patted her knee. "I can't believe I let it go so long. I have to apologize to you. I seldom broadcast the news that Thomas is my brother. A few locals know, but I just don't want to deal with accusations of nepotism or any sort of favoritism."

Pony nodded, her terror softening under Bebe's kind gaze. "I can understand that," she replied quietly.

"By the way, this is Peabody," Bebe said, indicating the sleek gray cat with golden eyes that had leapt into Thomas's lap. "He lives here and just dotes on Thomas for some weird reason."

"We need to get down to business," Spence said, reaching into a nearby briefcase open on the floor next to his chair. He pulled out a sheaf of paper and stared seriously at Pony. Seriously may have been the type of gaze, although Spence did not look the part of an expensive, hotshot lawyer. He was dressed in faded jeans that had a sizable rip at one knee, and his dark-blue T-shirt looked like an advertisement for an upstart brewery. He had a full though closely trimmed beard and mustache, and his long, sandy blond hair was twisted into a man bun atop his oval head. "I hope you know that TWEI and even the Feds could have had a field day with you concerning the falsification of your documentation."

"But the only thing—"

Spence waved one hand, the late afternoon sunlight flashing on the heavy silver ring he wore on his middle finger. "I know. Your credentials are all real. I checked when I had your actual name."

"I need to tell you why I used a different name," Pony said but was interrupted again.

"You were pretty smart," Spence told her quietly. "Using an abbreviation of your real name to set up the DBA 'E. Vernon' was genius. This way the Feds don't need to be involved and your tax documents are covered. No fraud is involved."

"How did you know to do that?" Thomas asked curiously. He absently caressed Peabody's ears.

Pony sighed and spread out her injured hand. She took another sip of the coffee then rested the cup on the tray. "I just did a deep search about how to use a new identity for protection. Doing business as E. Vernon helped hide my real name. That way there'd be no paper trail for Donna to follow. And I cut off all access avenues on my web pages. I truly hoped that she'd lose interest when she couldn't find me easily."

Thomas looked at Spence and screwed up his mouth. "Our comptroller will be pissed when he finds out," Thomas said with a chuckle. "Won't he, Spence? Because of the extra work and the fact that he missed her listing a DBA on her paperwork?"

Spence just nodded as he laid the papers on the coffee table. "He might get a kick out of it, you know, because of how smart it was."

"Maybe. I'm glad we're keeping this in-house, though. It could reflect badly on the company."

"It became public when we filed the protective order on her as an employee. And it'll be on the court docket as though it's already happened," Spence said. "Someone may see it, but maybe not. It's under the DBA name as well, so maybe no one will associate it with her. With Pony."

"I'm so sorry. I never meant for this to happen," Pony said, dropping her chin to her chest. Bebe took her hand and pressed it, trying to comfort her.

"What about the staff? Did you put the photo of that woman up?" Thomas said.

Spence nodded. "I did it already. I put a note on it just asking for anyone who sees her to let Beebs know."

"Will the protective order keep her away from me?" Pony watched each man expectantly.

"Well, we filed an emergency order with Judge Ben Harris on a felonious stalking charge. And that one means that this… er, this Donna can't come near you anywhere, at work or at home. Or even in a restaurant, any public place."

He paused and took a deep breath. "Now, if you decide to make it permanent, New Mexico law states that she will have the right to state her case, as will you, but in a court of law. Harris said he would try to get you onto his court docket but couldn't promise. The main thing is, if you want a permanent order, which lasts for years before needing renewal, you will need to provide proof of the physical violence against you. Do you have anything like that? Photos? Hospital records? Psychiatric records?"

Pony hung her head and stared at their clasped hands. "I don't. I never sought treatment."

She glanced up and saw Spence rub his bearded chin thoughtfully.

"Okay, then. I recommend that you just leave this order in place. We can renew it a few times and then revisit it later. Sound good?"

Pony nodded. "Yes, thank you. Again, I'm so sorry that my troubles had to visit your door." She directed her comment to both men.

"Okay, here we go." Spence handed her some documents. "I've explained everything to Judge Harris and he has already signed off on the name change, including making it retroactive to your employment date. You just need to sign them."

"Name change?" Pony was worried. *Another name change?*

"Oh, sorry. We need to start using your real name." He held up a staying palm. "I know, I know, but we'll protect you. All of us will."

Thomas spoke up. "That was me. You've accomplished a lot as Pony Dakota, and I want that to be known. I want to proudly share that you are part of my company. Hiding your accomplishments under Emma Vernon just isn't fair to you, or to TWEI."

"So…so I still have a job?" She was incredulous. This afternoon had not turned out as she had expected.

Thomas laughed and Bebe pulled her close in a sideways hug.

"Of course," he said. "Until you decide to leave us."

Spence indicated the documents and handed Pony a pen, eyeing her bandaged knuckles. "Here, sign up, if you can. I have a handball game scheduled at the gym."

CHAPTER FIFTY-SIX

Thomas and Bebe

When Spence left, Bebe closed the door behind him and cleared away the coffee tray and cups. "Chinese, Thomas?"

Thomas leaned back in his chair. "Do you have enough?"

Bebe laughed. "Chinese food? When have they ever scrimped on servings?"

"Well, sure, I'll take some," he said, shooing Peabody to the floor. "So, Pony, did you and Beebs have a good time in Virginia?"

Pony, still a little shocky, managed to smile and talk about her much loved but crazy Irish family. She told him about introducing Bebe to Old Coot, Old Bono, and described the town of Hillside Gap. He seemed to think the tales about his sister's timidity were hilarious and teased her about it.

"You've got to go there, seriously," Bebe said, placing the microwave-warmed food and a stack of empty bowls on the large dining table outside the kitchen. "It's a beautiful place. Okay, come and get it."

Thomas stood and offered a hand to Pony. Pony took it gratefully, knowing that she would always honor this man who had gone to bat for her. And she felt he would continue to do so, helping protect her from the woman who had haunted her for so many fearful months.

Bebe had emptied the restaurant containers into large ceramic bowls for heating, and as the three of them seated themselves, she passed them around.

"Are Mom and Dad okay?" Bebe asked her brother. "I forgot to ask."

"You need to call them as soon as you can," he replied, dishing up more vegetables. "Mother was horrified."

"You know I have a ton of vacation time," Bebe protested.

"You're preaching to the choir, sis. How dare you go to Virginia and not stay in DC to visit the monuments?"

Bebe paused and wrinkled her nose. "She said that? Seriously?"

She turned to Pony. "You're gonna just love meeting our mother," she said sarcastically.

Thomas guffawed, almost choking on some rice. He pointed his chopsticks at Pony. "Put it off as long as you can," he advised.

Pony let her eyes widen. "Oh, I will," she exclaimed comically.

"On another note, didn't I tell you I was working on things? Didn't I tell you that you could trust me?" Bebe asked Pony.

"I was so torn up about it," Pony said, sighing and laying her chopsticks aside. She looked at Thomas. "I just knew I was fired if Ralph told you—omigosh, Ralph!" Alarm raced through her. How could she go back to work with Ralph looking over her shoulder, making his sly passes and innuendos?

"History," Thomas said, loading his mouth with broccoli.

Bebe grinned at Pony. "He's gone. He finally revealed his true colors and Thomas shoved him out the door."

Pony felt relief and glee intermingle in her chest. "Oh, I am so glad I won't have to work with him."

"Me, too," Bebe agreed.

Pony looked at Thomas, hoping her gratitude showed in her gaze. "I can't thank you enough for understanding about the name thing. I wasn't trying to be deceptive. I was just hiding out."

"I'm gonna show her," Bebe said to Thomas. "She'll find out eventually, and I know we can trust her not to say anything."

Thomas lifted his shoulders defensively, then nodded.

Bebe wiped her hands on her napkin and laid it next to her plate. She rose and crossed the room to a bookshelf against a window wall. "Ah, this one's my favorite," she said, bringing a book to the table.

"Which one?" Thomas asked curiously.

"I've told you. *Love's Deepest Desire.*"

"Really? Cool," he said.

She handed the paperback book to Pony. The cover was a bit lurid but lovely, with the profiles of a man and woman face-to-face with a beautiful sunset in the background. Pony grinned as she examined the book. She turned it and read the back cover. She looked at Bebe. "I didn't know you liked hetero romances."

"It's mine," Thomas said, brushing grains of rice from the tabletop into his hand.

"Ah, so *you* like romance novels. Me, too. I read them from time to time."

Bebe laughed heartily. "He wrote it, Pony."

Pony's reality shifted. "Wait. What?"

"Pony, I'd like you to meet *New York Times* bestselling author Tara Vale. Also known as my brother, Thomas, but only in *very* select circles."

"Right," Thomas added. "This has to be our little secret. No one can know. My parents don't even know about it."

"Oh, man," Bebe said, placing her face in her hands as though fearing the thought of her parents finding out his secret.

Pony felt shocky once more. "I swear, I won't say a word," she managed to stammer out. She lifted the book and, sure enough, Tara Vale was touted as a bestselling author. The blond, female author photo looked nothing like Thomas. "How did you—"

"I like to read. *Everything*," Thomas said with a shrug. "And I get bored easily. One day I sat down at the computer and wrote *Love's Heyday*. That was, let's see, twenty-four books ago?"

"Twenty-six if you count the anniversary editions."

Thomas looked at Pony with a raised eyebrow. "She's my editor, so she should know."

Pony frowned. "I swear. I think I've stepped into an episode of *The Twilight Zone*."

"Okay, let's get this mess cleaned up. I'm exhausted from the two of us driving all night. Thank goodness tomorrow is Sunday. Seems like we always need to recover from vacations, doesn't it?"

Thomas lifted his bowl and one of the larger bowls, but he paused to look at Pony. "Kind of makes you understand how I feel about using another name now, doesn't it? Can you imagine the cred I would lose if my employees or any of our scientific publishing clients found out about this?"

Pony knew she must have the stupidest, most stunned look on her face, but she nodded in understanding.

After the table was cleared and the dishes washed, Thomas left the two women alone. Bebe locked the door. "You'll stay, right?"

Pony smiled warmly as she turned off the overhead lights. "Of course."

"Come on, Peabody, beddy byes," Bebe said.

"Can I ask you a question?" Pony said as Bebe handed her a nightshirt once they were in the large bedroom suite.

"Sure."

"If Ralph is gone, who's our new boss gonna be?"

Bebe pulled Pony down to sit beside her on the edge of the bed. "Well, Ralph really wasn't your boss, no matter how much he liked to pretend he was. He was editorial and you're with software engineering. Technically, he was my boss and Dam was yours."

"Oh, right. That's true. So has Thomas chosen a new boss for editorial?"

Bebe sighed. "Yep. Me. He wants me to head editorial."

"Oh, Bebe, congratulations. That's like a big promotion."

"Yep, I get the corner office and everything. Thomas says they've already moved my stuff across the hall."

Pony was swamped with sadness as she realized what that meant. "I'm sorry we won't be sharing an office anymore."

Bebe stood and moved into the bathroom. "Looks like you'll have it all to yourself now. After all, Thomas's new journal designer-slash-troubleshooter will need all the space she can get. You even have a new drafting table, and Thomas said he set you up with three—yes *three*—huge monitors and gosh knows how many machines. Must be nice to be brilliant."

Pony stood and stared wide-eyed at the bathroom doorway for more than a minute. Had she heard her correctly? "Wait. What did you say?"

Bebe returned to the bedroom and smiled seductively at Pony. "Congratulations, sweetheart."

Pony didn't hear the words Bebe said because Bebe was dangling her nightshirt from one index finger, her entire body bare and breathtakingly beautiful.

Bella Books, Inc.

Women. Books. Even Better Together.

P.O. Box 10543

Tallahassee, FL 32302

Phone: (800) 729-4992

www.BellaBooks.com

More Titles from Bella Books

Hunter's Revenge – Gerri Hill
978-1-64247-447-3 | 276 pgs | paperback: $18.95 | eBook: $9.99
Tori Hunter is back! Don't miss this final chapter in the acclaimed Tori Hunter series.

Integrity – E. J. Noyes
978-1-64247-465-7 | 28 pgs | paperback: $19.95 | eBook: $9.99
It was supposed to be an ordinary workday...

The Order – TJ O'Shea
978-1-64247-378-0 | 396 pgs | paperback: $19.95 | eBook: $9.99
For two women the battle between new love and old loyalty may prove more dangerous than the war they're trying to survive.

Under the Stars with You – Jaime Clevenger
978-1-64247-439-8 | 302 pgs | paperback: $19.95 | eBook: $9.99
Sometimes believing in love is the first step. And sometimes it's all about trusting the stars.

The Missing Piece – Kat Jackson
978-1-64247-445-9 | 250 pgs | paperback: $18.95 | eBook: $9.99
Renee's world collides with possibility and the past, setting off a tidal wave of changes she could have never predicted.

An Acquired Taste – Cheri Ritz
978-1-64247-462-6 | 206 pgs | paperback: $17.95 | eBook: $9.99
Can Elle and Ashley stand the heat in the *Celebrity Cook Off* kitchen?

Printed in the USA
CPSIA information can be obtained
at www.ICGtesting.com
JSHW021351210524
63541JS00001B/3